Lo⸱⸱
School of Dance

Annette Hannah is a Liver Bird who relocated to leafy Hertfordshire in the 80's and now lives near a river with her husband, two of their three grown up children and a crazy black cocker spaniel. She writes Romantic comedies in settings inspired by the beautiful countryside around her and always with a nod to her hometown. She worked in Marketing for many years as a qualified Marketeer which she loved as it tapped into her creative side. As an avid reader, she began to review the books she read, became a book blogger and eventually plucked up the courage to fulfil her life long dream of writing a book. For four years she was a member of the Romantic Novelists' Association's new writers' scheme, during which time she wrote a book a year. After signing a two book deal with Orion Dash in 2020 she graduated to full member of the organisation and is also their Press Officer. She loves long walks along the river, travelling to far flung places and spending time with her friends and family. You can follow her on twitter @annettehannah, www.sincerelybookangels.blogspot. com, www.annettehannah.com.

Lottie's
School of Dance

Annette Hannah

First published in Great Britain in 2023 by Orion Fiction,
an imprint of The Orion Publishing Group Ltd.,
Carmelite House, 50 Victoria Embankment
London EC4Y 0DZ

An Hachette UK Company

1 3 5 7 9 10 8 6 4 2

A CIP catalogue record for this book is
available from the British Library.

ISBN (Paperback) 978 1 3987 1846 3
ISBN (eBook) 978 1 3987 1002 3

Typeset by Born Group
Printed and bound in Great Britain by Clays Ltd, Elcograf S.p.A.

www.orionbooks.co.uk

For my beautiful nieces Camilla and Darcy,
the stars are shining for you...

Chapter 1

The chime of wedding bells echoed through the church, bounced off the rafters and drowned out the conversation beyond the wooden door she now stood in front of. The sun shone through the stained-glass windows, reflecting the red, blue and gold of religious scenes onto the white of her dress. Lottie hadn't been inside a church since her mum's funeral nine years ago when she was just seventeen and she wished more than anything that her parents could be with her now, although she was unsure whether they would entirely approve of her choice.

Her fiancé Chad had proposed after a day of drinking on his parents' yacht, and she'd accepted without a second thought. He was handsome, exciting, rich and, most importantly, he made her feel like the most beautiful girl in the room. What more could she want?

He'd hardly noticed her at school but then nobody did; she was grieving the loss of her mother for most of it. She knew who he was, but then it would have been hard not to – he was the popular guy that all the boys wanted to be and all the girls wanted to be seen with. It was years later that he'd asked her out after seeing her dance at a party with her dance troupe. She could hardly believe it. He hadn't even remembered her from school, she'd been that forgettable, and now as she stood in the foyer of St Michael's Church, she could hardly believe that the girl standing there in the wedding dress was her. Lottie Daniels, soon to be Lottie Mills.

His mother Greta had taken over the planning as soon as they'd told her the news, which was why Chad's dad Albie was walking her down the aisle and not her older brother, Blake, who lived in England now. Lottie had tried to protest politely but was guilted into agreeing because Albie didn't have any daughters of his own. Lottie had always sensed an underlying disapproval from Greta but Chad dismissed any such suggestion when she raised it.

As if summoned by her thoughts, Blake appeared in the church foyer with his fiancé Camilla. Lottie's breath caught in her throat and her heart began to race; he looked so like their dad when he'd been younger that for a minute, she almost believed it was him. He gave Lottie a hug, trying not to crumple her dress or catch her veil and, holding her gently by each arm, he stepped back.

'Well, will you look at you, my little sis looking so beautiful . . . Mum and Dad would be . . . well—' His words caught in his throat.

'Stop or you'll get me started,' said Lottie, overwhelmed by the love and pride in his voice and the tears in his eyes. The last time she'd seen him cry was at their mum's funeral. She dabbed at her eyes with a tissue. 'I don't know how you manage it, Blake, but even at twenty-six, you still manage to make me feel like a dorky younger sister.'

'Oh yes, I forgot to say beautiful *and* dorky, but I love you anyway,' he replied, his brown eyes twinkling.

Lottie smiled through her tears. 'I love you too.' He wasn't just a brother; at ten years older he was like a father to her. He had always been her protector and kept her safe. Dealt with all her teenage tantrums, getting drunk and hanging out with the wrong crowd.

'Oh, come here,' said Camilla, her calm voice cutting through the emotion like a hot knife through butter. She pulled a packet of tissues out of her bag and handed one to Blake before folding one into a point and dabbing at a few dots of mascara under Lottie's eyes.

'There we go, all better now. He's right though – you look absolutely stunning. Is that a vintage dress? It looks so expensive.'

Lottie ran her hands along the material, feeling the hand-stitched pearls and sequins. 'Yes, I would have liked something more modern, but this was Greta's dress when she got married and she insisted I wear it. Chad loved the idea, so . . .' She stopped talking and noticed Camilla looking deep into her eyes.

Camilla blew out a long, deep breath. 'Are you OK?' she asked.

'Yes, of course, I've just got pre-wedding jitters, that's all.' She shook her head and laughed. 'I'll be fine. Anyway, how are you and how's my little baby niece or nephew doing in there?'

'I'm fine, thank you, and all good with our little cupcake.' She patted her tummy.

'Ah that's so cute – I can't wait to meet him or her and I'm coming to England as soon as you go into labour.'

'That will be lovely, and you're welcome anytime.'

'By the way, thank you so much for offering to make the cake but Chad's mum had it all under control. I'm sorry.'

'No problem, I'll make you a special one when you visit,' she smiled.

'You must be the brother,' said Albie as he appeared through the door holding his hand out.

'Yes. This is my brother Blake and Blake, this is Albie,' said Lottie, pointing from one to the other.

'The future father-in-law,' said Albie, shaking hands with Blake, 'and who might I ask is this delightful creature?'

'This is my fiancé, Camilla,' said Blake.

'Pleased to meet you, Albie,' said Camilla sweetly.

Lottie had to stifle a giggle when she saw Camilla use her tissue to wipe Albie's sloppy kiss off her hand; many a time she'd had to discreetly wipe her cheek after one of his greetings.

Camilla took her hand and squeezed it. 'Well here goes – I'll see you on the other side when you're Mrs Mills. Good luck, darling.'

'Thanks Cami,' said Lottie.

'Ah Lottie, you look almost as beautiful as my Greta in that dress. Come on then, let's get you wed and our son off our hands.' Albie held his arm out for her to link it and her heart cracked open on seeing the look on Blake's face. Even though he'd said he was fine when she told him that Albie had been asked to walk her down the aisle she could see how much it hurt him to actually see it.

'I'm sorry, Blake, I wanted you to . . .'

'I know,' he said, 'it's all OK. I'm here for you anyway, always. May you be as happy as Mum and Dad were,' he said, and pulled her close to him. 'But if you have any doubts, it's still not too late,' he whispered in her ear, his beard tickling her cheek.

He pulled away again, winked at her and followed Camilla into the church.

Lottie's eyes opened wide, and her stomach lurched; she didn't know if she'd imagined those words or whether he'd really said them. He'd only met Chad a couple of times and while he hadn't said he disliked him – I mean how could he? Chad was charm personified – he had made several references to the fact that they hadn't been together long. Lottie felt she had made a mistake once by moaning about Chad to Blake and he told her that he sounded like a spoilt little rich kid terrified of losing his inheritance. Maybe Chad was immature but they had fun, so much fun, didn't they?

She remembered how her mum always said that she had an angel on one shoulder and a devil on the other and that every once in a while, she should listen to the angel. Lottie knew that Chad was definitely the devil's choice.

Rachel, her best friend and bridesmaid, appeared and began titivating her veil.

'You look gorgeous – you're gonna knock him dead in there.'

'Oh, thank you, so do you. Is everybody ready to go?'

'Yes, don't worry, it's all going as planned so far.' She pulled out a lip gloss from a little satin bag dangling from her wrist and began applying it to Lottie's lips. 'By the way, I thought you were still waiting to hear back from that job at Winters Dance School?'

'Yes, the head dance teacher one. I am.'

'Well, that's strange because I've just been talking to Jodie and she said that she knows the person who got it and they said you'd been offered it but had turned it down.'

'What?' Lottie's eyes opened wide and her stomach almost dropped to the floor. 'No, I haven't heard from them.'

'She said you emailed them to say you wouldn't have time now that you're getting married. Here, blot.' She placed a tissue between Lottie's lips and Lottie did as she was told.

'But that's ridiculous, that's my dream job.'

'That's what I thought. Oh well, we can sort that out later. Here goes.' Rachel blew her a kiss and wished her luck.

'Are you ready?' Albie interrupted her thoughts, they moved forward, and the organ began playing 'Here Comes the Bride'.

All eyes of the congregation were on Lottie and Albie now; a sea of joyous smiles greeted them and a quiver of excitement ran through her body. She saw a couple of her dance troupe friends who gave her the thumbs-up and butterflies began to multiply in her stomach. It was almost time for the surprise for her husband-to-be; she was so nervous she wondered if she should call it off but when the music stopped, and she heard the loud noise of a needle scraping across a record, she knew there was no going back.

Chapter 2

The uplifting beat of Bruno Mars singing 'I think I wanna marry you' resounded around the church and Lottie's bridesmaids began to dance. Two of them approached Albie and danced him up the aisle, much to his confusion and Lottie's relief; she'd decided if she couldn't have her brother giving her away then she'd have her friends instead.

Lottie broke into her dance routine and more of her dance troupe friends joined them to rapturous cheers from the congregation. Two of the guys cartwheeled down the aisle to her and lifted her, whilst others held circular frames to the side of her, two bridesmaids danced like dressage horses at the front and two more guys twirled large white spoked wheels alongside her. The overall effect was as though she were in a carriage; she felt like the leading lady in a Broadway musical. As they neared the end, they mimicked the door opening and another dancer helped her step down, then each member of the troupe twirled her then bowed before moving on.

Lottie's heart sang with joy as she caught sight of Blake and Cami, who were clapping and dancing along with most of the congregation. She was so looking forward to catching up with them properly afterwards.

She turned to face Chad, only to see him and his mother exchange a glance and roll their eyes. Instead of the look of joy she expected to see on his face, she saw anger and possibly embarrassment. The butterflies in her stomach turned into a swarm of angry wasps, the scratched record sound happened again and 'Here comes the bride' resumed from where it had left off. Lottie's heart raced and her breathing felt shallow.

Chad insinuated by jerking his head that she should get a move on. She looked down at the dress, beautiful but not hers, then at the engagement ring on her finger, expensive but bulky and not her at all, not chosen by the man she loved but inherited from his grandmother. As much as she loved the sentiment, she realised that apart from her brother, the only bit of her that she'd brought to this wedding was this dance. Her heart palpated and as the music came to a stop, she almost felt she could hear it beating out of her chest. A wave of nausea washed over her and Rachel's words began swarming around in her head. A little niggle began to intensify in her head; Chad had been using her laptop lately but surely he wouldn't have infiltrated her emails. There must be another explanation – he knew how much she wanted that job. She'd already turned down a job on a cruise ship because he didn't want her to be away for so long, but this job was local and it was perfect.

Chad called her in a loud whisper through clenched teeth. She couldn't move forward, as though a forcefield were stopping her. Her head began to feel woozy, and she took a couple of steps back.

'Are you OK, Charlotte?' asked the priest.

His concerned face swam before her and she worried that she was going to faint.

'Lottie, what are you playing at?' said Chad, his voice gruff.

'I'm sorry, but I'm afraid I don't think I want to marry you!' she said, shaking her head.

Chad's jaw dropped and she thought his eyes were quite literally going to pop out of his head.

'Did you intercept my emails? Did you turn my job offer down?'

The look on his face said it all and her pre-wedding Prosecco almost made a reappearance, as she shook her head.

'Look, we can talk about this later. You don't need a job — it's not like it pays anything worthwhile,' he sneered.

'That may be so, but having that job would have made me feel worthwhile. Winters is one of the most prestigious dance academies around. I can't believe you did that.' The shock was turning to anger and tears stung the backs of her eyes. The angel on her shoulder looked like she was about to say I told you so, but then seemed to think better of it and shouted 'Ruuuun!'

Lottie didn't need telling twice. She shoved her bouquet in Albie's hand, lifted her dress slightly at the front, turned on her heels and ran as fast as a greyhound after a rabbit. She heard loud gasps and people calling her name as she ran. It all seemed like a dream, and she half expected to wake up and for everything to be OK again but there were two things she knew for certain: one, she was not marrying Chad Mills and two, she was never going to humiliate herself by dancing in public again.

Chapter 3

A couple of days later, Lottie got out of the taxi and walked up the path to Cupcake Cottage. She took a deep breath and with a shiver of trepidation, she knocked on the front door.

'Surprise!' said Lottie, doing jazz hands as the door opened.

'Lottie, what are you doing here?' said Camilla as she pulled her into a hug.

'Blake, look who I've just found on the doorstep!' she called.

Blake joined her and welcomed her into the house with a hug and a smile.

'Well, you did say I could visit anytime and after you left to come back here, I just felt like I didn't want to be at home anymore, not for a little while anyway. I mean, I should have been on my honeymoon to Bali, but to be honest, I'd rather be here with you.'

'You can stay as long as you like,' said Camilla. 'Blake, can you put the kettle on and I'll take Lottie upstairs.

'I'm sorry, we've been using it as a storage space until the baby comes but we can clear some things out to make you comfortable,' said Camilla as she opened the door to the spare room. It's such a small house; Blake would like to move somewhere bigger but I love this cottage – I'd rather extend.'

'Oh, it's gorgeous, Camilla, so cosy, and I love the colour you've chosen for the walls too.'

'Thank you – it's called Lemon Delight,' Camilla replied. Lottie took in the single bed, small bedside table, chest of drawers and mirrored wardrobes. Not for the first time, she wondered whether she had done the right thing in coming over. It felt a bit selfish now.

'Here, let me move this.' Camilla picked up the clothes horse and carried it through to her bedroom.

'Where would Madam like her luggage?' said Blake as he entered the room carrying Lottie's suitcases.

'Just next to the bed will be fine, thank you. I'm sorry for being a pain and I promise I won't trouble you for long. I'd like to stay in England a little while so I'll find my own place soon and be out of your hair.'

Blake put his arm around her and kissed the top of her head. 'You might be a pain but that's OK because you're our pain and we love you. Besides, isn't that what little sisters are for?' he joked.

'Come on, Blake, haven't you moved that cot box yet – the poor girl has hardly got room to swing a cat in here.' Camilla stuck her head in the door and winked.

'Yes, come on, Blake, stop shirking,' Lottie added, using a word her mum had said a lot.

'Oh no, I can see I'm going to be completely outnumbered here once you two start picking on me. OK, I'll get on with this if someone else makes the tea.'

'I'm already on it,' said Camilla as she made her way down the stairs. Blake grabbed the box and slid it under the bed. 'There you go, I'll just take these other boxes into our room and you just make yourself at home.'

'Thank you.' She smiled at the familiarity of him, feeling warm and safe from the connection they had to their parents. She could almost hear her mum's voice calling them for dinner. She realised how much she'd missed him since he'd moved in with Camilla. Maybe the wedding fiasco was a blessing in disguise; she'd been stuck in a rut and now she could see she hadn't wanted to get married at all but had been carried along with the arrangements. A fresh new start was just what she needed.

'You're going to be OK you know, kid,' said Blake before leaving the room. She saw a hint of their beloved dad in his eyes, full of kindness and care. It hurt her to wonder what he would have thought of the mess she'd made had he still been around; everyone always said she was the apple of his eye, although she felt rotten to the core at the moment. She tried not to dwell on it too much.

She picked up a soft toy that had fallen on the floor, a little elephant, and stroked it with her thumb. 'So soft,' she whispered. 'You know it's really hit me seeing you and Camilla together here waiting for the baby. Mum and Dad should have been looking forward to their first grandchild being born.'

'I know, life can be very cruel but we make the most of what we've got. I mean he or she is going to have the best auntie in the world and an amazing mum and dad of course.' He put his arm around her shoulder and gave her a squeeze.

'I must admit, the thought of a new niece or nephew is keeping me going. I'm going to give this baby so much love on behalf of myself and our parents.'

'Even when you need to change a diaper?' he asked, screwing up his nose.

'Even the smelly diapers! I could help around the house and babysit,' she smiled as a vision of a chunky little baby sitting on her lap popped into her mind; she loved him or her so much already. I promise you I'll be an auntie to be proud of.'

'Tea and cake's ready,' shouted Camilla from downstairs. Lottie headed out the door and Blake raced her down the stairs just like he used to.

'Still a torment, I see,' she laughed.

'Me the torment?'

'Yes, that's what Dad always called you.'

'Only because he never saw you hounding me and then I'd be the one who got the blame when you ran complaining to him,' he laughed.

Lottie put her thumb on her nose and waggled her fingers at him whilst sticking her tongue out. 'Ooh, this cake looks delicious.'

'I can assure you it tastes even better than it looks,' said Camilla. 'My assistant Angela made it and dropped it in as a welcome back present.'

'It's divine,' said Lottie, tucking in. 'Is that toffee I can taste?'

'Yes, it's a millionaire's cake,' Camilla laughed. 'Chocolate, vanilla and toffee.'

'I wish I could bake like this but I'm no good at it at all.'

'Mum always used to say it was because you're too impatient,' said Blake, 'although I can't see what patience has to do with it.'

'Ah, let me guess, oven door opener by any chance?' Camilla guessed.

'Oh yes,' Lottie replied. 'Every five minutes and they would sink like deflated balloons every time! I still do it now.'

'Never say never! Maybe you could come and help out sometime – I'll pay you, of course. Angela is an amazing baker now, but you should have seen the burnt offerings she brought in for her interview. Luckily, we got on so well I forgot to check them before I gave her the job.'

'Well, I'd be happy to help out where I can, and I wouldn't want paying.'

After a pot of tea and two pieces of cake, Blake offered to show her around the area.

'No, don't worry, I'm sure you've got plenty to be getting on with. I'll pop out myself – I could do with walking that delicious cake off. She gathered her things together and after a quick glance at the map on her phone, she set off. She decided to start as she meant to go on and become the sensible, independent woman that her parents would have wanted her to be.

Chapter 4

After a pleasant walk along paths between rolling fields where the only sounds she could hear were birds singing, Lottie arrived at Bramblewood station; she recognised the historical signal box that had been converted into a café from photographs that Blake had sent her. It was so quaint and unique that for a minute she felt as though she had stepped through the photo into another world, so different to what she was used to. She wished she hadn't eaten so much cake already as she would have loved to go in. She continued up the high street to a bridge with slopes either side leading to the towpath along the river. She stood leaning against the wall of the bridge and admired the view. Ducks, geese and swans swam gracefully below her, leaving ripples in their wake that disturbed the glassiness of the still water and distorted the reflection of the willow trees whose branches skimmed the surface. Colourful narrow boats lined the banks and the towpath buzzed with runners, cyclists and walkers. She pulled out her phone and took some pictures, though this sight would be hard to forget.

As she walked over the bridge she could see more of the high street and at the end, opposite a mini roundabout, stood a clock house that was completely different to any of the surrounding buildings. The clock was wrong, she noticed, checking her watch, but the building looked steeped in history, including what looked like a dovecot or bell tower on top of it and the wall surrounding it. She headed towards it and passed shops and restaurants with bubble windows and beams, a playhouse and a sign for Hummingbird Lane, which was just off the high street. She stopped to take another photograph with the clock house as the main focus and the scene was like something from an old-fashioned Christmas card. She felt like she'd stepped back in time and two words that she'd never had occasion to use before popped into her head. 'Quintessentially British', The road forked just in front of the clock house; she turned left and walked along a path protected by trees which grew either side, high enough to join above, creating an archway of multiple shades of green. A row of thatched cottages and a church soon gave way to more rolling hills and fields with shire horses in one and allotments with mismatched sheds and various rectangles of vegetation in another. When looking down to the bottom of the fields, she realised she was walking parallel to the river, which looked so pretty, and soon came across a dusty road leading further up the hill and followed it. She could feel the burn in her calves and relished the pain in her dancer's legs as the muscles woke up again.

A strange sound broke the silence and she strained to figure out what it was; it sounded like an animal in pain. She eventually came to a gate leading to a thatched farmhouse with a sign saying Bramble Farm on the side of it. The house was surrounded by various outbuildings, the closer she got the louder the noise became and her heart beat rapidly. She closed the rickety gate behind her and ran to the sound, which appeared to be coming from the field. She scanned the area quickly and immediately saw a bit of the fence had come down at the far end so headed in that direction. When she saw what appeared to be two long pointy fluffy grey ears sticking up from the ground, she picked up speed and ran to them. She discovered a muddy ditch just beyond the fence and saw that the ears belonged to a small donkey who let out another loud eeyaw sound as his hooves scraped at the side of the trench, his eyes pleading to her from underneath rather impressive lashes.

'Hello boy, looks like you've managed to get yourself in a bit of a scrape here.' She sat down and reached over to stroke the coarse hair between his ears; the ditch was too deep to help him out straight away so her immediate reaction was to make him comfortable until she could get help. She reached into her bag, pulled out her water bottle and tried to pour it into his mouth, but she struggled as he got agitated and most of it went to the floor. She spotted a rusty bucket at the far end of the field near a manger and a tap. She ran to it and turned the tap, as the bucket filled, she saw a tatty wooden sign nailed to the fence with the word *Denni* burned into it. There were no other animals in the field, so she assumed that was his name.

Once full, she made her way back to him as carefully as she could, though not without sloshing some of the water over her shoes and bashing her shin with the bucket. She hoped there would still be some water left in it. Her heart pounded as he wailed again and when she reached him, she put the bucket down and eased herself into the ditch before grabbing the bucket and putting it next to him. He drank thirstily while she had a good look at him to search for any obvious injuries.

'You're OK now, Denni, don't worry,' she said as she stroked him and patted him gently. She swatted a fly from her cheek before realising her hands were caked in mud from sliding into the ditch, so wiped her face on her shirt and her hands on her jeans.

'Hello?' she heard a man's voice call.

'Hello!' she shouted. 'I'm over here in the ditch.'

She put her hands on the ground and tried to pull herself back out but her feet couldn't get any proper purchase and she slid back down again, leaving Denni looking bewildered.

'Do you need a hand?' the man said, in an accent that sounded Mediterranean though she couldn't pinpoint exactly where. She looked up to see a pair of brown eyes full of mischief, his black hair flopping over his forehead and his smiling mouth revealing beautiful white teeth. She blushed as she realised what a state she looked. He offered her his hand.

'No, it's OK, I'm fine, thank you,' she said, attempting to climb out again. She managed to get the top half of her body out and, after a few attempts to swing her leg out, she was taken aback when he grabbed both of her hands and plucked her from the ditch in one movement. He looked at his hands and brushed off some of the dirt before wiping them on his jeans.

'That takes me back to pulling potatoes up from the farm.' He winked at her and laughed. 'Erm, you've got a little something here.' He gestured to her face, which was now burning with embarrassment. She tried to clean her cheek with her forearm.

'Oh, thank you very much, though I wouldn't be resembling a potato if you had looked after your poor donkey a bit more carefully,' she retorted, trying to ignore how dangerously handsome he was.

His face turned serious.

'Is he OK?' He jumped effortlessly into the ditch and ran his hands over the animal.

'Apart from a few grazes, I think he's fine,' she said, straightening up and brushing herself off. 'But you really need to get that fence fixed, he could have been really hurt.'

He pulled himself out of the ditch with ease and stood in front of her.

'Are you OK? Did you hurt yourself?' he asked.

His thick black lashes and the accent were so distracting she almost didn't answer, but then realised he was still looking at her.

'No, I'm fine, thank you.'

'So, you're not from round here with that accent?'

'I could say the same about you.'

'Touché,' he replied. 'But I must say that if we are going to be saving a donkey together, then surely we should introduce ourselves. What's your name?' he asked.

Oh, here we go, she thought – the last thing she needed was to get involved with this devilishly handsome man and OK, it might seem innocent enough, he'd only asked for her name after all, but she recognised the look in his eyes, and she was far too much of a sucker for a good-looking man, which is how she ended up where she did with Chad.

'I don't really think introductions are necessary – the only thing that matters is Denni's safety.' She maintained her haughty manner in an attempt to distance herself from him.

'I'm only asking for your name, not your hand in marriage,' he said, laughing. 'I know what it is. You have one of those ridiculous names like Esmerelda or how you say Ermintrude, is that what it is?'

She laughed at his attempt to pronounce both those names.

'OK, you win, it's erm, Minnie.'

'Ah, I get it,' he said, 'beautiful and funny. In that case, Minnie, my name is Mickey, I'm pleased to meet you.' He shook her hand then wiped his on his jeans again.

'How are you going to get him out?'

He shook his head. 'I've no idea. Let's go and see if there's anyone in the house.'

'I saw your Land Rover on the way in – maybe you could just use that with some rope. Or maybe you have some other suggestions.'

'Yes, we could certainly try that,' he replied and began heading towards the cottage.

'Don't worry, Denni, you'll be out of there soon,' she said, allowing him to nuzzle her hand. His ears twitched and he eeyawed again.

She caught up with the man and was surprised to find him knocking on the door. 'Oh, did you forget your key?' she asked.

'Something like that,' he replied before pressing his face against the window.

'Oh no,' he said and banged on the window. 'Hello!' he shouted before following with 'Oh *merda.*'

'What is it?' asked Lottie, picking up on his urgency. She ran round to the back door and looked in the window; her heart leapt when she saw an old lady lying on the floor.

'Oh no,' she spluttered before following him to the back door.

'Luckily it was open,' he called from inside the house. 'Call 999.'

Lottie pulled out her phone and dialled the number.

'Ambulance please,' she replied to the operator as she entered the room. 'Yes, we've just found an old lady lying unconscious on the floor of her home.' She turned away from the phone. 'Is she breathing?' she asked.

'Yes, thank God,' he replied. He reached to the couch for a crocheted blanket to cover the old lady up when she opened her eyes and tried to sit up.

'Of course, I'm still breathing,' she said. 'Who the bloody hell are you and what are you doing in my house?'

'I think you've had a fall,' said Lottie, 'and it looks like you've hurt your leg. I'm just going to make you a cup of tea.' She went into the kitchen and found a letter with the address on which she read out to the operator before saying goodbye.

She brought the cup of tea to the old lady who was called Doris, judging by the letters and a plaque on the wall saying Doris's Kitchen. Mickey had carefully picked her up and laid her on the couch with plenty of cushions behind her to prop her up.

'I'm just going to step outside to make a few calls and see if we can get Denni out of his little spot of bother and I'll see if I can fix that fence too whilst I'm waiting,' said Mickey waving his phone at her.

'What's happened to Denni?' Doris frowned. 'Oh wait, I remember now, his fence was damaged in the storm we had yesterday and he managed to get out and fell in the ditch. I came running in to ring for help and slipped. I was in some pain but I can't really feel it now.' She moved to get off the couch but winced, her face screwed up in pain. Lottie gently touched her arm.

'Don't worry about Denni, he'll be fine, but I think you should stay here for now, just until the paramedics have checked you out.' She passed her a plate of biscuits that were on the table.

'Here, your boyfriend's a bit of a looker, isn't he? I thought I'd died and gone to heaven when I opened my eyes and saw that gorgeous face,' said Doris between mouthfuls of KitKat.

'Oh no, he's not my boyfriend, I thought perhaps he was your grandson,' Lottie replied, feeling her cheeks burn again. She could see him outside the window talking animatedly into his phone and brushing his hand through his silky black hair.

'Oh no, dear, I never had any children.' She shivered and Lottie reached for another blanket for her and placed the tea in her hands.

Doris seemed to be with it but after having a knock to the head Lottie wasn't sure if the poor old lady had concussion or whether she really had no clue who Mickey was, and if that was the case, she had some apologising to do after blaming him for neglecting Denni. She bit her lip; it was kind of him not to mention her mistake.

'Is there anyone we can call to let them know what's happened?'

'No, I'm fine, I'm perfectly self-sufficient, thank you, dear, and I'll soon be up and running again. I've never relied on anyone in my life and I'm not going to start now.'

'OK well, I'll just stay with you until the ambulance comes,' she said.

'I hate hospitals, you only ever go in them to die.'

'No, you don't, you'll be in safe hands,' Lottie said reassuringly.

'Well, my mum went in and died, same with my dad. And old Malcolm, who used to help me out on the farm. Went into hospital, next I heard he was dead,' said Doris, bursting into tears.

'I'm really sorry to hear that, Doris, but you're going to be fine, I promise you. I know lots of people who've been into hospital and they've been fine.' She tugged a couple of tissues out of a box on the table and handed them to Doris.

When they heard the siren approaching, Lottie stood up and watched as Mickey moved a bike that hadn't been there earlier away from the gate so he could open it for the ambulance. She opened the door for the paramedics and sat back down near to Doris.

'You will come with me, won't you, dear?' Her red-rimmed eyes pleaded.

It broke Lottie's heart to see the fear in her eyes despite proclamations of self-sufficiency and she didn't have the heart to tell her that the same thing happened to her parents – they went into hospital and never came home again.

'Of course I will,' said Lottie.

As the paramedics wheeled her to the ambulance on the trolley, she never let go of Lottie's hand as she walked beside her.

Mickey waved a man driving a tractor through the gate. 'Don't you worry about anything, Doris, we'll have Denni sorted in no time, he's been fed and watered so you've nothing to worry about.' He winked at Lottie and she smiled, feeling mortified that she'd blamed him for Denni's misfortune, yet he seemed like a great guy.

Chapter 5

'I'm afraid that as you live alone, we can't let you go home without someone to look after you,' said the doctor as he studied Doris's X-rays.

'But . . .' said Doris.

'No buts, I'm afraid,' said the doctor. 'Due to your age, this is going to take a little while to heal.'

'But this is my granddaughter Lottie – she's come all the way from Canada to look after me,' said Doris.

Lottie looked from one to the other and noticed Doris pleading with her, her rheumy eyes filled with tears. 'But, but I've got no nursing experience,' she muttered. 'I mean, I did work in a care home for a while back in Canada but—'

'Oh, you won't need nursing experience as the nurses will pop in regularly and see to that sort of thing,' said the doctor. 'Just a bit of TLC is all that's needed.'

'That's settled then, and I'll pay you to be my live-in carer,' added Doris and gave Lottie a huge wink. 'You were saying in the ambulance that you were looking for somewhere to stay so why not move in with me? I've been ever so lonely since Malcolm passed.'

Lottie tried to think of an excuse as to why she couldn't do it and couldn't really come up with one. She could move out and wouldn't be such a burden on Blake and Camilla. It seemed like the answer to all of her problems and the best thing about it would be that she could see Denni whenever she wanted to and to top it all off, she would show Blake that she could be responsible. Even as a grown woman, she hated to think that he was disappointed in her.

'OK Doris, as it's such a squeeze at my brother's house with his new baby coming, I'll move in with you as your lodger for a little while. I'll happily look after you but you are not paying me and we tell the doctor the truth – that I'm not your granddaughter, I'm your lodger. How does that sound?'

Lottie almost burst into tears at the look of gratitude on Doris's wrinkled little face.

'That would be absolutely perfect, my dear,' she whispered.

Once the taxi dropped them off at the cottage, Doris clapped her hands on seeing Denni looking much happier in his field with the fence all mended. 'Oh, you've got a good man there, you know. I must pay him for his work.'

'He's not my man, Doris, but yes, it was very good of him to sort everything out here for you.'

'You've got to admit, he's bloody gorgeous though, isn't he?'

'He's not bad, I suppose,' she replied as she felt a warm glow spread across her cheeks.

Lottie got Doris comfortable on the couch with a bowl of soup, a cuppa and a sandwich. 'Are you not having one?' she asked Lottie.

'No, I'll grab myself something later in town.' She hoped Doris couldn't hear her stomach rumbling.

'Oh no, all your meals are included — I insist. You must help yourself to anything in the cupboards.'

'That's very kind of you. OK, I'll join you for a quick sandwich then I'm going to get a taxi to pick up some of this equipment that the doctor recommended and I'll get some shopping in too,' said Lottie.

'Oh, I don't need any of that — it's only a fracture. I'm sure I can hop around OK without a wheelchair. In a few days I'll be as right as rain,' said Doris.

'The wheelchair isn't for you — it's for me,' said Lottie. 'I don't want us to be cooped up indoors all the time so this way we can go for walks, you can get a bit of sun on your face and I can get some exercise.'

'I might get a bit tired pushing you around, but I'll give it a go.' Doris smiled at her.

Lottie laughed, she could tell already that she and Doris shared a sense of humour. 'There's also some other useful things, like a stool for the shower and a special toilet fitting, which will help with privacy and comfort.'

'OK, but you're not getting a taxi — you can use Petal. Just pass me that phone a minute and let me have your driving licence details.'

Lottie handed her the green Bakelite phone and checked her phone for the licence details she'd stored on there. 'Who or what is Petal?' she asked.

'My vintage Land Rover. Well, I can't use her so you might as well. You go and make yourself a quick sandwich while I sort out the insurance details.'

Lottie felt as though she could have had a whole phone conversation, in the time it took for the first number to go round on the dial of the old phone, so she made herself a quick cheese and tomato sandwich from the crusty homemade loaf. She washed it down with a coffee just as Doris came off the phone.

'OK, you're all sorted for driving Petal now – the keys are in the hall.'

'OK, do you need anything before I go?'

'Just that blanket, dear,' she yawned. 'I might just have a little nap.'

Lottie placed a cushion under her head and covered her with the blanket; she wrote her phone number on a scrap of paper and put it on the arm of the couch. She found the keys hanging up in the small square hall and noticed a piece of paper crumpled in the letter box. She pulled it out and saw it was a folded piece of lined paper with Minnie written on it.

As she unfolded the scrawled note, she couldn't help smiling.

Hi Minnie,

Denni is fine, we got him checked over by a vet and the fence is all fixed. Hope Doris is OK.

Give me a ring sometime.

Mickey x

★

She looked at his number and her stomach flipped. Oh, how easy it would be to have a fling with a handsome guy, but she'd had her fingers burnt and was still untangling herself from the mess she'd made with Chad. In the long run, complications always set in and her life was complicated enough. Hiding away and looking after Doris would be the best thing for everybody; she didn't want to be a hindrance and wanted a chance to prove that she was a responsible adult. Although seriously tempted, she wouldn't be ringing him.

Chapter 6

Not having driven for ages, as Chad had always done most of the driving in their relationship and that was mostly speedboats and jet skis, it took a little while to get used to driving Petal. Being a Land Rover, the body seemed to wobble a bit, especially when going round corners, which made her feel a bit queasy at first but she soon got used to it and imagined she was the TV detective Vera, driving round in a beaten-up jeep and solving murders.

It didn't take long to pick up the things she needed to help Doris and she used the sat nav on her phone to find her way back to Blake's. She'd texted them from the hospital to explain the situation and asked Blake to bring her bags downstairs so she could pick them up. She arrived at Cupcake Cottage and they both came to the door to greet her. 'Was it something I said?' asked Blake jovially.

'Of course not, I just wanted to do something good for someone and I could do with having my own space and giving you yours. I think I'll enjoy it – Doris is a real livewire.'

'Well, by the sound of it, she's very lucky you turned up when you did. I dread to think what would have happened to her,' said Camilla.

'I'm sure she would have been fine as someone else turned up not long after me,' said Lottie, not wanting to take all the credit. 'But yes, it's a good job we did as the doctors thought she must have been lying there for hours.'

'Well, I think you saved her life so you have hero status as far as I'm concerned,' said Camilla, giving her a hug. 'Make sure you still visit us lots − I was so looking forward to spending time with you here.'

'Me too,' said Blake. 'Right, that's the cases loaded in the car. Make sure you text us the address so we can find you if we need you.' He cuddled her. 'I'm proud of you, sis.'

'Will do and thanks to both of you.' It warmed her heart to hear him say that, as she often thought his opinion reflected what their parents would have thought had they still been around.

She jumped up into Petal and waved to them both as she drove off.

Chapter 7

The next few days were spent in a whirl, finding her way around and working out what her new responsibilities were. The spare room was huge and had everything Lottie could need in it: a double bed covered with a floral quilted eiderdown, honey-coloured wardrobes and a dressing table with an old-fashioned arched mirror above it. Lace doilies protected the shiny wood from ornaments of farmyard animals. She was overjoyed when she looked out of the window to see Denni chomping on his fresh straw.

Although the bed appeared a bit lumpy at first, Lottie was astonished at how comfortable it was and she slept well in it. Her other life seemed like a million miles away now. She realised she could be anyone she wanted to be and totally reinvent herself if she wished.

She quickly found that Doris was a very selfless woman who wouldn't accept her breakfast until she knew that her animals had been fed, so Lottie's first job in the morning was to feed and water Denni and the chickens, aka the Beatles. Lottie had laughed when Doris explained that she loved the Beatles but her dad would never let her play the music in the house or name any of the animals after them, so years after he died, when she was given four chickens, she named them John, Paul, George and Ringo.

'You gave them boys' names,' laughed Lottie.

'Well, yes, I couldn't get cockerels as they don't lay eggs!'

Lottie loved checking for eggs in the henhouse, which she collected in a little basket and cooked for herself and Doris. There was nothing like dippy egg with soldiers to start the day well according to Doris, and as Lottie dipped the toast, dripping with butter, into the orangey yolks, she had to agree.

Lottie had organised Doris's medication into a pill box and set alarms on her phone to remind her which pills Doris should take and when. Although Doris had originally said she didn't want to go in the wheelchair, she soon got used to it and relished the freedom it gave her.

She was able to sit at the kitchen table and shout instructions to Lottie as to how to make bread, with helpful phrases such as 'give it some more welly' and 'pretend it's someone you hate and punch it'.

When Lottie tasted the bread, infused with hand-picked rosemary from the herb garden, which she had made with her own fair hands, she served it up to Doris absolutely bursting with pride. Thinking of Chad and his mother had helped the kneading process along very nicely and released a lot of her pent-up frustration and anger.

The cottage smelt delicious as the fresh bread smell mingled with a casserole in a crockpot in the oven. Lottie sat side by side with Doris and together they'd peeled potatoes and vegetables from the garden and cubed the meat taken from the freezer the day before. Lottie remembered her mum trying to get her to show an interest in cooking but to no avail as Lottie preferred to practise her dancing. Looking back, she realised what wonderful memories she could have had and how bonding it was to prepare a meal together. Doris asked Lottie to save some of the cubed carrot for Denni and explained that cubes were better than rounds for donkeys because of choking hazards. Doris had the carrots in a bowl on her lap and Lottie pushed the wheelchair out to the fence and took some carrot from the bowl. She reached her hand out to Denni and jumped back at first, almost dropping the carrot as his strong lips nibbled on her hand.

'There, that's a lovely treat isn't it, Denni,' said Doris.

'What other treats can they have?' asked Lottie as she tickled Denni between the ears and stroked his soft muzzle.

'He can have swede, turnips, bananas with the skin on, chopped or grated apple, but he should never have potatoes or sprouts, broccoli or cauliflower as they're bad for him.' She stopped talking to scoot away a chicken. 'Once when he wasn't well, the only way I could get him to take his medicine was on a jam sandwich.'

Lottie laughed.

'Anyway, young lady, I've decided to give you the day off tomorrow as I'm not having you looking after me seven days a week – I've arranged for a home help to come in to give you a break.'

Lottie was a little taken aback; she'd been so absorbed in the farm and enjoying Doris's company that it hadn't felt like work at all.

'That way you can have a lie-in and go exploring and, I don't know, go on a date with your handsome man, so you don't end up an old spinster like me,' she chuckled.

Lottie would love to have probed Doris about her life but didn't want to be intrusive or seem nosy.

'Are you sure, Doris, because I really don't mind.'

'I'm positive, my dear. She's arriving at six in the morning so you can turn your alarm off. You deserve a rest as you've been working non-stop.'

Lottie relished the opportunity of doing a bit more sightseeing; Doris hadn't yet wanted to venture out very far and she still hadn't explored everything Bramblewood had to offer. The next morning her alarm went off as usual as she didn't want to sleep in, just in case the helper didn't turn up but once she heard her voice, she knew Doris was safe and she managed to roll over and go back to sleep for another couple of hours.

Once awake, she helped herself to tea and toast and took it outside to eat on a bench overlooking Denni's field. Denni approached her and she stood on the fence to nuzzle her face against his; he fluttered his huge eyelashes at her and his ears twitched as she tickled him in his favourite spot. He'd certainly wormed his way into her heart as had Doris, Lottie realised; she could get used to this slower but much more rewarding pace of life.

Feeling the need for some exercise, she decided to walk into town and then along the river. She waved to Doris and the helper and made her way through the rickety gate. After about half an hour she reached the clock house and knew she needed to turn right into the high street. As she got to the playhouse, she saw a couple of young women mid-conversation and handing out flyers.

'He's so arrogant though and he loves himself,' said the first girl.

'I don't care, he's just so dreamy I could look at him all day. I almost don't want to hand these flyers out so I can increase my chance at the audition.'

Lottie's ears pricked up at the word audition and she waved her hand to decline the leaflet. A queue had formed by a serving hatch called The Posh Pannier; she joined it and had a look at the menu. When it was her turn, she bought a prawn and mango salad wrap, a sweet potato chocolate brownie and a coffee. Her mouth was already watering just at the thought of it. The food came in a cute little paper bag that she carried in one hand, the coffee in the other. She crossed the bridge to the slope and made her way down to the river, walking past a pub garden with benches outside.

She walked along the towpath waving to passengers on narrowboats as they cruised through the water and marvelled at a group of colourful kayakers gliding along together. She passed houses and apartments with wonderful views and kept going until there was only greenery to keep her company and the odd rabbit hopping away from her. She stopped for a rest at a wooden bench and decided it was the perfect place for her picnic lunch. Across the river between the trees, she caught a glimpse of a marina which reminded her of Chad, but she quickly pushed the memory of him away again. He didn't belong here.

She devoured the wrap followed by the delicious coffee and brownie. The view was hypnotising, and she felt more relaxed than she could ever remember feeling. She was about to put the rubbish in the bag when she noticed something colourful inside. She pulled it out and found one of the flyers from the playhouse had been put in there anyway. She threw the waste in a bin next to the bench and unfolded it.

She skim-read the leaflet and saw that auditions were opening up for a dance competition called *Truly Dance*. The local competition was to find a partner for someone called Marco Abruzzo, a local actor currently working on a film called *Latino*. The winner would go on to compete with other celebrities in London. Lottie had missed her regular dance classes but the humiliation of the wedding dance still hung over her. She crumpled up the leaflet and stuffed it in her pocket. As far as she was concerned, the only dancing she would do in future would be in the privacy of her own home.

However, she was in a private spot here and her legs were itching to move as the advert had put salsa music in her head. She scrolled her phone to find her favourite tunes, her heart fluttering as she jumped up and began dancing, kicking dust up on the ground as she moved faster to the rhythm. She turned the music up and felt it reach every cell in her body. She spun her head round, her thick black hair whipped around her shoulders, and her legs and arms moved in perfect co-ordination. After her almost-wedding, she swore she'd never dance again but she knew deep down that she'd never be able to resist swaying her hips to the samba beat.

'Wow, that was impressive.' A man's voice cut through her concentration.

She stopped mid-step and almost toppled over as she wondered where the voice had come from as there was no one else on the towpath.

'Is that you, Minnie?' he asked.

She couldn't quite believe her eyes as she saw the man who had already had to rescue her out of a ditch now balanced on a paddleboard in the middle of the river looking at her as though she were an apparition in the desert.

'Mickey, what are you doing here?' she replied, her face hot enough to light a candle, with having been caught in the act.

He shrugged his shoulders gesturing to the paddle and the board.

'Erm, would you believe me if I said I was riding a bicycle?'

For some reason this tickled her and she laughed so hard she had to sit down. He laughed too and eased the paddle through the water, steering the board towards her.

'How's Doris doing?' he asked. 'Did you get my note?'

'She's fine, thanks, has to take it easy for a few weeks but she'll be OK. Sorry yes, I did, I meant to text you to let you know but you know . . .' She shrugged, not really wanting to tell him that she saw him as a potential danger to her heart.

'Has she got someone to look after her? I got the impression she lived alone.'

'Yes, she has, she's got me – she only went and told the doctor that I was her granddaughter so they would release her from hospital.'

'Ha, I expect she had him wrapped around her finger.'

'What makes you think the doctor was a him?'

'Of course, how sexist of me, then I expect she had *her* wrapped around her little finger.'

'Well actually the doctor was a he so I'll let you off just this once and yes, I think Doris is a real charmer. She was hoping to pay you back for the fence and what she owes you for the vet. She was so grateful for everything you did.'

'She doesn't have to do that; the tractor driver was a friend of my cousin and he hoisted Denni out of the ditch and helped me fix the fence. The vet just charged a call-out fee. It was my pleasure but if you want to thank me, then maybe we could go out for dinner some time?'

'What, so you want Doris to pimp me out to thank you for saving her donkey?' she laughed and so did he.

'Hmm, I realise it does sound bad when you put it like that. Don't worry, I can take a hint. How is my friend Denni anyway?'

'He's really good, I get to see him a lot now I'm living on the farm and I think I've fallen in love with him.'

'Then Denni is a very lucky Asino.'

Lottie rolled her eyes and tutted.

He laughed, 'So I couldn't help noticing you dancing earlier – do you always dance in the wild?'

'As a matter of fact, I have danced in the wild a number of times with my dance group back in Canada. We regularly do flash mobs – we quite often do shopping malls or zoos for wedding proposals or special birthdays.'

'That's amazing – have you ever done a wedding?'

Lottie's stomach twisted. 'Er yes, I have actually, but the last one didn't go down too well.'

'Why, what happened?'

'That's a long story for another time maybe.'

'OK, well did you know that paddleboarding is really good for dancers?'

'Erm no, in what way?' she asked sceptically.

'It's good for balance, you know for your core. Come, jump on and I will show you.'

The good angel on Lottie's left shoulder whispered in her ear to end the conversation now and go home but the little devil on the right spoke up for her insatiable sense of adventure.

'I can't get on there – I'll fall off,' she said, though she was very tempted.

'You won't, I promise you. Here, I'll help you.' He held out his hand to her and Lottie brushed away the little angel and reached her hand to his.

'Hold on, I'll get on my knees first just to balance the board.'

'Oh really, Mickey, you don't have to beg me.' She laughed and squealed as the board jiggled when she put her foot on it. She looked into his eyes as she concentrated on getting her other foot in place and couldn't help noticing a cheeky sparkle in them. After a wobble, she balanced perfectly, and he carefully rose up onto his feet. The board almost tipped sideways, and she squealed again, grabbing hold of his jacket.

'It's OK,' he said, 'I've got you. Don't worry, this is a two-person board – you'll be fine. Now I think you should try and face the other way – I know I'm good-looking but I don't think you want to travel backwards, do you?'

She flushed as she couldn't deny his looks were getting the better of her; maybe she should turn round.

With a little help, she manoeuvred herself round to face the front and he gave her the extra paddle. 'That's it, just do it gently and there you go, we're on our way.'

'Yes!' she shrieked as they glided through the water. 'This is amazing!'

'Do you want to try your dance steps now?' he joked.

'No way,' she laughed. 'I imagine I'd get a good soaking if I tried that. Talking of dancing, have you heard of a thing called *Truly Dance*?'

'Yes, I have actually, in fact . . .'

'Aaargh,' she screamed as she almost lost her balance, electricity rippling through her body as he steadied her with his hands on her waist, letting go as soon as

43

she got her balance. 'Oh, where was I? Oh yes, *Truly Dance*, they were giving out leaflets at the playhouse, some guy called Marco is in it. He's meant to be some famous actor, but I've never heard of him.'

'He's obviously not that famous then,' he replied.

'One of the girls said he loves himself,' she replied.

'He sounds like an ass,' he said. 'You should do it though – it sounds like fun.'

'Who, me? No way. I'm finished with dancing and besides, I'm much too busy now looking after Doris.' She stopped paddling and pulled her phone out of her bag. 'This scenery is just gorgeous – say cheese,' she said, eager to change the subject, taking a selfie with him in the background. Her stomach flipped at how wickedly handsome he was, especially when he smiled.

'I love your accent. Whereabouts in America are you from?'

'Canada.' She laughed

'How long have you been over here?' he asked as they whipped through the water at a steady pace.

'Believe it or not, I'd not long landed when I met you.'

'What, you landed straight into that ditch?' he laughed.

'Pretty much, yes – I'd only been in the country a matter of hours when you found me.'

'When I found you covered in dirt like a potato,' he laughed again. 'What brought you to England?'

'Oh, you know how it is, I got to a stage in my life where something needed to change. It had all come to a head and my brother suggested I come and stay with him and his fiancée in Bramblewood. I said no at first and then I thought, why not?' she shrugged. 'Then I met the man of my dreams in a ditch so now I can never leave.'

'I have that effect on most people,' he teased. 'Oh wait, you're talking about Denni, aren't you?'

'Of course, he's the love of my life,' she chuckled.

'He is irresistible, but Minnie, you have broken my heart.'

'So where are you from then and what brings you to Bramblewood?'

'I'm from a little place in Italy called Ventimiglia and I have family here, my cousins, Gabe, Holly and Franco. I came to visit years ago and forgot to go home.'

'It's a beautiful place and I can understand why you wouldn't want to leave.'

'Does that mean you intend to stay here too?' he asked.

'Hmm, I haven't really planned ahead that much but I think a couple of months should do me. Just before I left, I applied for my dream job in Canada but unfortunately there was a misunderstanding which I've explained to them. If that job came up again, I would go back in a heartbeat but jobs there are very few and far between.'

'And what is your dream job?'

'Dance teacher, it's what I trained for and maybe one day in my wildest dreams I could open my own dance school, but lately I've been doing ad hoc dance jobs. Before my dream job came up, I had a brilliant opportunity to dance on a cruise ship but well, I blew it.'

'Oh no, what happened?' A large ripple rocked the board and he steadied it.

'My fiancé at the time didn't want me to go. So stupidly, I turned it down. Apart from my almost-wedding, it's one of the dumbest decisions I've ever made.' She realised she was opening up to him because he was behind her and it felt easier to talk.

'I'm sorry to hear about that and the almost-wedding that I'm assuming didn't go to plan. Do you want to talk about it?'

'That's kind of you, but it all seems a bit ridiculous now and I'm sure you don't want to be bored with the details of my failed and embarrassing love life.'

'I'm a good listener and a bit of a failure in that department myself.' He bent his knees to steady them again, Lottie yelping as a ripple rocked the paddleboard.

'You're very sweet,' she replied. 'Oh no, what's your story?'

'Well, I'm afraid that will have to wait for another time because look . . .' His arm came from behind her and he pointed ahead.

'Oh wow, it's the bridge to the high street – that was such a quick journey.'

'Yes, if we aim to the left now, we can climb out here and I'm parked in the pub car park. Do you want a lift back?'

'No thanks, I'll be fine, but thank you so much for the ride – it was a wonderful experience.'

She carefully stepped up onto the mooring after taking his proffered hand. He kissed hers gently, which sent shockwaves right through her. 'I thought so too,' he said. 'Bye Minnie.'

'Actually, my name is . . .' she said, turning round, only to see him swallowed up by a group of friends who were helping him pull the paddleboard out of the water. He hadn't heard her, so Lottie crossed the bridge and headed back to the farmhouse.

Chapter 8

Lottie walked into the house and was greeted by the warm smell of cinnamon in the air. The home help had dug out the slow cooker from the back of the larder so that Doris could prepare a melt-in-the-mouth moussaka and she had thrown some Charlotte potatoes in the oven, which had roasted to a perfect crisp.

Doris asked Lottie to grab a bottle of wine from the rack in the utility room. 'Is this homemade?' she asked after seeing the blackberry label with 'Bramble Wine' written on it in marker pen.

'Oh yes,' said Doris, 'that'll put hairs on your chest as my dad always used to say, though why that was considered tempting, I don't know,' she chuckled. 'It'll knock you to sleep though and give you sweet dreams, I can promise you that.'

Lottie pulled down two glasses from the dresser, opened the bottle and poured the blackberry wine, then stopped to inhale the rich, full-bodied smell. 'The colour is gorgeous, and it smells divine,' she said.

'It's my own secret recipe and now that I've finished my antibiotics, I'm going to bloody well enjoy it. At least I can't get drunk and fall over, seeing as I can't stand up yet anyway.'

'Cheers,' said Lottie as she clinked glasses with the older lady. She was pleasantly surprised as the burgundy liquid slid smoothly down her throat and warmed her up from within. She smacked her lips together and lifted the glass up to the light. 'Wow, that is amazing. Delicious, with a kick like a mule.'

'Or even a donkey,' added Doris, taking another swig. 'Here's to our gorgeous Denni, who brought you into my life,' said Doris.

'To Denni, and to the lovely Doris, I'm sorry you had to be in pain but I'm so glad to have met you.' Lottie raised her glass.

'You too, my love,' said Doris. 'And cheers to Mickey too for helping Denni and fixing his fence.'

'Cheers to Mickey,' added Lottie, a warm feeling sweeping over her and this time it wasn't the wine. She picked up her fork and began to tuck into the food.

'I saw Mickey today actually and he gave me a ride on his paddleboard.'

Doris stared at her, frowning. 'Is that a euphemism?'

Lottie's eyes opened wide and she nearly choked on her moussaka. 'No,' she laughed. 'It really was on his paddleboard. Here, look, I took a picture.' She put down her knife and fork, found the photo and handed it to Doris.

'Ooh, let me have a closer look.' She grabbed her glasses, which dangled from a chain around her neck and put them on. 'Ah I see, so it looks like a surfboard and wow, just look at him.' She took her glasses off and held the phone about an inch away from her squinted eyes, 'What is it you young people say these days? Hot, isn't it? Well, he's volcanic hot like lava!'

'Oi, behave yourself, Doris, before you blow a gasket,' Lottie laughed. 'You're meant to be looking at the paddleboard, not the paddleboarder.'

'Spoilsport, 'Doris replied with a twinkle in her eye. 'So how does it move then?'

'Can you see that stick? Well it's called a paddle, which is just like an oar. It was so serene paddling along the river like that, I really enjoyed it. He said the balancing would help with my dancing.'

'Oh, you like dancing, do you?'

'I love it, or should I say I loved it. It was the one thing I knew Mum and Dad were always proud of me for. I wasn't so good at schoolwork; well, I mean I probably could have done better if I'd tried, but it didn't really interest me, whereas with dance I could have filled the house with my dance trophies I had so many. I was only young when I lost my parents, still a teenager.'

'Oh, I'm so sorry to hear that, darling,' said Doris, squeezing her hand. 'That must have been awful for you.'

'Yes, it was really. I had my older brother, but he couldn't really cope with me.' She looked down, unable to make eye contact with Doris. 'I went off the rails a bit, but he stuck with me and steered me back into dancing. He encouraged me to go to a dance school and I graduated with honours. When I danced, I could escape it all and just enter other worlds, be totally absorbed in the character, and focus all my energy into it. I applied for a job as a dancer on a cruise ship not so long ago but my ex, Chad, didn't want me to take it so I turned them down. I regret that now.'

'Well, if you had got it, you wouldn't have come here and we wouldn't have met. In fact, I might still be lying on the floor,' said Doris.

'No, you wouldn't because Mickey wasn't far behind me.'

'You know, I always wanted to learn how to dance but when I was younger, I was obviously smaller than I am now, but still quite stout, and my mum always told me I was the wrong shape for ballet. My dad used to call me his little dumpling and said I was more suited to rugby than dance. I did manage to get to a dance school once but I felt so out of place with the perfectly petite little dancers that I just burst out crying and never went back. My mum just filled me up with homemade chicken and vegetable pie and jam roly-poly and custard to make me feel better.'

'That does sound delicious, I have to admit,' said Lottie. 'But I'm sure it didn't help with your distress.'

'If I had a bucket list, which I don't by the way, then learning to dance would be on it.'

'That's no problem – I can teach you,' said Lottie, jumping up and pirouetting around the room.'

'Oh, I'm far too old for all that business,' said Doris, waving her hand dismissively.

'You're never too old for anything! Look, we can even get started right now with you in the wheel-chair – it will be really good exercise for you even just doing the arm movements. Come on, just give it a go.'

Doris just about managed to put the last forkful of food in her mouth before Lottie gestured to the handles of the wheelchair.

'May I?' she asked, and following a nod from Doris, she wheeled her chair into the middle of the room.

'OK, so I'll do the full movement and you just do the arms. Are you ready?'

'As I'll ever be,' said Doris.

Lottie watched her face light up as she attempted the movements, then she got mixed up.

'Oh, I just feel silly now,' she said.

'You shouldn't feel silly – you're doing great, Doris, and it will do your heart good to get that blood pumping round your body.'

'I'll go slower – let's try again.'

Lottie's heart lifted at seeing Doris's smile when she managed to get it right as they continued to practice.

'You're a beautiful dancer, Lottie – you should see if there's anywhere round here you could put your talent to good use.'

'Ah, thank you, Doris, that's really kind of you to say. Funnily enough, I saw a flyer today for auditions for a dance show at the local playhouse.'

'Well, that sounds perfect – you should definitely do that.'

'Oh, I don't know . . . I'd need to really brush up on my ballroom etc. and I'd need a space to do that; besides, after being quite humiliated, I don't think I can ever face dancing in public again.'

Doris looked thoughtful and strummed her fingers on her lap. 'OK, well, if it's space you want then I've got something to show you. Can you give me a push please? Oh, and grab a torch from the kitchen drawer.'

Intrigued, Lottie found the torch and took hold of the handles of Doris's wheelchair.

'You just lead the way,' she said.

Doris directed her towards the smaller of the two barns. Lottie unlocked the heavy bolt and opened the door wide. There's a light switch just on your right there,' she said.

Lottie flicked the switch.

'Oh, wow, now this is not what I was expecting.' Lottie scanned the room, expecting it to be rustic, but the floor was covered in lino and it looked like living room furniture underneath dust sheets. Along the far wall stood old furniture and pieces of farm machinery. A window to the right was boarded up and a wet bar at the far end had a sink, cooker and a fridge with a breakfast bar separating it from the rest of the room.

'What is this place?' Lottie asked.

'This was where I lived when I was younger. I wanted to do so many things, travel the world, get a job in an office in London like my friends were doing, but I was always needed on the farm. I sulked a lot, as you do when you're younger. Then one day my dad surprised me with this conversion; he said I could have my independence and play my loud music but still help out where I was needed. I loved it in here. My friends could come round, and I even sneaked in the odd boyfriend now and then.' Doris's eyes sparkled as she appeared to get lost in her memories. 'Oh yes,' she sighed. 'I had a great time in here – it was all self-sufficient, you see.'

Lottie pushed Doris further inside and walked towards a wooden staircase. 'May I?' she asked, pointing upwards.

'Yes, of course – that was the old hayloft, which eventually became my bedroom, it was really cosy. Dad did a full conversion for me with radiators and plumbing and everything. When Malcolm worked here; he updated the wiring and I used to hold our women's group meetings here.'

Lottie loved the bedroom area, which had a little window overlooking the farm. It was empty apart from a chest of drawers – she could see the mattress and bed leaning up against the wall downstairs.

'Were you close to Malcolm?' she asked.

Doris gave a furtive glance around the barn before answering, 'Yes, we were lovers.' She whispered the last word loudly.

Lottie nearly choked on her own saliva – she certainly wasn't expecting that.

'You're full of surprises you are, Doris.'

Doris giggled in response.

Lottie came back downstairs and squeezed the older lady's hand.

'I'm so sorry, Doris, you must really miss him.'

'He was wonderful company but there's no point in crying over spilt milk.'

'I think losing the love of your life is a lot worse than spilt milk, Doris.'

'Oh, he wasn't the love of my life, but I did love him.' Lottie's eyes opened wide.

'Don't you have your women's group meetings anymore?' It had occurred to Lottie that Doris hadn't had any visitors since she had been there and she hadn't gone out either, apart from visiting a small local farm shop for supplies.

'No, that all stopped a long time ago, after Malcolm died. I didn't really want to see anyone and my old friends eventually gave up inviting me places.'

'That's such a shame. Don't you hear from them at all?'

'Not really. Well, I do get the regular hand-crafted Christmas card and I presume the women's group still goes ahead because the card is signed from all at the Bramblewood Women's Group.'

'Well, why don't you go back to it? It will do you good to get out and about again.'

'Oh no, dear, I'm quite happy staying here with the animals and with you.'

'Well, I won't be here forever, Doris – I need to go back to Canada one day.'

'Oh, must you?'

'I'm afraid so, but it will make me feel so much better knowing that you have your friends around you. Why don't you let me contact them and I'll go with you?'

'Would you really?'

'Yes, of course I will, it will be my pleasure.'

They went back downstairs, and as Doris looked around the large room and smiled, Lottie imagined she could see her friends there and hear the chatter as memories came back to her.

'I'll think about it,' she replied. 'Anyway, open that door over there?'

Lottie did as she was told and made her way over to it, trying not to trip over various obstacles, and discovered a toilet, shower and sink.

'Oh my god, this place is a real hidden gem, isn't it?'

'So, what do you think? Do you think you could practice here?'

'Yes, definitely!'

'For the auditions?'

'Well, no, because I'm not auditioning, but I'd be able to dance in private here to keep fit, and I can teach you to dance. I mean, I'd obviously have to clear all this stuff out of the way but it would be perfect.'

'I'll let you into a little secret. After I lost Mum and Dad, I tried to teach myself from some videos I'd sent off for, but I realised I was and always would be that little dumpling who couldn't keep up with the pretty girls. So, I drew the curtains, moved back into the bungalow and that was that.' Her voice wavered and she swiftly brushed a tear away from her eye. Lottie bent down and gave her a hug. Doris patted her hand.

'Well, I'm here to teach you whenever you want. In fact, you'll be doing me a favour.'

'Oh well, I don't know about that, but there's nothing else going on with this place so help yourself. Maybe you could even get that nice young man round to help.'

Lottie rolled her eyes and laughed as Doris nudged her with her elbow. She looked around the barn. 'You're impossible, Doris, but I have to say I've got a really good feeling about this.'

'Come on then, wheel me back in and we can watch *Strictly* to get some ideas.'

Chapter 9

The next couple of weeks were a whirlwind of feeding and tickling Denni, feeding and de-egging the chickens – Lottie always thanked them for their produce – and looking after Doris, which included driving her to hospital for her physio appointments and going on shopping trips, usually for food. Any spare time she had was spent clearing out the barn, which some-times involved catching a couple of unwanted guests, which had sprung out at her. Fortunately, Doris got that sorted out with the help of the local pest controller.

She had moved the farm machinery out into the larger barn using a wheeled trolley that Doris kept in the shed. Now she had to work on a way of getting the wardrobes and bed back up the stairs; the mattress was destroyed, her furry friends had seen to that, so she'd arranged for the council to collect that along with some other bits.

She began pulling the wardrobe towards her when she tripped backwards, and it fell on her, pinning her to the couch. Luckily, she wasn't in too much pain – she just couldn't find the purchase to push the damn thing off her. There was no point in shouting for help, so she tried wriggling to manoeuvre herself from under it when she heard voices.

'I think she's still in here,' said Doris, as the door was flung open. From under the wardrobe, she could just about make out Doris holding a huge bunch of flowers and a man standing next to her who looked damned sexy even from this weird sideways angle.

'She was here a minute ago . . . Wait, what's that wardrobe doing like that?'

Lottie contemplated not saying anything but eventually gave in. 'Er hello, I'm here,' she muttered.

Mickey sprinted over to her and lifted it off her in one fell swoop, pulling her up by the hands. 'Are you OK? If you wanted a dancing partner, you could have asked me instead of waltzing with the wardrobe.'

'Ha-ha, very funny,' she said, brushing off the dust and trying to dislodge a cobweb that had landed in her hair. 'I'm fine, thanks, nothing broken thankfully.'

'I'll leave you two to it then,' said Doris, who was a dab hand at pushing her wheelchair now.

'Where do you want it?' he asked, in his smooth Italian accent.

'Pardon?' she asked, after hoisting herself out of a daydream about him.

'Where do you want the wardrobe?'

'Oh, the wardrobe, well, I'd really like it upstairs, if possible.'

'Anything is possible as long as you want it enough.'

Lottie cleared her throat and couldn't look at him.

'Here, it's easy – look.' He walked the wardrobe to

the bottom of the stairs then made his way up a few stairs whilst gently laying it on the steps facing upwards. He came back down. 'OK, you go up and just guide it when it gets to the top and I'll push.' She followed his instructions and tried not to notice his muscles flexing under his skin or his black hair flopping over his eye as he pushed the wardrobe up the stairs, but she was having difficulty concentrating.

Soon the wardrobe was lying on the bedroom floor. He jogged up the stairs to join her and moved it to where she wanted.

'What a fantastic place – are you moving in here?'

She looked around it again – it wasn't a bad idea actually. 'Er no, I'm just clearing it out for Doris – she said I can use it to practise for the auditions,' she laughed.

'So, are you entering the auditions?'

'No.' She tutted and rolled her eyes. 'I'll be going back to Canada soon – I think it's a tactic of hers to get me to stay but I'm going to give her some secret dancing lessons instead. Shush, she doesn't want anyone to know.' She held her finger to her mouth, and he repeated the gesture.

'That's a great idea,' he whispered.

'Thanks,' she whispered back. 'It's something she's always wanted to do.'

'Well, good luck to her. Just let me know if there's any more heavy lifting and I'll come back,' he said, turning to leave.

'I will, thank you. Actually, it's Doris's birthday coming up and I'd love to surprise her.'

'What with?' He stopped and faced her again.

'It might sound a bit crazy but to fulfil a childhood dream of hers, I'd love to put up some mirrors and maybe a barre along this part of the wall.' She gestured with her hands and walked along to the area she was talking about. 'That way she won't be able to turn down my offer of dancing lessons and when I've gone back she can have a little private dancing space just for her.'

Mickey tapped the wall with his knuckles. 'That certainly sounds doable – I can ask around if you like. My cousin is very involved with the local playhouse; in fact, they had to replace some of their mirrors recently so he'd know the best place to get them from.'

'Oh, that would be brilliant, yes please.'

'OK, great, I'll let you know what he says. Bye then.'

She opened the door to let him out and he waved. 'Bye.'

'You know where I am if you need me.'

'Do I?'

'Yes, I gave you my number, remember?'

'Ah yes you did, I think it's on Doris's noticeboard.' It wasn't – it was tucked safely in her bedside drawer, but he didn't need to know that.

Chapter 10

Doris was soon on crutches and there was no stopping her; the doctors were really pleased with her recovery.

'I suppose that's it then, you won't be needing me anymore,' said Lottie. 'You'll be pleased to get your independence back. I guess I should start planning my move back home or check with my brother if it's OK to stay with him for just a little while longer.' Lottie's heart broke at the thought of leaving Doris, especially as she was looking forward to teaching her to dance but she didn't want to outstay her welcome, after all this was Doris's home.

'What are you talking about?' said Doris. 'It's not just a case of needing you here – it's wanting you here too. I know I told the doctor a little white lie about you being my granddaughter but honestly, you are the granddaughter I never had. I've absolutely loved having you here, my dear, and you've been a brilliant help to me. Lord only knows where they would have carted me off to if I hadn't had you around . . . I know it can't have been easy living with an old biddy like me cramping your style . . .'

Lottie went to interrupt but Doris held her hand up. 'No arguments. I would like to offer you the option to stay on here. I was even thinking you might want to move into the barn now that you've had a good old sort-out. It would be lovely for me to see new life breathed into it again.'

Lottie's heart leapt for joy; she'd fallen in love with the little house in the barn and couldn't remember a time in her life when she'd felt more settled in a place, not since her mum and dad were alive. She had to give it to Doris – she was very good at dangling the proverbial carrot and delaying Lottie's departure.

'Well, that's certainly given me something to think about, hasn't it? I would absolutely love to move in there, Doris, but only if I pay the going rent. If I stay any longer, I'm going to have to apply for a National Insurance card so I can work here and look for a temporary job.'

'Ah, of course, because you're Canadian.'

'Well, actually I was born here so I have dual citizenship.'

'Well, there's still plenty of jobs around the farm that you can do, which will free me up to do some more enjoyable things, if you don't mind. But if you really want to pay, then you can pay me in kind. I've been thinking and I'd really love to take you up on your offer of dance lessons. In fact, I can't stop thinking about them.'

'Oh, Doris, you've made my day now. Of course, it would be my absolute pleasure but let's check with the physio at your next appointment. He did say you'll soon be good to go.'

The knowledge that she was moving into the barn gave Lottie even more energy as she swept and dusted. Doris had insisted on inviting Blake and Camilla round for dinner and they helped Lottie move the bed upstairs for which she'd ordered a new mattress. They bought her some bedding and a thick fluffy rug to put next to her bed as a housewarming present. Lottie had bought some cheap pale-pink fleecy throws to throw over the worn but perfectly comfortable three-piece suite. Blake also gave her his spare flatscreen TV.

Blake helped Lottie to remove the board from over the window and Camilla helped her to mop. The last job was polishing the windows, which Lottie did with extra vigour. She'd had the curtains dry cleaned and they'd come up a treat.

When they'd finished, they flopped down onto the couch together, just as Doris hobbled in with a small vase of flowers she'd picked from the garden and a tote bag over her arm.

'Oh, it smells lovely in here, really fresh and clean. Well done everybody.' She popped the vase on the little coffee table that Lottie had bought from a charity shop and retrieved a bottle from her bag. 'Now I think this calls for a toast with a bottle of my finest.'

Lottie hugged her. 'Thank you for the gorgeous flowers and well, for everything, this is all so amazing.'

'Nonsense, dear, you've earned your place at my table, that's for sure, and for you, Camilla, here's a bottle of my bramble cordial.'

Lottie gathered some glasses together, filled them

with the wine and topped Camilla's cordial with water as they toasted to new beginnings. Before they left, Lottie took Blake and Camilla to see Denni and he rushed over to them, eager for Lottie's tickle between his ears. She'd saved some cubes of carrot as a treat for him, which he devoured.

When she looked up, Blake was smiling at her.

'What?' she asked.

'Nothing,' he replied, his smile now more of a beam.

'Why are you looking at me so weirdly then?'

'That's not weirdly – this is weirdly.' He pulled a funny face.

'You know what I mean.'

'I'm just winding you up. The thing is, you look so happy, happier than I've ever seen you, well, since Mum and Dad were alive. I'm so incredibly proud of you.'

'Thanks bro, that means a lot and yes, I feel happy. I love it here.'

'It's done you the world of good. I'm glad you came.'

'Me too,' she replied.

'Me three and four,' added Camilla as she patted her bump.

'Eeyaw,' bellowed Denni, his lips parting to reveal his large teeth.

Their laughter rang with happiness as it caught on a light breeze and drifted off over the fields.

Chapter 11

The first night in the barn could only be described as blissful. After Blake and Camilla had gone, she couldn't resist performing a dance routine and her whole body tingled as that familiar rush of adrenaline hit. To finally have the space to move about like that was thrilling and her body welcomed the familiar movements like an old friend. She had a shower, dimmed the lighting to just lamps and wandered about the room, topped up her wine glass and sat on the couch watching dance videos on the telly whilst enjoying her drink. Every now and then she would jump up and try a step she hadn't seen before, repeating it until she had mastered it.

By nine o'clock, she could stifle her yawns no longer; the excitement of moving in, mingled with the alcohol, had knocked her out. She pulled the curtains shut and after brushing her teeth, she went upstairs to bed.

Lying there bathed in the moonlight via the hayloft window, she felt at peace. Having been undecided whether to text Mickey her number, she thought she probably would – the little devil on her shoulder was jumping up and down urging her to do it, and surprisingly, the angel on the other shoulder nodded her approval. Satisfied that she'd only done it for practical reasons, she snuggled under her cosy duvet and drifted into a deep satisfying sleep.

Sunlight filtered through the curtains the next morning and at first Lottie wondered where she was, but threw the quilt back and jumped out of bed when she remembered she was in her own little home. She reminded herself that it was only temporary and that she needed to go back to Canada at some point, but she couldn't deny that the reasons for returning were dwindling. She made a decision there and then to stay at least until the baby was born so she could meet her niece or nephew. That thought filled her heart with deep joy. She snuggled her toes into the warmth of her new fluffy rug, pulled on some old jeans and a battered sweatshirt, and ran downstairs. She opened the door and stepped into the wellies caked in dried mud that stood outside the door, threw on a bobble hat and headed to the larger barn to get fresh straw for Denni. He jumped around when he saw her and showed off with a little gallop around the field whilst she topped up his water. She cuddled him, nuzzling her face into his coarse hair and he did that funny thing with his lips that was so endearing as it looked like he was laughing.

She picked up his brush and swept it through his coat, ensuring there were no knots in his fur. She often wondered if he was lonely out here in the field on his own. Doris had said she had a dog that he used to get on well with, but sadly he'd died the year before.

She had visions of a little dog, maybe a rescue running around the field with Denni, but realised she was getting ahead of herself. Doris didn't need any extra responsibilities and Lottie didn't even live here. Once she'd finished with Denni, she opened the chicken coop and topped up their feed. She liked to sing to the chickens, Beatles songs of course, and hoped it helped with their egg production. She grabbed a brush and shovel and scooped out all the old dirty bedding and replaced it with fresh. It wasn't her favourite job but she felt it was the least she could do for Doris and it was so satisfying knowing they had a lovely clean home. Once she'd finished, she collected the eggs, thanking each of the chickens as she did so.

She carried the basket to the main house and let herself in. Stepping out of her wellies, she put the basket on the table, washed her hands, filled the old-fashioned whistling kettle and put it on the gas hob. She poured water into a pan and put it on to boil. Once the water was bubbling Lottie put four eggs into the water and turned the egg timer over. She cut thick slices from the bread she had made yesterday and put them in the toaster. Once the egg timer had finished, she took Doris's eggs out and turned the timer over again as she preferred hers a lot less soft than Doris did. She made a fresh pot of tea and poured some orange juice into two glasses.

She placed Doris's eggs in the eggcups.

'Breakfast's ready,' she shouted. The toast popped up noisily and she spread it with lashings of fresh butter from the farm down the road; they had an understanding and traded eggs and bread for the delicious creamy fare.

Doris entered the kitchen singing and limping slightly but without her crutch.

'Look at you, you're practically skipping in here,' said Lottie as she placed the plates on the table.

'I know, I'll be dancing the light fandango before you know it,' she chuckled as she cut off the top of her boiled egg and dipped a fat soldier dripping with butter into the soft orange yolk. 'I have the most excellent news.'

Lottie looked up at her expectantly but didn't want to speak with her mouth full.

'The physio has signed me off and said as long as it's not too strenuous, I can start my dance lessons if you're ready,' Doris continued.

'Are you kidding me? I was born ready. Do you want to start now?' She laughed as she saw the look of panic sweep across Doris's face. 'Don't worry, I'll go easy on you.'

Doris breathed a sigh of relief. 'Thank you, darling. How about sometime next week after we've got all our jobs done?'

'That sounds great and I can't wait,' said Lottie.

'Oh, look you're a poet and you didn't know it,' smiled Doris. 'I'll see you over at your little school of dance then, shall I?'

'Lottie's school of dance – that's got a lovely ring to it, hasn't it?' replied Lottie. 'It's a date.'

After helping Doris with the dishes, she drove over to Cupcake Cottage where Camilla greeted her with a warm smile and a hug. 'Come in, I've just finished for the day.'

'Oh, it smells delicious in here – what have you been baking?'

'Try one and see,' said Camilla as she put the kettle on and placed some beautifully iced cupcakes onto a plate.

'Ooh strawberries and cream, how lovely,' said Lottie as she bit into one and laughed as she got buttercream on the tip of her nose. They went through the orangery to the garden and sat in the sun, Camilla carrying two mugs of coffee.

'Is Blake at work?' asked Lottie.

'Yes, he's excited about a new building project he's taken on.'

'That's good and how are you?'

'I'm really well, thank you. Ooh, what are you up to in there, little one.' She shifted around to get in a better position. 'Would you like to feel the baby kicking?'

'Ah, is it happening now? I'd love to.'

Camilla placed Lottie's hand on her bump and moved it round until she could feel the movement. She was surprised at how firm her stomach was and then she felt the little kick and then a much bigger one. Lottie's eyes filled with tears, and she could feel her heart bursting with love for this little person she was yet to meet. 'That's just beautiful. Have you got any names yet?'

'No, nothing yet. I guess I still can't quite believe it. Anyway, how are you? What have you been up to?'

'I've been healing, I think.' Lottie was surprised to hear the words coming out of her mouth; she hadn't quite realised that being tucked away at the farm had allowed her to come to terms with herself. 'The guilt I felt at ditching Chad at the altar has dissipated and I've come to realise that I'm not a bad person. I've been able to put others before myself, which is something I haven't been used to doing.'

She recognised that Doris had provided her with a loving home and that was obviously just what she needed.

'That's fantastic, Lottie, I'm so happy for you and you shouldn't feel guilty about Chad. It's better you broke up than being in a marriage you knew wasn't right.'

'Thank you and I know. But I haven't even told you my other news yet. I've decided to stay here until you have the baby.'

Camilla's face lit up and Lottie noticed a little tear in her eye.

'That's the best news I've heard in a long time. I can't wait to tell Blake, although you do know he'll try and make you stay for longer!'

'Well, I am beginning to wonder what I've got to go back for, but I suppose my life is there really.'

'But your family is here,' said Camilla.

'And it's growing,' said Lottie.

Her phone pinged with a text from Mickey telling her to go to Bramblewood Playhouse and ask for Gabe Sellers. He still had the old mirrors.

'Excellent,' said Lottie, clapping her hands and she texted back her thanks.

'More good news?' asked Camilla.

'Yes, just a little surprise I'm planning for Doris. Oh, that reminds me.' She looked at her watch. 'I must go, but before I do, do you mind if I use your printer, please?'

'Of course not. Come through and I'll show you where it is.

Lottie had giggled as she'd worked on the design for her sign but as she tried to print it, she discovered the printer had other ideas and called out to Camilla.

'I'm so sorry, Lottie – sometimes I want to throw this printer out of the window,' said Camilla after trying it herself. 'I'll drop it into you next week if that's OK.'

'Of course, no worries,' said Lottie, kissing her future sister-in-law goodbye.

Chapter 12

Lottie drove to the Playhouse and had to park in a car park just off the high street as all the parking bays reserved for the theatre were taken, as were the ones outside the shops.

People were milling about in the foyer and the receptionist was busy on a call, but there were several people holding clipboards so she approached one of them.

'Hi, I'm here to see Gabe Sellers,' she said.

'Name please,' asked the young woman.

'Erm, Lottie Daniels,' she replied.

'Lottie Daniels,' she repeated as she wrote it down. 'Phone number please?' Lottie looked around her, hoping to see Gabe. Lottie reeled off her number. 'Oh um, I'm just here about the mirrors.'

'That's fine. Here's your number,' she said, placing a sticker on Lottie's chest. 'If you can just make your way through there.' She pointed to some double doors where lots of other women were heading.

'Is this some sort of auction?' she asked, as that was the only explanation she could think of as to why so many people would turn up for some mirrors, or maybe there were more items up for sale.

The clipboard lady laughed politely and turned to a woman who'd been patiently waiting behind Lottie. 'Name please?'

Lottie felt she had no choice but to follow the others through the double doors, down a corridor and into the theatre. The atmosphere buzzed with the sound of excitable chatter and music coming from somewhere, then she thought she had a fleeting glimpse of someone who might be Gabe, but who then disappeared again just as quickly. Maybe it was an auction.

Another woman with a clipboard stepped up to the stage. 'Can you all take a seat please,' she announced through her headset mike. Stewards led people to the tiered seating and one ushered Lottie to sit down. 'Excuse me, I'm just here to see Gabe Sellers,' she said.

'That's fine, he'll be out shortly. Would you just like to take a seat,' said the young man.

A pretty girl with long thin braids tied in a thick ponytail tapped Lottie on the shoulder and gestured to the empty seat next to her. 'Is anyone sitting here?' she asked in a loud whisper.

'No, help yourself,' Lottie replied.

'Thank you.' She settled herself into the chair. 'Are you nervous?' she asked.

'Yes, a little bit, I'm just here to buy the mirrors but I've never been to an auction before and I hope I don't end up buying something ridiculous by accident.'

'Oh, is there an auction?'

'I assume so. Isn't that what this is for?' She pointed to the numbered sticker.

74

'I'm so nervous. In fact, I feel a bit faint actually.'

'Oh no, would you like some water?' Lottie rummaged in her bag and handed an unopened bottle to her.

'Are you sure?'

'Yes it's fine I have a spare?'

'Thanks.' She opened it and sipped it slowly.

'OK everyone, quiet please,' announced Gabe as he stepped out onto the stage. 'Has everyone got a seat? Are you all sitting comfortably? Then let's begin. Thank you for attending the auditions for *Truly Dance*.'

Lottie's hands flew to her burning face and her stomach tied itself in a collection of knots a seaman would have been proud of.

'I think I've made a mistake being here,' she said, wiping her sweaty palms on her trousers. She stood up as nausea swept over her.

The girl grabbed her arm and gently coaxed her back into her seat. 'Hey, don't worry, that's just your nerves trying to trick you into saying you're not good enough but you've got this. You have just as much right as anyone else to be here so just give it a chance. I mean, we might both get knocked out in the first round but we'll never know if we don't try and if we do, at least we can go to the pub down the road and drown our sorrows together. What do you say?'

'But you don't understand – I haven't come for an audition.' Lottie bit her lip, her fight or flight impulse on high alert, but she looked into the friendly face of the girl sitting next to her who appeared terrified.

'Oh, please stay with me. Come on, you're my best friend here, you can't leave me on my own. How about you stay with me for the audition and I'll help you find the auction afterwards?'

Lottie looked round and realised it would be quite embarrassing to walk out now as the place was packed and it would also be quite rude whilst Gabe was making his announcement. She may as well listen to what they had to say as she was here. She exhaled and smiled at her. 'OK bestie, I'll wait with you for a bit to make sure you're all right, but I'm not auditioning. I need to see that man,' she pointed to Gabe. 'About a mirror. I do like the idea of going to the pub afterwards though,' she laughed.

'It's a deal,' said the girl. 'My name is Mia.' She held out her little finger to Lottie and Lottie linked it with her own. 'I'm Lottie, pleased to meet you.'

'OK everyone,' continued Gabe. 'We'll be calling you down in groups of twenty. We would like you to perform your piece altogether and the judges will be milling around to watch you. At the end of each round we will be calling out the numbers that are going through to the next stage, in no particular order. If your number is not called out, then you must leave the stage. Thank you for coming and better luck next time.'

Lottie looked down at her number 108 and then at Mia's number 114. The music began as the first batch of dancers were called to the stage and the rhythm beat its way through her body like nothing else. She couldn't sit still; she noticed that Mia was the same, as was most of the audience. Maybe she could just have a little dance for old time's sake? At least no one knew her here, well, apart from Gabe and now Mia, but no one else. What harm could it do? She had no chance of getting the part and she'd probably be back in Canada by the time it came round so she really had nothing to lose and a really good excuse to dance.

'Uh-oh, here we go,' said Mia as their numbers were called. 'Come on, you're not going to make me do this by myself are you?'

Adrenaline ran through Lottie's veins like an express train. She jumped up. 'Come on then, let's do this.' She said before she had a chance to change her mind.

'Break a leg, bestie,' said Mia.

'You too.' Lottie took a deep breath and made her way to the stage with her new friend.

As the music played, Lottie chased away her inhibitions and danced as though she were the solo performer on the stage. She imagined that she was still in the barn at Doris's place or in the field with only Denni, as the audience and her nerves soon crept away as she became absorbed into the music. When it stopped, she panted as she waited to hear the numbers called. She glanced to the other side of the stage and saw Mia also out of breath. She held up her crossed fingers to Lottie and winked at her; Lottie crossed her fingers too and held them up to her mouth. She cheered as she heard number 114 called out and saw Mia blowing out a sigh of relief.

'And the final contender going through to the next round is number 108,' said the announcer. Lottie

77

double-checked the number on her sticker and gasped, her hands flying to cover her open mouth. She became overcome with a light-headedness and worried she might float off like a helium balloon until Mia grounded her with a congratulatory hug.

'We got through!' she shouted. 'Well bloody done us!' They raised their water bottles up and clinked them together. 'Congratulations Lottie. I'm so glad you didn't back out.'

'I must admit that was exhilarating and has certainly woken my body up,' said Lottie. 'I haven't danced like that for months. I'm just as nervous for the next round, whatever that is.'

She soon found out as they were ushered to a smaller practice room and taught a quick dance routine by a choreographer called Pixie. On the way, she noticed a café called It's a Wrap, heaving with people. She did a double-take as she thought she caught a glimpse of Mickey, but whoever it was, he was soon swallowed up in the crowd.

Lottie tried not to let her nerves get the better of her and fell into step next to Mia as Pixie issued the instructions. 'This part of the audition is to see how quickly you can pick up last-minute instructions and new dance moves.' Soon the adrenaline was pumping around her body, chasing away the nerves, and she felt alive. Trying out new steps woke up both her muscles and her brain. Some of the moves went against everything she'd ever learnt, but she revelled in learning something new.

'OK, take a quick break to rehydrate and then we go back on the big stage to show those judges what you're made of,' Pixie shouted. Lottie joined Mia at the edge of the room and they both drank thirstily from their bottles.

'I wonder if we'll get to meet Mr Gorgeous today?' said Mia breathlessly after glugging all her water. 'I heard a rumour he might be at the audition.'

'Who's Mr Gorgeous?' asked Lottie. She held her hand out for Mia's bottle so she could fill it up from the water fountain as she'd done her own.

'Oh thanks,' said Mia, handing it over. 'You know Marco Abruzzo, the masked dancer, he's one of the professionals in *Truly Dance* – one of us could literally be dancing with him in the show if we get through. I love him so much; I saw him in a show here a couple of Christmases ago – he was spotted, went to New York and he has a movie coming out soon.'

'Oh, that's right, I remember seeing his name on a flyer – I've no idea what he looks like though. I keep meaning to look him up but where I'm staying doesn't have any Wi-Fi.' Lottie handed back the water bottle after resealing the top.

'Thank you,' said Mia, immediately taking another sip. 'Oh my god, I can't believe you don't know what he looks like. Hold on, I'll show you.' She riffled through her bag for her phone but stopped when Pixie clapped her hands together and ushered them all out of the room.

'I'll show you later but not only is he gorgeous, I've also heard he's hung like a donkey.' Mia elbowed Lottie gently and laughed, her hazel eyes sparkling.

'I'm joking.'

Lottie threw her head back and shrieked with laughter. 'Oh Mia, that's so funny, I've got a friend who's got a donkey but I've never noticed that,' she giggled.

'What? You've got a friend who's a donkey? I didn't think you could go up any further in my estimation. Please say you'll introduce me to him – I love donkeys.'

'Of course I will. His name's Denni.'

The noise in the main theatre was deafening so Mia joined her two forefingers and thumbs into a heart shape and moved them up and down over her heart.

The next couple of hours were exhausting but exciting as they both managed to get through to the final round. Every muscle in Lottie's body ached and she fantasised about relaxing in a hot bath, which she'd have to do in Doris's house as she only had a shower in the barn. They now had to prepare for the last dance; each of the finalists were to be partnered up with a professional dancer. Lottie's guy was quite good-looking and introduced himself as Simon. The music started and each couple danced in perfect sync to begin with. Judges with clipboards wandered around tapping contestants on the shoulder and subsequently ending their dreams of being on the show. Lottie enjoyed the feeling of the music vibrating through her body as her partner swung her round. She saw a couple being tapped and felt a little unsettled as the girl began crying and asking for a second chance. She saw Pixie put her arm around her and try to comfort her as she led her off the stage. The beat of the music intensified and a roar of cheers came from the dancers who sat in the audience.

As Lottie twirled, she saw a man in a black Venetian mask with a hat and cape which swished around him as he danced. His muscles were evident through his see through fitted black shirt and the way he moved was mesmerising. She almost missed a beat as she couldn't tear her eyes away from him. Then her heart sank to the floor as she felt the rough tap on her shoulder; she saw the puzzled look in her partner's eyes too and then heard someone say sorry. Her partner didn't miss a beat though and spun her round; she then realised that the tap wasn't from the judge but another couple had accidentally bumped into them. She watched as the judge tapped them on the shoulder and they left the stage. The relief swept through her body like a fireball and she felt as though she were floating on air.

The dance continued and when they got to a part where all the couples had to spring apart, she noticed the masked man dance with each of the finalists, swirling them round before moving onto the next. When he got to her, she felt a rip of desire tear through her body as he pulled her into his embrace, his rock-hard body pressing firmly against hers. He let go of her and she very reluctantly loosened her grip of his hand. Just before he spun away, she saw him wink at her through his mask. She did a double take and blinked wildly as she felt abandoned, and even after such a short time, she missed the warmth of his body, which had sent fireworks through her, some of which were still fizzing and popping.

The masked man had left the stage as quickly as he'd appeared.

'OK, congratulations everyone,' announced one of the organisers. 'I have to say the calibre of the dancing today has been truly magnificent and you have been whittled down to the final nine. One of you will be going through as a contender on *Truly Dance*. We won't be announcing the winner tonight, but we will call you when the final decision has been made. Thanks everyone, you're all free to go.'

The room once again filled with chatter and Lottie and Mia sought each other out again and hugged whilst jumping up and down congratulating each other. 'Let's go for a celebratory drink in the bar,' said Mia as they grabbed their bags.

'Yes let's,' agreed Lottie. 'I take it that was the magnificent Marco in the mask?'

'Isn't he amazing? I just wanted to rip it off his face with my teeth,' said Mia.

'He was unbelievably sexy, I have to agree,' said Lottie, her heart fluttering at the memory of his touch.

Once in the bar, Mia grabbed a table whilst Lottie went to order the drinks. As she picked up the glasses, she heard a familiar voice behind her.

'Hello Minnie.'

She turned around and smiled instinctively.

'Mickey, what are you doing here?' As she spoke, her eyes roamed down his body and she took in the familiar see-through shirt and black trousers with sequins down the sides. 'Wait, hold on . . . it's you. The masked dancer.'

'Guilty as charged,' he replied, holding a hand out to her. 'Marco.'

'Oh my god, I can't believe it's you.' She shook his hand gently. 'I'm Lottie.'

'Good to meet you, lovely Lottie. I didn't know you were auditioning.'

'I wasn't – it was all a big misunderstanding. I came here to see Gabe about the mirrors.'

'Ah good, what did he say?'

'Well, that's just it. I assumed they were auctioning things off and when I realised what it was, I was too embarrassed to leave. So I haven't spoken to him yet.'

He grinned at her. 'Well done for getting through – I just hope I can be as good a dance partner as your wardrobe.'

She felt her cheeks flush at the memory.

'Thank you, and I'm cringing now, thinking about what I said about you.'

'What, about me being arrogant and handsome and probably in love with myself?' He laughed a deep, sensual laugh. 'Don't worry, that's all true.'

Lottie blushed and laughed as well. 'Well, I didn't say that, but those girls did who gave me the flyer.' She could see over his shoulder Mia covering her mouth with her hand as if stifling a scream and then she held both hands about a foot apart like a very proud fisherman boasting about his latest catch and began pouting and made kissy faces at her. Lottie let out a shriek and almost spilt her drink.

Marco looked behind him and looked amused as he saw Mia waving at him. He waved back at her and she swooned.

'Why didn't you tell me?' asked Lottie.

'I was going to, but then you nearly fell off my paddle-board and distracted me,' he replied. She blushed as she remembered that intimate moment of just the two of them gently gliding down the river. She'd loved it so much.

'How's Denni and dear old Doris?'

'Ah, they're both really well, thanks for asking.'

'It's my pleasure. I was thinking that Denni's shelter looked a little ramshackle and maybe I could fix it up for him. Do you think that would be OK?'

'Oh yes, I'm sure Doris and Denni would love that. There used to be a guy who worked at the farm called Malcolm but he died a little while ago and I think he used to keep up to date with all those sorts of jobs.'

'OK, well, things are pretty hectic here but as soon as I get a chance, I'll pop over.'

'That will be nice . . . for Doris, I mean,' she added.

'Marco! Marco!' a man shouted from the other end of the bar, gesturing with his arm to join him.

'Sorry, I've got to go. Good luck with the results and just so you know, I don't have anything to do with the judging but your dancing was impeccable – that wardrobe of yours taught you well,' he teased. 'Bye Lottie.' He winked at her and walked off. She gave him a gentle wave.

She enjoyed the sound of her name coming out of his mouth. Her heart was pounding so fast it reminded her of a little ping-pong bat she had when she was younger, where the ball was attached with an elastic. She had no intention of dating anybody anyway but couldn't deny the chemistry between them was intense.

Mia was trying to hurry her over by gesturing with her hands and she eventually joined her and handed her a drink.

'Thanks. OMG, what did he say to you?' said Mia, clinking her glass against Lottie's before taking a huge slurp of juice.

'Well, it turns out we know each other,' replied Lottie, also taking a much-needed drink.

'What? You know him? Why didn't you say? Oh my god, are you two . . . you know?' She made a circle with her forefinger and thumb and went to put the other forefinger through the circle it made.

'Nooo,' shrieked Lottie, her voice reaching glass-smashing pitch. She laughed as she pulled Mia's hands apart to keep them separate.

'Thank God for that, after what I said about the donkey thing,' Mia blushed.

Lottie put her hands to the top of her head like tall ears and eeyawed, which had them both cracking up laughing until tears poured down their cheeks.

'One day I'll tell you about how a donkey brought us together but for now let's just enjoy our success because I'm knackered but very happy,' said Lottie. 'However, this is as far as I'd like to go. I've had a great time but I can't really commit to anything else . . . You can have Marco and *Truly Dance* and I'm happy to stick to my donkey.'

'To donkeys,' said Mia, holding up her drink.

'To donkeys,' repeated Lottie, still chuckling. Having a friend to laugh with again felt good.

Chapter 13

After a couple of drinks, Lottie said goodbye to Mia and she went looking for Gabe. She found him in reception changing the poster board.

'Hi Gabe.' He stopped and looked round.

'Ah hello, you're Marco's friend, Lottie.'

'Yes, that's right, I came to see you about the mirrors hours ago but ended up on a little, shall we say, detour.'

'I saw you got through to the final. Congratulations, you must be thrilled.'

'Er yes I am, thank you.'

'OK, so I'll show you the mirrors – they're in storage at the moment.' He locked the poster frame and tucked the keys into his pocket. 'We were going to bin them as it happens, as they're a little bit damaged at the top.' He led the way to the back of the theatre and unlocked the door, a musty smell escaping the room as he opened it. He reached in and turned on a light. Lottie looked around to see an array of fascinating items: an old piano covered in dust, props from various shows made from papier mâché and polystyrene.

'Ah, here they are, some of them broke as they took them down and some of them are damaged at the back but only at the very top. Marco said you'd only need the panels to be about six feet so I can get a friend to resize them for you if they're any good.'

'Oh yes please, they'll be perfect for what I need, how much do you want for them?'

'Absolutely nothing – you'll be doing us a favour by taking them off our hands.'

'Are you sure?'

'Positively sure. Now, is there anything else I can help you with?'

Lottie looked around at the Aladdin's den of goodies. 'What about that red curtain? Don't you need that anymore?'

'No, there's only one there, the other one was damaged when we had a leak in the ceiling a few years back so we had to replace the whole lot.'

'That's a shame,' said Lottie. 'I was thinking it could look quite theatrical if we used it to cover the mirrors when they weren't in use.'

'Here, let's have a look,' said Gabe, opening it out and giving it a good shake, releasing a cloud of dust into the air. 'It's massive, I think you'll probably need to give it a trim.'

'I can do that,' said Lottie. 'I think this will be perfect.'

'Fantastic, I'll drop it off tomorrow if you like.'

'That would be amazing, but let me give you something for the delivery or your time.'

'Not necessary at all – any friend of Marco's is a friend of mine.'

'You're very kind, thank you. You know the address, don't you?'

'Yes, it's where Denni the donkey lives, isn't it?'

'That's right, you helped Mick . . . I mean Marco to rescue him.' It was going to take her a little while to get used to his real name.

She said goodbye to Gabe and headed back home with just one thing on her mind – to snuggle up in bed, preferably for a week, to relax her recently awakened and aching muscles. But when she saw Doris's light on, she felt a renewed burst of energy and couldn't resist telling her the news. When she saw Doris was making a supper of beans on toast, her stomach rumbled and reminded her that she hadn't eaten since lunchtime.

'We had to dance like this . . .' She moved round the room, recreating some of the performance she gave and Doris clapped her hands. 'And I'm not sure how I feel about this but I got through to the finals so I'm waiting for a phone call.'

'That's brilliant love, I'm so pleased for you.'

Lottie wished she felt more excited about it, but it wasn't really something she wanted to be involved in and besides, if she did get it, she'd probably have to turn it down as she would be returning to Canada soon. She retrieved her egg from the pan and sat at the table to crack the top off with her knife.

'Oh, I met a new friend called Mia so that was nice, and oh my god, you'll never guess who I saw there, dancing like a sexy Zorro?'

Doris dangled her soldier dripping with yolk inches from her mouth whilst she thought about who it could be. 'Ooh I don't know, was it Anton Du Beke?'

'Nope!'

'Engelbert Humperdinck?'

'Engelbert who a dink?'

'Sorry, much before your time. I don't know – the suspense is killing me. Who was it?'

'It was Mickey, except his name is actually Marco and it turns out he's a little bit famous.'

'Oh, you mean the donkey rescuer, well it had to be, didn't it? I mean, he is very sexy,' she cackled. 'I bet he could teach you a move or two.'

'Doris, you're so cheeky,' laughed Lottie, feeling her cheeks grow warm as she remembered Mia's donkey joke.

'What? I meant dance moves; I can't possibly imagine what you're talking about.' She winked and Lottie noticed a mischievous glint in her eye. 'So, what's the next step?'

'I just have to wait for the call to find out whether I'm in and then I suppose I'll have a decision to make.'

'Well I'm sorry but I hope you do get it and that you stay here for ever, Good lu—' Her hands flew to her mouth. 'No, I mean break a leg, although not literally like I did.'

'Thanks Doris but it might be better if I don't. I'm happy to have got this far.' Her insides twisted as she felt torn between wanting the job and needing to go back to Canada.

Chapter 14

The next morning her alarm reminded her that chickens and donkeys wait for no woman so, wearing pyjamas and wellies, Lottie hobbled tenderly out to the field to feed her feathered and furry friends.

In the middle of topping up Denni's water, she heard a vehicle approaching and turned to see Marco hopping out to open the gate whilst Gabe drove the van into the grounds. She looked down at herself with horror and contemplated standing still in the field with her arms outstretched and hope they'd mistake her for a scarecrow, but no such luck. Marco waved to her so she had no choice but to approach them.

'Hi.' Her head was facing down but her eyes looked up at Marco, a sense of awkwardness had come over her now that she knew who he was. He smiled back at her, but he too had lost his air of confidence. Gabe was his normal happy and positive self.

'Right then, where do you want these mirrors?'

'Have you had them resized already?' asked Lottie.

'Oh yes, my mate works nights, doesn't hang about, and it didn't take him long. He also has an industrial steamer so me and my man Marco here have steam-cleaned your curtain too.'

'Oh wow, that's amazing, thank you so much.'

'All part of the service,' Marco saluted.

She led them into the barn.

'This is where they need to go but I'll just tell Doris that you're dropping off stuff to fix Denni's shed – these are a surprise for her birthday.'

She whizzed over to Doris's house to let her know; she could hear her singing in the bath so shouted the message up the stairs.

'Rightio, darling,' she replied.

Lottie got back to find Marco and Gabe had already fitted two of the mirrored panels. 'Wow, I'm impressed, that was quick. Coffee?' she offered.

'Yes please, black no sugar,' said Gabe, as he held the panel whilst Marco stood on a stepladder and drilled the screw into the wall.

'White no sugar for me, please,' said Marco, flashing her a smile.

'I found this rail for you,' said Gabe. 'I thought it might be useful for the curtain.'

'Oh yes, that would be perfect, thank you.' She made the coffees and passed them over.

'Do you want us to put it up while we're up here?'

'Only if you don't mind?'

'Here, you can have a go,' said Marco, handing her the cordless screwdriver and she climbed up the stepladder. Marco reached up and placed his hand over hers; it felt warm and comfortable there. He directed the screwdriver to the screw in the wall. 'That's it, get the fittings in place with that hand and go.' He pressed her hand so her fingers pushed on the trigger and she screwed it till it stopped turning.

'That's it, now we'll move the ladder along and do the other side.'

Lottie inserted the other screws and tested it to make sure it wasn't moving. 'There that's it, all done.'

Marco offered his hand for her to climb down the stepladder and she took it graciously then stepped back to inspect her handiwork.

'Does that look wonky?'

'Just a little bit,' said Marco, holding his finger and thumb a centimetre apart. 'Not quite the Leaning Tower of Pisa, but it's fine, you won't notice it once the curtains are up.'

'The mirrors look fantastic, thank you so much. Doris is going to love them,' said Lottie as she unravelled the red velvet curtain onto the floor. 'Have you got a tape measure?' she asked.

'Yes, there's one here in the toolbox,' said Marco, retrieving it and handing it to her.

'Thanks.' She began measuring up.

'Did you still want to have a barre installed?' he asked whilst drinking his coffee.

'Well, that would be the icing on the cake, I think, but I wouldn't know where to get one from.'

'I could get some banister rail and make you one, if you like.'

'Oh, I wouldn't want you to go to any trouble.'

'It's no trouble at all. I'll just need to pick up my car and I can grab it.'

'Well, I'll be getting off now so I can drop you home if you like,' said Gabe.

'OK great,' said Marco. 'Let me just measure the width and I'll go to the DIY shop.'

'That would be great and thank you both for doing this for me – you've absolutely transformed the place. It seems so much bigger in here.'

'You're welcome, it does look really cool. I hope Doris likes it. Thanks for the coffee.'

'My pleasure,' said Lottie. 'Here take these.' She handed over the basket of eggs she'd collected; she knew Doris wouldn't mind as they had plenty.

Gabe's face lit up. 'Thank you, Poppy will love these.'

Once they'd gone, Lottie raced upstairs for a quick shower and got dressed before running round to Doris. She could still hear her singing in her bathroom and knew that she had a fondness for topping up the hot water regularly while luxuriating in the bath.

'Doris!' she shouted up the stairs again. 'Is it OK if I borrow your sewing machine? I'm making Denni some blankets.'

'Yes of course, dear, help yourself.'

'Thanks,' she shouted back. She wasn't exactly lying as there was plenty of material left over to keep Denni warm too.

She took the sewing machine over to the barn and began hemming the curtains. Marco came back with the pre-varnished banister and drilled some new holes in the wall.

'I was thinking of unpicking this gold braid and adding it to the top like a little pelmet and down the sides.' She held it up to him. 'What do you think?'

'Er, I think it sounds complicated but I'm sure it will look very good.' He drilled holes in the wall for the brackets to hold the barre in place. It was strange for Lottie to see the sexiest dancer she'd ever seen in her life now in jeans and a T-shirt doing DIY in her house. It would certainly take some getting used to, merging Mickey and Marco together.

'I didn't know you could sew,' he said, holding screws between his lips as he moved to the next bracket.

'Yes, although I haven't done any for ages. My mum taught me when I was quite young. I went through a phase of making my own clothes as a teenager, you know, finding my look and probably looking like a right weirdo.' She smiled as she fed the material through the sewing machine. 'My poor mum tried to get me to show an interest in so many things but nothing grabbed me, apart from dancing, of course, and dressmaking.

'My mum couldn't dance for toffee, although she was my greatest supporter so dressmaking was our thing. I started off with a little toy machine but that frustrated me as the stitches were never tight enough. I remember converting a pair of denim shorts into a bag and I was mortified when it burst open whilst I was out shopping. My mum then bought me a real sewing machine for my thirteenth birthday and I sewed everything that wasn't nailed down. Mum and I used to sit together in her workroom discussing patterns and refashioning everything in our wardrobes. The sound of the machine is so comforting to me – it's the sound of my childhood; it could drown out any problems I had at school, I just had to turn on the little light and watch the needle go up and down. It's very soothing.' She laughed as a memory resurfaced. 'I remember making my dad a tie, it was the most ludicrous material with flamingos all over it, ideal for a young girl but for a grown man's tie, not so much. But my dad wore it – he was a good sport.'

She looked up to see that Marco had stopped what he was doing and was listening intently to her.

'I'm sorry,' she said self-consciously. 'I'm going on a bit, aren't I.'

'Not at all, you talk about them as much as you want. You must miss them – Canada is a long way away.'

'Oh no, well yes, I do miss them more than anything but they're not in Canada, they both died – my dad when I was fifteen and my mum two years later.'

'I am so sorry, how stupid of me for putting my foot in it.'

'You weren't to know. Being honest, I usually try to block them out of my mind, as it hurts too much to face up to the truth that they both left me. I think that's why I ended up . . .' She paused. She didn't want to go into her relationship with Chad; he had helped to blot out the pain for a while but she had eventually come to realise that he wasn't the answer.

'How do you feel now?'

'I feel comforted. It's amazing how sounds and smells can take us back to happy places. I haven't sewn since I lost my mum so right this minute, I feel happy, just like I did when I was younger.'

'That's good, this place definitely feels like home.'

'Have you still got your parents?'

'Yes, I'm very lucky. They still live in the house where my mother gave birth to us and my dad still works in the restaurant. They argue like dog and cat over everything that it's possible to argue about, but they love each other. They make the best olive oil in the whole of Italy, according to my father of course. Next time I come over I will bring you some.'

'Thank you, I'd like that,' Lottie smiled. She imagined they were so very proud of him. 'OK, how's this looking?' She held up the curtain.

'It looks fantastic – the gold makes it look very luxurious.'

'Thank you, there's enough braid for some tiebacks and some to go on the blankets for Denni too.'

'He will be the poshest donkey around.' Marco swished the curtain around himself like a bullfighter's cape. His dark eyes twinkled as he laughed.

'I could put some round your hat that you wore yesterday, if you like.'

'I always thought that hat needed a little extra something,' he laughed.

'How did you get into dancing?'

'I had a lot of girl cousins who went to dance classes and my friends just wanted to box and fight all the time, but my mama said that I was too pretty to fight and too bothered about my hair looking good! She's a huge fan of black and white films and I used to watch them with her and help her peel potatoes for the restaurant – buckets and buckets of them that I'd picked from the farm. Sammy Davis Jr. was our favourite and Fred Astaire; I used to copy the dances to entertain her friends and then my cousins' dance teacher took me on. I was like an Italian Billy Elliot except I was no good at ballet. My family hoped I'd forget about the dancing and take over the restaurant and other stuff, which I won't bore you with, but my cousin Gabe needed a flatmate so I came over here and never looked back. I do miss home, but this place reminds me so much of it, I really like it here.'

'Me too, My friend tells me you're in a film, how did that come about?' she asked, he looked up at her, his dark hair flopping over his eye.

'I was in a play called *Latino* in New York, Gabe wrote it and it was one of the best experiences of my life. Then it got picked up by a Hollywood producer and they wanted me to star in it. It will be out next year.'

'What do you prefer, the theatre or film?

'I loved them both, the theatre because you are pretty much looking into the audiences eyes and every night is slightly different but with the film, although there are sometimes lots of takes, the final product forms an everlasting product, a piece of history.'

'It sounds absolutely fascinating, so you're a talented dancer, a famous actor but how are you at doing jobs around the house? It looks like it's time to inspect your handiwork.' She stood up and held the barre, which was now firmly fixed to the wall. She adopted a ballet pose, walked a few steps on tiptoe and then clapped her hands together.

'This is brilliant, I'm so excited for Doris to see it. Thank you.'

'You're welcome. Come on, I'll give you a hand with getting these curtains up – Gabe brought some spare curtain hooks in a tin.'

Lottie located them and threaded them onto the curtains whilst Marco stood on a chair and began fixing them.

Once they'd finished, Lottie pulled the string at the side and watched them swish open and closed.

Marco shook her hand, 'Looks like we make a good team.'

'Yes, it does,' replied Lottie, who couldn't help but smile. 'You're a good friend.'

Chapter 15

Doris went through every emotion during the first week of her dance lessons, from tears of frustration to indescribable joy when she got a step right and compete euphoria when both her arms and legs moved in the right direction. Lottie's heart burst with pride on seeing her protégé literally come on in leaps and bounds.

It all started with Doris's birthday. Lottie had invited her over for presents, tea and cake and as soon as she walked in, she commented on how fancy the curtains were.

'I've got a surprise for you,' said Lottie.

'What is it?

'Just stand here next to the string while I get my phone, and when I nod you can open the curtains.'

'Ooh, I feel like a mayoress – I just need a chunky gold necklace. It's not a portrait of me, is it?' she laughed and moved into position.

'Mmm, something like that.' Lottie pressed record and began singing happy birthday, and as she got to the *hip, hip hooray* bit, she nodded and Doris pulled the string, the curtains sliding smoothly along the track.

Doris gazed open-mouthed in surprise; her hands covered her mouth. She looked at Lottie through the reflection in the mirror and broke down crying.

Lottie ran to her and hugged her, tears starting to flow down her own cheeks.

'You did this for me?' Doris managed between sobs and pointed to her own chest.

'Yes, Doris for you, for your special dancing lessons.'

'I can't believe you did all this for me . . . I feel a bit giddy.'

Lottie took her hand and led her to the couch. 'Well I did have some help from Marco and his cousin Gabe. Here, let's have a sit-down and a cup of tea – you can open your other presents and have some cake. Then I'll show you some basic ballet steps, but don't worry, nothing too adventurous for your first time.'

Doris squeezed her hand and kissed her on the cheek. 'You're an angel, you are darling – thank you from the bottom of my heart.' She bit into the cake that Lottie handed her. 'This has been the best birthday of my whole life. Thank you, thank you.'

Lottie breathed a contented sigh as she chatted with a totally overwhelmed Doris whilst enjoying tea and cake. She knew Doris would love the mirrors but she hadn't been quite prepared for this level of emotion.

Chapter 16

On the following Monday, at 2pm precisely, Lottie heard knocking on her door. She checked the room was ready and answered it to see Doris laughing on the doorstep.

'Oh, I love the sign,' she said.

'I thought it would make you laugh. I meant to put it up last week but Camilla only dropped it off yesterday,' said Lottie as she looked at the laminated paper on the door with *Lottie's School of Dance* printed in colourful letters with an image of a cartoon donkey dancing in front of a barn.

'We thought it was hilarious,' said Doris.

'We?' asked Lottie.

'Yes, I told my friend Ruby about my dance lessons and she asked if she could come.'

Lottie stuck her head out of the door to see a little lady with a carrot-coloured rinse on her hair. She couldn't help smiling as Ruby curtsied.

'Of course, you're welcome, Ruby – come on in!'

Ruby's face lit up and she entered the room with Doris.

'I'll pay,' she said.

'No, there's no need for that.'

'Yes, there is,' said Doris. 'It's decided. You need to earn money and we want to learn to dance. It's the perfect solution.'

'I insist,' said Ruby. She took ten pounds out of her purse and put it on the coffee table. 'You can put it towards our tea and biscuits at the end.'

'No, honestly, I'm not taking money off you, this is a thank you for letting me stay on, so why don't you put it towards a nice afternoon tea out or something.' Doris winked at Lottie and Lottie grinned back. What had she let herself in for? she wondered.

Lottie clapped her hands. 'OK ladies, let's start with a few stretches and a little warm-up.' She connected her phone to her speaker, put on some music and started by getting the ladies to shake their hands and feet and roll their heads from side to side; she could hear a fair bit of creaking and cracking as the ladies woke up their muscles and, in their words, their 'creaky old bones'. She stood with her back to the mirror and instructed them with some gentle ballet moves to get their joints going. When their cheeks were rosy, she suggested they had a drink of water before the more energetic dancing began.

'OK, so I'm just going to teach you a few basic salsa steps and by the end of the session, we should be able to do a little routine. Are you ready?'

'Yes,' said Doris and Ruby simultaneously. Lottie started the music and began slowly showing them the first step. Doris almost tripped over her foot and Ruby had to ask where the toilet was. 'Sorry, too much water and jigging about.'

'No problem.' Lottie pointed to the door and once it had closed, she whispered to Doris, 'So you got in touch with your friends then?'

'Just Ruby for now,' Doris nodded. 'It felt a little overwhelming to meet everyone back at the women's group and I bumped into Ruby's son in the farm shop the other day and asked him to get her to pop in for a cuppa.'

'That's lovely and I'm so proud of you. Has it been nice?'

'Oh yes, dear, it's been marvellous. We chatted as though we'd never been apart. Poor Ruby lost her husband and has had a hard time of it lately, so I feel bad that I haven't been around for her.'

'You've had your own sad journey to go on, Doris, and besides it's the present that counts. We can't rewrite the past.'

'You've got an old head on young shoulders, you have.' Doris kept practising as she spoke and Lottie guided her until she found her rhythm.

'That's it, you're doing it!' Lottie clapped.

'I'm doing it, Ruby, look,' she said as Ruby joined them again. Ruby followed suit and soon she was in the rhythm as well.

'That's great, shall we move onto the next step now then?' asked Lottie.

'Oh, can we just keep doing this one for a while in case we forget how to do it?' asked Doris, flushed and slightly breathless.

'Yes, of course,' smiled Lottie. 'We're going at your pace. There's no rush.'

After a few more minutes of doing the same step, Lottie urged them to take another sip of water and helped get them to get going again.

'OK, ladies, this is the same step, but you're now going to get that sexy wiggle on and use the arms, like this.' She demonstrated to them what she was talking about and they giggled as they tried to emulate her moves.

'This is like trying to pat your head and rub your stomach at the same time!' laughed Ruby, but she eventually got the hang of it.

Lottie looked at her watch and realised the hour was almost up. She put some slower music on and taught them a Hawaiian dance move, gently swaying from side to side as they moved forwards and back again, their faces etched with concentration. She eventually got them to stand still and perform the neck rolls again to far fewer creaking noises. She then clapped her hands, 'Well done, ladies, that was amazing, give yourselves a round of applause – you did really well.' She gave each of them a hug then went to put the kettle on and opened some biscuits.

Both of her students were flushed and happy as they chatted animatedly to her and practised the steps in between dunking biscuits in their tea. She felt a huge sense of fulfilment just seeing the obvious joy on their faces, the sparkle in their eyes and the excitement and energy they exuded. After they'd left, Lottie danced like she had at the audition until her muscles ached and her workout top was drenched in sweat. She felt able to take on the world.

Chapter 17

The next week was spent practising and doing chores around the place. She showed Denni her dance moves as she filled up his hay and he seemed fascinated by them, judging by the way he threw back his head and pranced around the field with excitement. Lottie showered and got the place ready for the next dance class and could hear giggling outside the door before she heard the knock.

'It's only us,' shouted Doris. Lottie's face broke into a huge smile and she opened the door to five elderly women, including Doris and Ruby.

'Hi, I'm Edie,' said the first. 'I won a dancing trophy at Butlin's once when I was younger.'

'Lovely to meet you,' said Lottie, shaking her hand and noticing a mischievous glint in the woman's eye. 'Maybe you could teach me a thing or two,' she added.

'Oh,' Edie giggled, 'I very much doubt that, though me and my husband could pull off a good waltz in our time. I've missed dancing since he died though, so this is perfect.'

'Well, it's lovely to have you here,' said Lottie. 'Here, let me take your jacket.' She helped the old lady out of the jacket and hung it on the coat rack near the door. The other women followed suit.

'I'm Frances, are you sure it's OK for me to come? I don't want to be a burden, you see,' said a woman with short grey curls.

'Very nice to meet you, Frances, and it's a pleasure to have you here.' Frances smiled shyly, which endeared her to Lottie even more.

'And last but not least, here's Peggy,' said Doris.

Lottie's heart leapt, and she teared up as she looked into the smiling face before her. The jade green eyes were so like her late mum's that she almost felt she was standing there in front of her. Peggy's dark grey hair with tiny white flecks here and there was immaculate. Lottie gave into an overwhelming compulsion to hug her and Peggy reciprocated gladly.

'I can see you and I are going to get on brilliantly,' said Peggy into Lottie's shoulder.

'I can feel that too,' said Lottie as she reluctantly parted from her.

'I hope you don't mind, but Ruby and I were telling everyone at our Ladies Lunch about our dance lesson and they wanted to join in,' said Doris.

'No, that's absolutely fine, the more the merrier,' said Lottie. She winked at Doris to let her know she was impressed with her venturing out to meet her old friends again.

'OK everyone, my name is Lottie and welcome to my little unofficial school of dance. Just so you know, I'm a qualified dance teacher and I also have certificates in first aid. So, first things first, did you all bring some water as we need you to keep hydrated during the session?'

Peggy's hands flew to her mouth, 'Oh no, I've left mine at home,' she said whilst the others jiggled their water bottles for Lottie to see.

'Not a problem,' said Lottie, moving over to the fridge. 'I've got some spares.' She took one and handed it to Peggy, who mouthed a thank you to her. 'OK, so to begin with, I just need to know whether anyone has any injuries or problems that I need to be aware of?'

'I've got a touch of arthur-itis in my hands,' said Edie, 'but I can still knead bread with the best of them.'

'That shouldn't be a problem,' said Lottie, smiling at the mispronunciation, 'but if you find anything painful or uncomfortable then do let me know.'

'Will do,' said Edie.

'I have a twinge in my back occasionally,' said Frances, rubbing at the affected area and it goes straight down my leg sometimes but I've been so looking forward to this, I hope that doesn't mean I can't join in.' Her mouth was downturned and she looked as though she might cry.

'No, don't worry, it should be fine,' Lottie reassured her. 'Just stop if it hurts and we'll keep an eye on it.' She smiled as Frances's face lit up.

'OK, let's get started.' She walked over to the mirror and stood with her back to it. 'If you can all spread out and we'll begin with some warm-up exercises first and by the end of the session you should be able to perform a short dance, but don't worry if you can't keep up – just keep up your own pace and just watch first if you find the move a bit tricky.' She noticed Ruby had her hand up. 'Yes, Ruby?' she asked.

'Can I go to the toilet please?'

'Yes, of course, you don't need to ask,' said Lottie.

'Oh, I think I might need a tinkle as well,' said Frances. 'I think it's my nerves.'

Lottie smiled. 'There's absolutely nothing to be nervous about – just take your time and don't worry.' She turned to the rest of the group. 'OK ladies, we're going to start with some neck rolls followed by gentle side to side steps.'

Everybody proceeded to follow her instructions and within the first five minutes, everyone had gone to the toilet, 'Just in case.'

'I've heard of a Mexican wave, but that was like a Mexican wee,' joked Lottie as the final student rejoined the class.

Lottie ran through some simple salsa steps and watched as one by one, her students picked up the rhythm. Doris almost tripped as she and Ruby crashed into each other during a grapevine, but nobody was hurt.

'And now everyone, have a quick drink because it's time to put everything together,' shouted Lottie over the music, 'and don't forget to wiggle those hips, you sexy ladies.'

She shouted instructions and pointed in the directions they needed to go in as Shakira blasted out of the speaker. Apart from a few hiccups with Edie facing the wrong way at one point, and Frances being completely out of sync with everyone else, it went pretty well. When the dance finished, Lottie encouraged them all to clap themselves. 'That was amazing, ladies! At this rate you'll have your own dance troupe.' She looked at the huge smiles on flushed faces and felt a sense of pride in herself and a rush of affection for these older women, who seemed to be having a ball. She cooled them down with gentle stretching exercises and put the kettle on to make tea, which she produced along with a plate of biscuits.

'That was amazing, thank you so much,' said Frances, placing ten pounds on the coffee table. 'Can I come again next week please?'

'Yes of course, but I can't take all that, it's too much,' said Lottie, blushing.

'No, it's not, it's perfectly reasonable for the wonderful activity you've just provided for us. There's not much else to do round here for us oldies, so this is brilliant,' added Edie as she placed her ten-pound note on top of the others. 'Same time next week?' she asked, looking hopeful.

'No, I can't take money as this isn't an official dance lesson and yes, same time next week if you'd like to. I'll even get some posher biscuits for you all,' Lottie said, returning the money.

'Right, well, I'd better get off home to my Bella and Bertie – they'll be wondering where I've been,' said Edie as she put her jacket back on. Lottie helped her get her second arm in as she struggled.

'Are they your grandchildren?' she asked.

'I wish,' said Edie. 'No, they live far away; Bella and Bertie are my Liver Birds, my pet parrots and I love them.'

'Oh, I love the sound of them,' said Lottie. 'Hold on, my brother's fiancée told me a story about two parrots called the Liver Birds – she loves them too.'

'Oh, you mean Camilla, so Blake is your brother? Yes, I've known him for years, Camilla is like a granddaughter to me.'

'Just like this one is to me,' added Doris, kissing Lottie on the cheek.

Lottie's heart danced to its own joyful tune as she waved goodbye to her new dance students when they left en masse, chatting away to each other, and giggling whilst practising the dance steps they'd picked up quite easily. She found she was very much looking forward to their next session. Seeing them together, enjoying each other's company did make her miss her friends though; her best friend Rachel had come to wave her off when she left Canada and she longed to see her again.

Chapter 18

Doris was singing and dancing around her kitchen the next morning when Lottie turned up with their breakfast eggs. She popped them in the waiting pan and joined in with a samba step.

'Oh, you've really brightened up my world by coming here, Lottie – all the ladies were saying what a fab time they had at the dance class and I'm afraid that there's a few more interested in coming next week. I hope that's OK?'

'Yes, of course, I really enjoyed it too. It's the most fun way of exercising as far as I'm concerned.' She bit into a thick slice of hot buttered toast.

'I completely agree and it really lifts the mood too. Just being able to say I'm off to my dance class feels so liberating, especially for this little dumpling.' She poured two mugs of tea from the pot.

'I'm glad you're enjoying it, and stop being so hard on yourself – you're not a dumpling, you're actually very graceful in how you move,' Lottie replied, taking one of the teas.

'Oh, I don't think so,' Doris blushed and looked a little flustered as she scooped the sausages out of the pan.

'I'm serious. Do you think Frances looks graceful?'

'Well yes, but she's petite and elegant.'

'And so are you. I was only thinking yesterday how you two moved very similarly. You need to stop that little voice inside your head from telling you you're not good enough, because you are.' Lottie could see that her words had touched a chord with Doris, the same way that Mia's similar words had affected her.

'Anyway, have you heard from your audition yet? asked Doris, whilst swiping a tear from her eye.

'No, I haven't, which means I probably haven't got the part. I'm not bothered about it but looking back, I think it did me good having to dance like that – it showed me I'm bloody good and has chased away some of my insecurities after my wedding dance went so wrong.'

'Your wedding dance?' Frown lines appeared on Doris's brow. 'I didn't know you were married?'

'I'm not. It's a bit of a long story so I don't want to bore you, but I almost got married. I danced up the aisle and my groom didn't like it. I felt humiliated and ran away.'

'Ooh, what a horrible bugger – I bet you looked beautiful dancing up the aisle. He should have been grateful.'

'Aw thanks, Doris, I'm over it now. I think it was just the idea of being part of a family that appealed to me but when I saw Blake, it was like I woke up and came to my senses and it all went downhill after that when I found out I couldn't trust him. I don't feel like that person anymore.'

'I know how you feel. I've always wanted to be part of a family but it wasn't meant to be, but you're part of my family now and you're very welcome.'

'Aw, thank you, Doris, you've certainly made me feel very much at home here.'

'Anyway, I was wondering what you thought about getting whiffy installed, as my friends were raving about it.'

'Whiffy?' Lottie pursed her lips and tilted her head, not sure she'd heard correctly.

'Yes. They said they keep up to date with the women's group and everything. Apparently, I could even sell my bread and eggs on there too and play games with them like Scrabble but through the computer.'

'Oh, you mean Wi-Fi.'

'Yes, that's it, I knew it began with a w. By the way, that's what I need as well: a computer and a smartphone.'

'I think that's a great idea, Doris – do you want me to arrange it for you? I can set you up with an account so that you can see your friend's photos and things if you want. It can be a lot of fun.'

'Sign me up then, but do I have to look at all of their photographs?' she frowned.

'No, of course not,' Lottie laughed. 'Just the ones you want to. You can even block people you don't like if you want to.'

'If only we could do that in real life,' she laughed.

'If only,' echoed Lottie as Chad invaded her thoughts.

Chapter 19

A couple of days later after the Wi-Fi was installed, Lottie set about giving Doris a masterclass on the internet and social media, with a resounding cheer going up when Doris finally mastered the double click.

'So, let's go out in the garden and take your profile picture,' said Lottie, positioning the older woman in front of a pretty, flowering bush. Doris smiled shyly as Lottie took the picture and after a few more attempts, with Doris scrutinising the end results and alternating between holding the phone at arm's length and an inch away from her face, she finally settled on an acceptable shot.

Lottie uploaded it and explained to Doris how she could find her friends on there. Doris searched for those she liked that she could add as friends and also people she hated so she could have a nose at their lives too. 'Oops,' said Lottie as she had to stop Doris inadvertently liking a photo from someone on her hit list or, even worse, accidentally adding them as a friend.

Lottie also set up an account for the eggs and bread that Doris loved baking.

Doris quickly got into the swing of internet shopping, her first purchase being a laptop of her own so she wouldn't need to borrow Lottie's all the time.

'It's like magic,' she said when it turned up the next day. 'I don't know why it's taken me so long to get *with it*.'

'Just don't let it take over your whole life,' warned Lottie, slightly concerned about the shopping monster she appeared to have unleashed.

'I won't – I'm totally in control,' said Doris, her eyes peeping over the top of the computer. 'I'm just bidding on a smart new blanket for Denni and I'm winning so far.'

'Well, good luck with that,' Lottie smiled. 'Oh, by the way, talking of Denni, did I tell you that Marco said he'd really like to mend his little house? Is it a house or a stable for a donkey?' Her heart fluttered at the mention of Marco's name and she had a flashback to being in his arms. Doris's reply cut into her thoughts before her imagination carried her off to some fantasy world with a Venetian dancer in a mask. Perhaps she'd better stick to just thinking about Denni, he was the only male she was interested in at the moment and he'd already stolen her heart.

'I just call it his shelter, but yes, that would be lovely. It took a battering in the storm and will definitely need repairing before winter. Marco's friend covered it with tarpaulin when they rescued him from the ditch but it's only a temporary measure. Shall I see if I can buy a new one on the internet?'

'No, not yet – I think it's best that we see what he suggests first.'

'Yes, I'm sure you're right. Now then, Frances tells me you can play games on these things – can you show me how to do that?'

Lottie rolled her eyes. 'What are you like, Doris? You've become an internet fiend overnight.'

Doris laughed and ran her eyes over the list of games that Lottie was scrolling through. 'There that's the one, a bit like Scrabble but you don't have to be in the same room. I can play that with my old friend Gertie, she's a lovely woman but suffers with terrible wind. I always had to have the windows open when she visited. Jesus, it was everything I could do to stop myself from gagging; one time I had to put hand cream on my upper lip to give myself something nice to smell.'

Lottie was stifling a giggle but tried to keep it restrained out of respect for poor old Gertie – she just hoped she didn't want to come to dance class. She helped Doris get the game started and connect to Gertie before going back to the barn, where she showered, changed into her pyjamas and video-called her best friend in Canada.

'Hi Rachel, how are you?'

'I'm so good, thank you, I see you've got the internet installed now at last. Are you going to give me a tour around your little home? I mean, the pictures are great but nothing like a live tour.'

'Yes of course, here we go.' Lottie walked around with her laptop showing Rachel around her cute little barn.

'It's just gorgeous,' she said. 'It really suits you. You look really well, Lottie, but I miss you so much.'

'Me too,' said Lottie, 'but it's done me so good to get away, you know, from everything.'

'I know and I completely understand why you had to go, but I just wish things could have been different.'

'So do I, but it's my own fault for making stupid rash decisions. I mean, what was I doing marrying him? It was like I was just caught up in this whirlwind, well actually more of a tornado, and my feet couldn't touch the floor. I look back now and ask myself "What were you thinking?"' She shook her head and took a sip of wine.

'We all make mistakes, Lotts, so don't punish yourself anymore.'

'I know, but I just feel so stupid. Have you seen him lately?'

'I haven't. He finally stopped asking for your address.'

'I'm so sorry, Rach, for leaving you to pick up the pieces and fielding all my calls.'

'It's fine, you're always welcome to hide out at my place, hopefully Chad will grow up and be less reliant on his parents. The last I heard he was working and doing well.'

'I'm glad he's OK. We just weren't good together, especially with his interfering mother and lechy dad.'

'This way is better for everybody. Anyway, enough of all that – how is lovely Denni, has he been a good boy?'

'He's just gorgeous. Here, look, you can see him out of the window.' She turned the laptop and heard

Rachel calling him. For a whole hour Lottie relaxed in her friend's company and thoughts of Chad soon evaporated as Rachel told her all the latest gossip amongst their friends.

Chapter 20

The sound of her phone ringing jolted Lottie out of a weird dream, in which she was back in the church looking at Chad's mum's disgusted face and was just about to tell her exactly what she thought of her.

'Hello,' she answered groggily, her heart still pumping wildly from her stressful dream.

'Hello, is that Lottie Daniels?'

'Hi, yes, it is.'

'Hi, my name's Rie and I'm calling on behalf of *Truly Dance*. I just wanted to say I'm sorry you didn't get the lead but the calibre of dancing was so high that the choice was almost impossible.'

Lottie's heart stopped; she held her breath and leapt out of bed to pace the floor. The woman continued, 'We would like to offer you a position as one of the backing dancers in the show.'

'That's fantastic, thank you so much for letting me know.' Lottie's heart sank momentarily, she really hadn't thought she wanted the job but once she grasped how lucky she was to get one of the eight positions of backing dancers from the hundreds who had auditioned she admonished herself for being so ungrateful. She would have given anything to get a job like this back in Canada and this job offered her the perfect excuse to stay in Bramblewood a little longer.

'You're very welcome. We will email you with the finer details but just to let you know that the requirements are rehearsals four times a week and the shows are on the Saturdays, which will run for four weeks and start in a few weeks. Do you have any immediate questions?'

'I, er, can't think of any at the moment.' Lottie was trying to take it all in but her mind was racing. Hopefully she could keep the dance sessions on as Doris and her friends would be so disappointed if she didn't do them anymore.

'Well, just email me if you think of anything later. Oh, and are you free tomorrow to get measured up for the costume fitting, two o'clock at the playhouse?'

'Yes of course.'

'We'll see you then. Congratulations again. Bye.'

'Thank you, bye.'

She put the phone down on her bedside table and didn't know what to do first. She was desperate to tell Doris but needed to get her chores done, so quickly threw on her scruffy clothes and headed out to feed Denni.

'Well, Denni, it looks like you're the first person to find out my good news. I've got through as a backing dancer, what do you think of that?' Denni blinked his beautiful fairy-tale eyelashes and nibbled the chopped-up carrot from her hand; she stroked him between the ears and went off to sort out the chickens. She heard a vehicle pull up and the gate opening and when she turned to see who it was, she saw Marco waving at her before jumping back in the van and driving it up to the field. He jumped out, opened the back doors, and began offloading some wood.

'Good morning to you, Minnie, I mean Lottie!' he shouted.

She reluctantly waved back, knowing her scruffy joggers were covered in chicken poo and feathers. She could only imagine what state her hair was in as she hadn't brushed it yet. She hoped he couldn't see from where he was but despaired when she saw him heading her way. She put down the brush and quickly spread fresh hay down for the chickens that were now clucking around her. She stepped out of the coop as he approached and picked up the basket to collect the eggs. Her cheeks burnt as he gently kissed her on each one.

'How are you today?'

'Oh, you know, not bad thanks. Just getting on with my chores.'

'I used to do this back in Italy at my family's home. It was attached to the restaurant. I miss it. Do you mind if I help?'

'No, go ahead, I was just about to collect the eggs. Hey John, Paul, George, and Ringo – meet my friend Marco. Marco meet the Beatles.'

'You do know I'm going to have to think of Beatles songs and chickens now, don't you? Let me see, oh yes, how about I Want to Hold Your Hen? Or Here Comes The Hen?'

'The Ballad of John and Yolk-o,' Lottie joined in chuckling. 'Get it? Y.O.L.K.' she spelled out.

'Oh yes, that's a good one, I like that,' he laughed, 'very clever. I've got another: Eight Lays a Week.'

'How about I Saw Hen Standing There?' Lottie sang.

'Good one, I've got another, That'll be the Lay.'

'Erm nope, sorry that wasn't the Beatles.'

'Oh damn it.' He replied, 'Go on, you can have another turn while I think.

'With a Little Help From My Hens?' added Lottie

'OK, last one, and this is a cracker, oh did you see what I did there.' He joked and Lottie laughed. 'OK drumroll . . . Hen I'm Sixty Four.' He took a bow.

'OK, I can't think of any more now, but I'm sure Doris would love to hear those titles. She loves the Beatles and she's got me singing their songs too. My mum was from Liverpool, so it makes me feel as if there's a connection, albeit a small one.'

'I'm sorry you lost your mum.' He looked at her with empathy in his eyes.

'Thanks, me too.' She changed the subject, not wanting to lose the fun element they'd been enjoying. 'OK, so how have our fab four done today?'

Marco reached into the boxes, retrieving the large brown eggs, placing them gently in the basket Lottie was holding. She could smell his aftershave again, which had lingered on her skin from his kiss. The hint of lemon and bergamot awoke her senses and reminded her of sunny mornings and cloudless blue skies. The warmth of his face so close to hers was having a strange effect on her and she hoped he couldn't tell. She probably smelt of stale wine as she'd had a fair few glasses of the stuff whilst reminiscing with Rachel last night. She just hoped she didn't have a red wine moustache as she hadn't washed yet. She tried to keep her hand covering her face as much as possible.

'There's nothing quite like the taste of a fresh free-range egg, is there?' he said after filling the basket.

'You certainly can't beat one of Doris's dippy eggs.'

'Wait, a Doris what egg? Did you say dippy? What is dippy egg?' He was frowning but she could tell he was amused.

'You know, dippy egg, it's a boiled egg and you cut the top off and dip your soldiers in.'

'How do you dip your shoulders in? You English people have some funny traditions.' He shook his head and his eyes sparkled.

'Soldiers, not shoulders,' she laughed, whacking him on the arm as she realised he was winding her up.

'So, nothing beats the taste of Doris's free-range dippy egg then?'

'There is one thing that's equally as good, I think,' she replied. He looked into her eyes and she looked away immediately before she got lost in his sexy brown ones.

'What's that?' he asked.

'Doris's homemade bread, toasted, thickly spread with butter and dipped into the golden yolk is sheer heaven.' She looked back at him and saw he was focusing on her lips as she spoke.

'You make it sound like one of those Marks and Spencer adverts,' he smiled. 'This is no ordinary dippy egg, this is a Doris dippy egg with thick, toasted shoulders . . . I mean, soldiers.'

He grinned when he'd finished and his face lit up completely; he seemed to be waiting to see if she was amused or annoyed and when she put him out of his misery by laughing out loud, he joined in. They both turned towards the house as they heard a voice and saw Doris waving a tea towel out of the window.

'Marco, you must stay for breakfast!' she shouted. 'I've bought a new bacon crisper from the internet.'

'I guess you're going to find out just how extraordinary Doris's dippy egg is for yourself now,' smiled Lottie.

They both headed over to the house.

'Have you heard back from your audition yet?' he asked.

'Yes, I'm delighted to say I got the part of backing dancer.'

'That's brilliant and you'll be amazing. Does this mean you will stay here longer now?'

'I guess so, to the end of the show anyway. I need to send my details off for a DBS check and I've already applied for a National Insurance number so I can be paid. I mean, honestly, I would have done it for nothing but truthfully, I'd like to pay back some money to my ex's family.'

'Is that for the wedding that never was?'

She blushed as she remembered she'd confided in him about it.

'Yes, I paid towards some of the wedding and so did Blake but I feel awful because it was me who walked out on it.'

'I'm sure they'll survive – you did the right thing.'

'I just wish I'd listened to my doubts earlier on, but I thought they were just pre-wedding jitters. If ever there was a time I needed my mum, it was then. She always told me I had a devil and an angel on my shoulders and I should listen to the angel more.'

'The trouble is, the devil always offers the most fun choices but in the long run they turn out not to be the best decisions.'

'That sounds like someone with experience of being burned. What's your story, Marco?' They stopped walking and Marco looked deep in thought.

'My story is one of karma. My mama always told me to stop breaking the girls' hearts because I would get it back one thousand-fold. She was right – my ex tore my heart out of my chest and danced the tango all over it in scarlet high heels. I hadn't realised how much hurt I'd caused the women I left behind. I immediately contacted those I could and apologised to them and in my childhood sweethearts' case, I apologised to her parents too. They hoped we'd marry but I came to England instead to stay with my cousin.'

'That must have been a big change for you?'

'It was. I came from a small village where everybody knows everybody, so when I arrived here, I went crazy like a kid in a candy store. I'm ashamed of that now but Alexia paid me back. I made a pact with myself that the next woman I date will be the woman I marry. I want to settle here in Bramblewood, raise a family and be a husband and father to be proud of.'

'Oh wow, that's some serious talking there. But you shouldn't be so hard on yourself, Marco, we can't change what we've done in the past but we can adjust our behaviour and try to be better people in the future. I've made a pact with myself too – I think I need to learn to love *me* again before I can ever share my heart with anyone else.'

'That sounds like an excellent idea – do you mind if I share that pact with you?'

'Not at all. It's good, isn't it?'

'It really is. I mean, the one time I realised I really didn't like myself was . . .' He paused and looked down, his cheek pulled inward as though he was clenching his teeth.

'What?' she asked, intrigued as he seemed reluctant to make eye contact.

'Oh nothing, never mind.' He shook his head and spoke in a much lighter tone.

'I just have to do one thing when I find my future bride.'

'What's that?'

'Hide her running shoes,' he quipped whilst nudging her gently with his elbow. Lottie put her hands on her hips and pulled a fake stern face at him. 'Oi you.'

'What? Too soon?' he teased and ran towards the farmhouse. Lottie raced behind him and pulled on his jacket to slow him down. They arrived in the kitchen flushed and giggling whilst Doris ordered them to wash their hands as she dished up their breakfasts.

'Doris, Marco is being arrogant,' teased Lottie.

'I'm not, I promise, Doris, it's just that Lottie makes me feel nervous.' He smiled and she caught a glimpse of dimples in his cheeks that she hadn't noticed before.

'Right the bacon is crisping up nicely so now we just need those eggs. 'Lottie, my dear, I mean this in the nicest possible way, but you look like you've been dragged through a chicken coop backwards.'

Lottie ran her fingers through her hair and pulled out a piece of straw. Doris continued, 'Go on, we've got a guest. You've time for a quick shower before breakfast. Don't worry, Marco will butter the toast.'

She glanced at Marco and smiled like a naughty schoolgirl. She noticed a twinkle in his eye as his mouth curved into a slow smile, revealing his perfect white teeth, his black hair flopped onto his forehead. As he ran his fingers through it to brush it back, Lottie gulped, her throat dry, partly from the hangover and partly because the simple action had an interesting effect on her insides.

'That's why I love you, Doris, you always just say it like it is. Won't be long.' She kissed the older woman on the cheek.

'Doris, we've been thinking about Beatles songs – putting words to do with chicken in the title.'

'Oh, what like Chicken to Ride,' said Doris as she poured the tea.

Lottie stopped in her tracks and she and Marco looked at each other in total surprise before simultaneously bursting out laughing.

'You're an absolute queen, Doris,' said Marco.

'You really are,' agreed Lottie, 'you've just completely wiped out our suggestions.'

Marco winked at her as she left and her stomach flipped.

Ten minutes later she rejoined them, smelling fresh with wet hair in plaits and a clean T-shirt and shorts on. She'd been able to smell the freshly cooked sausages and bacon before she entered the house and her stomach was rumbling loudly.

Her heart flooded with emotion as she walked into the kitchen and saw Marco waltzing around with Doris in his arms, her head up high. Her cheeks were flushed and Lottie could see she was in her element. As the song on his phone ended, he twirled Doris around and bowed to her and she curtsied in reply. She began to dish the breakfast out as the next song began and he held his hand out to Lottie.

'Ah, this is perfect for the rumba . . .' As the music played, he led her around the room; she could feel the heat from his hand on her waist and kept up with him step for step, her heart rate quickening as he expertly positioned her hand just a little closer to eye level and he looked deeply into her eyes as they danced. Lottie found it very difficult to look away. When they'd finished, Doris applauded.

'Oh, that was just beautiful – you two look so good together.'

Marco smiled and Lottie blushed. She busied herself by grabbing the teapot and put it on the table with cups and saucers.

Marco sat where Doris gestured him to and she and Lottie sat in their usual places.

'Maybe you could help out at a session at Lottie's dance school in the future as I'm sure my friends would love that,' suggested Doris, her eyes filled with hope.

'I'd love that too,' said Marco. 'I didn't know you had a dance school,' he said to Lottie.

'Well, that was actually just a jokey sign I made for Doris and her friends.'

'Oh, I see, so what sort of dance are you doing?' he asked.

'All the sexy stuff like whatsername? Sharika with the hips,' said Doris.

'Shakira,' Lottie corrected with a smile. 'A bit of samba and salsa for now, but hoping to progress on to all genres eventually – it depends how long the ladies want to keep on going for and for how long I'm here for.'

'We're loving it so much I'm wondering whether we'll need to convert the bigger barn for it.'

'You really think there'll be that much demand?' asked Lottie.

'I guarantee it. All the ladies who lunch have expressed an interest and there's about thirty of them. They've asked if you can come along to one of our lunches to do a little mini session.'

'I'd be delighted to,' said Lottie, completely taken aback.

'They meet in a scruffy portacabin now since the council closed the community centre down. A few of them have been asking whether you teach younger children as their grandchildren are interested too – there's nothing like that around here anymore.'

'Well, yes, I'm qualified to teach all ages.'

'So shall we do the barn then?'

'I can help with that,' added Marco.

'Why don't we see how we get on first? I mean I'm not even sure how long I'll be staying in England for – I was only meant to be visiting.' She felt a bit flustered and overwhelmed at the permanency of everything.

'Sorry, that's my fault for getting overexcited, but really it won't take much for the barn clear-out – it's got a few bits of farm machinery in it but nothing too awful. I could probably sell them and make a bit of money. It would be doing me a favour if we did clear it out and as Marco has offered his big strong muscles, who am I to argue with that?'

'Well only if you're sure, but please don't do it on my account,' said Lottie, feeling slightly less responsible for it all.

'It'd be great to give the old barn a new lease of life and I can sell the bits and pieces on the internet. It's a win-win situation.'

'It sounds like a great idea,' added Marco. 'Let me know what I need to do to help.'

'Thank you, love,' said Doris.

Marco's phone pinged just as he put the last forkful of food in his mouth. 'Excuse me, ladies, this might be my cousin who's helping me with Denni's shelter.' He read the text. 'Yes, it is – he's just outside.' He stood up, pushed away his chair, and carried his plate to the sink. 'That was a delicious breakfast – thank you so much, Doris, a real baptism of dippy egg and the company was even better.' He made eye contact with Lottie and she smiled.

'I told you it was no ordinary dippy egg, didn't I?'

'You sure did and you were absolutely right.'

'You're more than welcome anytime, Marco. Give me a shout if you need anything – there are tools in the shed if they're any use to you. I'll pop over in an hour or so once your breakfast has gone down with some homemade cake and coffee. How does that sound?'

Marco did a chef's kiss with his hand. 'It sounds bellissimo Doris, thank you. Ciao!' He kissed her hand and Lottie smiled as she saw her cheeks flush.

Lottie walked out with him and over to see Denni, as Gabe approached them smiling. He patted Marco on the back and said hello.

'It's so good to see you again, Lottie,' said Gabe. 'I hope this one hasn't been giving you any trouble.'

'Not at all, he's been as good as gold,' replied Lottie, feeling her cheeks go even redder than Doris's had. 'It's great to see you too. Doris and I really appreciate what you're doing for Denni.'

'He's a lovely animal,' Gabe replied. 'In fact, I was wondering whether we could hire him for a nativity play we are putting on in the playhouse later in the year.'

'I'm not sure – you'd have to ask Doris. I believe he loves children though, from what she's told me.'

'I'm sure the show would be a sell-out with Denni starring in it,' added Marco.

'Anyway, I'd better be off. I've got a dress-fitting later,' said Lottie, who felt quite reluctant to leave.

'Lottie got through as a backing dancer in *Truly Dance*,' announced Marco.

'Oh, that's brilliant, congratulations – the competition was fierce,' said Gabe. 'You should be very proud of yourself.'

'I am actually,' said Lottie. 'I just need to find out whether my friend got through too or she may have even got the main part.'

'I feel sorry for whoever does get it; I mean, you do know this guy has two left feet don't you,' Gabe joked, digging Marco in the ribs with his elbow.

'This is very true,' Marco laughed along, as did Lottie.

'Well, it's time for me to go.' She ruffled Denni's hair between his ears and scratched his long snout.

'Goodbye then,' said Gabe, 'and good luck with the show.'

'Thanks, bye.'

She was too far away from Marco for him to kiss her on the cheek without striding over to her and both looked at each other awkwardly. She scratched her cheek where she imagined his kiss would have been and unfurled her hand into a wave. He waved back before bending to pick up the wood they needed for the shelter.

133

'I guess I'll see you at rehearsals,' he said.

'Yes, I guess you will,' she replied.

'Why are you acting all tongue-tied?' she heard Gabe ask him and she smiled to herself as they bantered whilst carrying on with the work.

A shiver ran through her entire body as she walked away from them as she self-consciously wondered whether he was watching her. She kind of hoped he was.

Chapter 21

When Lottie got back to her place, she picked up her phone to see a couple of missed calls from Mia. She called her back and settled by the window where she could watch Marco and Gabe work.

'I'm a backing dancer,' screeched Mia as soon as she answered the phone. 'Me tooooo!' replied Lottie, mirroring her excitement. 'Have you got to go in for a fitting today?'

'Yes, at two, what about you?'

'Same,' said Lottie.

'Shall I pick you up? Can we practise together some time? Oh, this is going to be brilliant.'

'Yes please, yes of course, and I know, it really is, isn't it.' She had decided to enjoy this amazing experience for what it was. Going through it with Mia was equally thrilling as she was such good company.

An hour later, Mia was sitting next to the window with Lottie and taking photos of Marco and Gabe with her phone, which she zoomed in on, telling Lottie exactly what Marco was up to and how gorgeous he was. 'And that's his cousin, you say?' she asked.

'Yes, that's Gabe,' replied Lottie. 'Now come away from the window before they see you!' she laughed.

'They're both so bloody hot! Can we go and see Denni?' she asked.

'No, not today, but next time though, I promise,' said Lottie. 'Come on, we've got to go – we don't want to be late.'

As she closed the barn door, Marco looked over and waved. Lottie raised her hand whereas Mia looked like she was in a waving competition, enthusiastically using both hands.

'Come on, let's go,' said Lottie, linking her arm through Mia's and marching her giggling towards her car.

'How can you not fancy him, Lottie?' asked Mia as she pulled out of the drive.

'I never said that,' she replied.

'Ah, so you do fancy him!' she laughed.

'No, yes, well, the thing is, obviously he's absolutely drop-dead gorgeous but I'm just coming out of a relationship I thought was going to be forever and I've only just realised what a disaster that would have been. I feel like I was blinkered or something and I've left it very messy so the last thing I need right now is another relationship. One day I'll tell you all about it but at the moment I need to forget it and concentrate on what I love the most.'

'You mean me, don't you,' said Mia.

'Too right I do, and of course dance,' she laughed.

'Soooooo, how would you feel if I was to turn my charms on him? You know, woo him with my womanly wiles.' She pouted and twisted a braid around her finger; thankfully they were waiting in traffic.

'I would wish you good luck, or maybe I should wish him good luck as you look like someone whose womanly wiles mean business.'

'Are you sure you don't mind?'

'Not at all – we're just friends. He's all yours.'

'Thank you so much, you're a true friend,' said Mia. She turned the music up full blast and they sang along unashamedly to the Jonas Brothers as they continued their journey.

Once at the playhouse, they were led backstage where the finalists of two more women and four men were introduced to one another along with Davina, the performer who had been chosen to be the main dancer. A costumier set about measuring them behind some curtains. The atmosphere was a heady mix of anticipation and exhilaration; Lottie felt alive again. She had loved working on shows in Canada but usually just to live audiences – she had never worked on a TV show before. After the measurements were taken, they had a quick meeting and Lottie and Mia, along with a couple of others, decided to have a late lunch at the playhouse restaurant. Lottie decided on a mozzarella and grilled peach wrap whilst Mia had tuna and grape.

'These fillings are a taste sensation,' commented Lottie between bites.

'I totally second that,' said Mia. 'It used to be a bit of a Greasy Joe's sort of place with uninspiring sandwiches.'

'Oh really? Well, I'm glad it's not anymore seeing as we're going to be spending a lot more time here. I can't tell you how happy I am to be working again. I missed out on a couple of dream jobs back home but this makes up for it.'

'I'm so glad to hear it. I wasn't sure if there would be complications with you being Canadian.'

'Well luckily for me I was born here and my mum was British anyway so it wasn't a problem.'

'Oh, that's good, and I'm really happy that your life is moving forward in the right direction for you.'

'Thank you, darling,' said Lottie, nudging her softly with her elbow. She loved that Mia didn't probe too much into her private life and seemed to have the ability to sense that Lottie didn't want to talk about stuff. 'I'm lucky and I just love it here. I've never felt happier, especially as I've started my little dance sessions too. What about you? Do you have another job?'

'No, but I've just come back from being an entertainer in a Spanish holiday resort.'

'Well, that sounds exciting.'

'Yes, it was, I loved it.'

'Why did you come back?'

'Oh, you know, reasons.' Mia shifted awkwardly in her chair and Lottie could have kicked herself for being nosy after just appreciating Mia's lack of invasive questions.

'Sorry, I shouldn't have asked that.'

'Don't worry, it's fine.' Mia waved away any awkwardness with her hand. 'Let's just say this job has come in just in the nick of time for both of us. Hey wait, is that Marco over there?'

Lottie's heart leapt out of her chest at the mention of his name but she calmed when she realised that Mia was referring to a photo on the wall.

'Let's go and have a look,' said Mia.

They walked to a brightly painted wall with colourful frames surrounding pictures from the various shows that had been performed there. Marco was dressed as a baddie in one photo with a cape swooshing around him.

'He looks devastatingly dark and sexy in this one, don't you think, Lottie? He's making my legs go funny just looking at him.'

'He's not bad,' agreed Lottie, 'although my legs are fine.' Her legs were fine but he was having an effect on other parts of her body that she didn't want to mention. 'Oh, look there's Gabe.' She pointed to another photo, desperate to change the subject. 'He's the one who was at my house today helping Marco.'

'Oh yes, another hottie in that genie outfit – he could make my wishes come true anytime,' smiled Mia.

'You're incorrigible,' laughed Lottie.

'I know, I think it adds to my charm, don't you?'

'Very much so,' Lottie agreed. 'And you're just the sort of person I need in my life right now.'

'Ditto,' said Mia as she linked arms with Lottie and they headed out.

Chapter 22

Mia's face dropped exaggeratedly as she pulled into Lottie's drive.

'Oh no, their cars have gone. Can I meet Denni though quickly before I head off?'

'Yes, of course, we can inspect their handiwork too. The shelter is looking brilliant from here.' The car came to a stop and Mia quickly undid her seatbelt and jumped out.

'Erm Mia, aren't you forgetting something?' Lottie gestured her head towards the car, which was still purring away.

'Of course, I need to switch my engine off. I'm just so excited to meet Denni.'

Lottie smiled at the childlike excitement on Mia's face.

Mia bent into the doorway and turned off the engine before slamming the door and heading off in Denni's direction, Lottie running to keep up with her.

They both pelted over the fence and into the field and Denni, resplendent in his new red velvet blanket, ran over to Lottie, bowing his head up and down to her.

Mia approached cautiously and waited for Lottie to introduce her. Soon they were both stroking him and Mia was able to hug him too.

'Oh Denni, I can see why Lottie loves you so much, you're just beautiful.' She stroked her face against his neck.

Lottie handed Denni some chopped up carrot from his manger. 'Just hold your hands out flat,' she said.

Mia did so and giggled as Denni's lips nibbled the chunks from her hand.

'They've done a brilliant job here – I must get them something as a thank you,' Lottie said from inside the shelter which now looked like a little house instead of the scruffy old aluminium and tarpaulin effort that was there before.

'You can offer me up as a thank you if you want,' Mia laughed, winking at Lottie.

'You want me to pimp you out for a donkey shelter? Can I see if they'll throw anything else in too?' Lottie joked.

'Be my guest,' she grinned. 'Oh Denni, it's been lovely but I have to go now.' She squeezed him gently and gave him a kiss.

'Thanks for the lift today and it was so nice to be with someone I know,' said Lottie.

'No problem – see you at rehearsals tomorrow. Shall I pick you up again?' She jangled her car keys.

'No, it's OK thanks, I'm going to visit my brother tomorrow straight after, so I'll make my own way.'

'OK, see you then.' Mia kissed Lottie on the cheek and Lottie watched her drive off. She smiled as the music boomed from the car as she went. Mia was a real breath of fresh air and gave off good positive vibes. She made Lottie feel as though she could achieve anything and she certainly felt less nervous when Mia was there.

Lottie hung out with Denni for a little while longer, took some photos of him in his new shelter, finished off her chores for the day and made herself a toasted sandwich for dinner before going up for an early night. As she drifted off to sleep, she tried to chase away flashbacks of seeing Marco tear down the old tatty shelter, his strong muscles rippling as he did so. She remembered the feel of his arms around her as he pulled her towards his firm body as they danced and she shivered as a surge of longing shot through her body like a rocket. Feeling totally wide awake now, she had to go downstairs for a glass of water and took a book up with her to read, which sometimes made her feel sleepy. Nothing could chase him from her thoughts though and the devil on her shoulder persuaded her it would be a good idea to text him a picture of Denni in his shelter. The angel on her other shoulder urged caution but she couldn't see any real harm in it, as long as she didn't put any kisses at the end of the message. Lottie decided to do it quickly before the angel had time to change her mind but accidentally added a kiss to the end anyway as she used them for full stops on texts. 'Damn it,' she hissed.

Marco replied immediately with '*Denni looks so comfortable, tell him he's welcome and so are you. Ciao x*'. She could imagine him saying the words in his sexy accent and eventually nodded off with the angel and devil on her shoulders arguing about whether she should be interested in him or not. She silenced them with the thought that if she were interested now, it didn't matter because even if Marco was emotionally available, Mia liked him and she was gorgeous so that was that.

Chapter 23

The atmosphere at the playhouse was electric as the dancers congregated and were paired up. Lottie's dance partner was called Stephen and Mia's Matthew. Four of the backing dancers made up two same-sex couples, which everyone found thrilling. The first rehearsals were back-breaking and Lottie worked harder than she ever had in her life. By the end of the day, she felt as though she had been in a washing machine on spin cycle as every single muscle in her body felt battered and bruised.

She understood now why the audition had been so gruelling because they had to have real stamina to get through this far. She had been really looking forward to visiting Blake and Camilla that evening but she couldn't face it. She sent him an apologetic text explaining how exhausted she was and that she needed to cancel, which he was fine about. She then helped herself to the plasters and antiseptic wipes from the first-aid box on the table to tend to her blistered feet.

Once home, she found that Blake had popped round to tend to Denni and the chickens and had left a flask of Camilla's homemade soup and a tin filled with cupcakes on the doorstep. Her eyes filled with tears at the lovely gesture and she managed half of the soup and two mini cupcakes before crashing out on the couch. She wondered, not for the first time, whether she had bitten off much more than she could cha-cha chew.

She needed far fewer plasters at the end of the next day's rehearsals and her face hardly winced with pain at all after the first full week, although that was more because she'd trained her brain to not receive the messages from her overstretched muscles and aching feet. The more she spun and kicked and shimmied, the more exhilarated she felt.

'I still can't believe I'm a part of this show, it's such an amazing dream come true,' she said to Mia at the end of another exhausting rehearsal.

'I know exactly what you mean, but as much as my body is finished, my mind feels totally alive.'

'Me too, it's like it's gone into overdrive. I think it's trying to remember every step in every sequence.'

'Yes, you've hit the nail on the head there – even when I'm dreaming, everything happens in sequences of eight. I don't think I've ever done anything this intense before.'

'Well, seeing as the show officially starts next week, this is our last Saturday off for a while, so how about we have a drink and something to eat? We need to replace some of those calories we've burnt off.'

'Sounds like a great idea,' said Mia. 'Let's go to the Grape Escape, I think it's tapas night tonight.'

'Ooh delicious, and I could murder a cocktail. Oh, but I'm driving.'

'That's OK, you can leave your car here and pick it up tomorrow I'll drop you off later.'

'Don't you want a drink?' asked Lottie.

'No, I'm up early tomorrow so I won't bother. I'll have one when I get home though.'

'Hi ladies, we're just off to the wine bar for a drink, do you want to join us?' asked Stephen. 'I'll buy you a drink, Lottie, to make up for standing on your foot earlier.'

Lottie looked at Mia and she shrugged her shoulders and smiled. 'Great minds think alike,' said Lottie. 'That's just where we're off to. And don't worry about the foot thing as I seem to remember getting a little too close to your face with my high kick. I forgot to account for those bloody heels I was wearing.'

'Ah good, so we're even then,' said Stephen as he took her hand and twirled her towards the door.

As they walked down the corridor, a door to one of the private dance studios suddenly opened and Davina stormed out. 'You did almost drop me, you idiot!' she shouted. Marco appeared behind her.

'Davina, please have a heart, the poor guy said he was sorry − you were perfectly safe,' Marco tried to calm her,

'Well, I don't see why I should have to dance with the ordinary dancers anyway, when I'm supposed to be the star of the show and just dancing with you.' She stroked his chest as she spoke and Marco took her hand and again tried to reason with her.

'That's what the show is all about − we're doing old-school musicals for the practice and if you watch the old films, you can see that the star of the show is always carried by lots of the male dancers. We need to work together to achieve this.'

'Well, I want him fired,' Davina spat indignantly.

'I think you're overreacting,' said Marco. 'Go home and get some rest – I'm sure you'll feel better by Monday.'

A man suddenly pushed past them, his face red, his shirt drenched in sweat. 'Don't worry, I'm leaving anyway. No amount of money is worth putting up with her for.'

'Good riddance!' Davina shouted to his back.

Lottie caught Marco's eye as he gave her companion the once-over. She smiled but he didn't reciprocate; instead he tried to coax Davina back into the room.

Matthew had run after the man. 'Con! Con, are you OK?' He put his hand on his shoulder. Con slowed down. He pulled off his shirt, stuffed it in his bag and threw a hoodie on.

'Hi Matt, I'm all right, don't worry. That woman is impossible, she thinks she's Beyoncé or someone. Such a diva.'

Matt encouraged him to go for a drink with them and they were soon sitting at a table in the wine bar just down the road.

'Don't let Davina the diva push you out, Con – you've earned your place in the show,' said Mia. 'I've heard a few things about her, that she makes all kinds of unreasonable demands.'

'Like what?' asked Lottie.

'Well, it seems to be her party piece trying to get other people fired. She apparently pushed to the front of the queue in the café and when someone told her to get in line, she said, "Don't you know who I am?"' Mia replied. 'Apparently she was an extra in some TV show so she thinks she's the dog's you know what's.'

'Yes, that definitely sounds like something she would do,' replied Con, taking a swig of his beer. 'I didn't nearly drop her; she threw herself into me on purpose, trying to hurt me.'

'Why would she do that?' asked Lottie, bemused.

'I can only think she wants to get me sacked. We've got history, you see.'

'Oh, I get it,' said Mia. 'A woman scorned and all that. What happened?'

'Nothing, and that was the problem.' He looked at the four puzzled faces and continued, 'We went out a couple of times, I thought as friends but it seems she thought it was something else. When I got together with my boyfriend, she said I had offended her and made her feel foolish. It seems she still hasn't forgiven me and wants me gone.'

'Well, that's just not fair,' said Lottie. 'Maybe you can talk to the organisers rather than leave altogether. She sounds like a nightmare.'

'That's the understatement of the year; she's more like nightmare on Elm Street than your common or garden nightmare.' He laughed along with everyone else and drained his glass before putting it down on the table. He stood up to go. 'The thing is, Marco really needs to watch out because I can see the hunger in her eyes. She's got her sights firmly set on him; she loves a scandal and lives in a world of make-believe – she'll do anything for attention.'

Lottie's eyes opened wide and her stomach churned at the thought. 'Well, that's tough because they're not allowed to have a relationship – it says so in the rules.'

'Davina the diva doesn't do rules and from what I've heard, Marco likes the ladies,' said Con.

'Well, she'll have to get through me first because the gorgeous Marco is all mine,' laughed Mia, hugging herself. Lottie almost choked on her cocktail.

'I swear Marco used to go out with some gorgeous redhead who used to be a dancer round here. Alexa or Alexia was her name,' said Stephen. 'My cousin really fancied him and I remember she saw the article in a magazine and sulked for weeks, so Davina the diva could be just his type.'

Lottie sucked on her straw, louder than she expected, as she approached the end of her drink. She realised everyone was looking at her and put the glass down. 'That must have been who was in the photograph with Marco that we saw in the playhouse,' she said.

'Oh yes, she was stunning,' said Mia.

'As long as he's not interested in personalities then she could be in with a chance, I suppose,' Matthew teased. Mia elbowed him. 'But there's no way he could resist the lovely Mia's charms over DD,' he added.

'To my charms,' said Mia, holding up her glass.

'To Mia's charms,' the others joined in.

Chapter 24

Lottie's eyebrows raised when she opened her door, a couple of days later, to see a gaggle of older women surrounding one man. Doris marched through the door first and the others followed like a caterpillar.

'Hi Lottie, we've brought Arthur today. He's got two left feet when it comes to dancing but wants to propose to his lady friend and we need you to help.'

Lottie beamed a welcoming smile. 'Come in everyone and find a space to stand. So, Arthur, what sort of dancing were you thinking of for the proposal? A tea dance maybe or ballroom perhaps?'

Lottie did a double take when he told her his thoughts. 'I'll see what I can do,' she told him, whilst wondering how in the world she was going to be able to pull that one off, especially as he stood on her toe even just shaking hands with her. She grimaced, turned on the music and began the warm-up session.

After everyone had gone, she decided to visit Denni and brush his coat. He greeted her warmly with loud eeyaws that seemed to echo for miles.

Staying at Doris's had provided her with a sanctuary and she had felt peace at first, but now she sometimes felt confused, especially about Marco. She was in no way ready for a relationship but she couldn't deny that she found him deeply attractive. A few years ago as a dedicated commitment-phobe, she would have just had a fling with him and got it over and done with but she'd never been fulfilled doing that and often wondered what her parents would think of her if they were looking down from above. Also she knew that Marco was looking for something much more serious than a fling and she couldn't offer that.

When she got back from the night out on Saturday, she'd decided to google Marco and Alexia and discovered that they were in an on-off relationship for a couple of years but it seemed what attracted them together also tore them apart. In one article he had referred to Alexia as a love like no other, but then Lottie herself had probably said the same about Chad to anyone who may have questioned her reasons for marrying him. Looking back now, she would probably refer to him as the most fun of her life or the most excitement of her life, but most definitely not love. She could see that now as clearly as the tuft of hair between Denni's ears.

'I thought I'd find you here.' She jumped as a familiar voice interrupted her thoughts. She quickly reached for a strand of hair that had come loose from her ponytail and hooked it behind her ear.

Denni lifted his head up and down a couple of times in greeting.

'Marco, hi,' she said. She wondered why she hadn't heard his car but then noticed his bike leaning against the wall next to the gate.

He jumped over the fence as though it were part of a graceful dance and nuzzled his face in Denni's fur.

'I've been ringing your number but no answer.' His hair flopped over his eye and he swept it back with his hand; she imagined how soft it would be beneath her fingers and how his lips would feel if he'd kissed her.

She patted her jeans pocket but the phone wasn't there. 'Oh sorry, I haven't turned it on this morning – I've been doing my chores and teaching my dance class.'

'Oh yes, how's that going?'

'Very well actually, thank you, and I have a children's class starting too next week, thanks to the grandchildren of my mature ladies and some advertising I did. I can start charging now too as I'm all legal, and above board and the seniors practically threatened to string me up to Doris's new curtain if I don't accept their money, most of which has gone on the insurance I had to take out.'

'That's amazing, well done. You deserve good things happening to you,' he smiled.

Her eyes filled up at that point and she felt ridiculous – what on earth was she feeling tearful for? The answer came to her straight away; she'd been so busy self-flagellating that she had *unworthy* set as her default mode.

'Are you OK?' he asked. 'You look a bit upset.'

'No, I'm fine, thank you,' she sniffed. 'Allergies, I think – some of Denni's hair went in my eye.' She pulled the mound of hair out from the brush as if to prove a point and let it drift off on a breeze.

'We used to do that when we brushed the donkeys back home on the farm,' he replied. 'My mother would say let it blow free so the birds can make warm nests to lay their eggs in.' He seemed lost in his memories for a few seconds.

'Would you like to have a go?' She held out the brush to him.

'I'd love to,' he replied. He took it from her hand and looked straight into her eyes as his hand brushed against hers for the briefest of seconds. Lottie almost heard the crackle of electricity that jolted through her body at his touch and she pulled her hand away quickly.

Marco began brushing Denni.

'You're not allergic to me as well, are you?'

'No,' she laughed, wiping her hands on her jeans, and feeling her cheeks burn up. 'It was just one of those static shocks.'

'That's good,' he said, 'because I'd like to make you an offer.'

'An offer?' Lottie couldn't imagine what he was going to say.

'Yes, that's why I've been ringing you and emailing you.'

Just then the clouds that had been building up all morning decided it was time to empty their coffers in one go. Denni trotted into his shelter and Marco and Lottie ran to her barn.

'Where did that come from?' Lottie closed the door against the elements. 'Here, make yourself at home.' She handed him a towel, which he took gratefully, and rubbed his hair. She filled the kettle and flicked it on.

'Tea or coffee?' she asked.

She turned to face him and saw him look at her chest for the briefest moment before averting his eyes; on looking down, she yelped when saw her T-shirt was almost see-through.

'Won't be a minute,' she said and raced upstairs to change into a different top.

'Milk and sugar?' he asked when she returned.

'Just a little milk please.'

She grabbed a towel and patted her hair dry whilst he finished making the drinks. He handed hers to her with a smile that took her breath away. He opened his mouth to speak when the door burst open and Doris ran in armed with her laptop.

'Oh my god, have you seen the news?' she said, flashing the screen at Lottie then slamming it shut when she saw who she was with. 'Oh, hi Marco, don't worry – I'll come back later.' She turned her back on them and headed for the door.

'What is it, Doris?' asked Lottie, intrigued after seeing Marco sigh, she looked from one to the other.

'It's OK, you can show her as it's partly to do with why I'm here anyway.'

Doris looked relieved and bustled over to Lottie and set up the laptop on the coffee table and the two women huddled together. Marco stood with his back leaning against the worktop and ran his hand through his hair.

Lottie's eyes opened wide and her hand flew to her mouth as she read the headline:

MUCKY MARCO COULDN'T KEEP HIS HANDS OFF ME! BY DAVINA DEVONSHIRE

'Oh my god is right,' said Lottie as her eyes scanned the article.

'It's not true – I can explain everything,' said Marco, looking deflated.

'Well, it doesn't look good from what it says here, Marco.'

'I promise you nothing ever happened with her apart from dancing but this woman has been a complete nightmare from beginning to end. The company have looked at the CCTV from where she alleges, we . . .' He hesitated and Lottie read out loud from the article.

'We had mind-blowing sex standing up in the alley at the back of the theatre, and I can tell you Marco's rhythm is not restricted to his dance moves.'

Lottie had to stifle a smile when she saw Doris give Marco the once-over. 'You know one of the guys said that Davina the diva had her sights set on you.'

'That's an understatement. She tried to get me to go out with her from the very beginning but number one, I'm a professional and we would have been disqualified immediately if that had been true, and number two, I've got feelings for someone else and I would never want to jeopardise that.'

Lottie suspected this was Alexia, the woman who stole his heart, and she felt a stab of jealousy in her own heart.

He paced up and down the small kitchen area, his hands gesticulating as he spoke. 'But don't get me wrong – in the past I was known for being what my cousin calls a Lothario. But I'm not like that anymore – I've grown up. I'm no longer interested in flings, especially not in the workplace. Once bitten and all that. I want to distance myself from the old me.'

'I believe you, Marco,' said Lottie, wanting to put him out of his misery, his face wearing a troubled frown. She stood up and put her hand on his arm. 'Why is she doing this?'

'The bosses had so many complaints about her that they had to let her go – they know this is just a publicity stunt from Davina; in fact, she's already been offered a role in a soap. She just used us to get ahead and that's fine, good riddance to her.'

'Sounds like you dodged a bullet with her. But I don't understand what this has to do with me.'

'Ah, I was coming to that. When they realised the situation with Davina had become untenable, the judges decided to reach out to the dancer who came second in the final auditions.'

'And who was it?' asked Lottie, still not quite getting it.

'It was you,' he said, his beaming smile showing his beautiful white teeth and his elusive dimples that not many people got to see. 'She only beat you by one point anyway, as it happens.'

Doris nudged her. 'Well done, Lottie.'

Lottie's mind was racing but her mouth wouldn't work for a couple of moments whilst the news sank in.

'I can't do it.' She slumped onto the couch, her eyes staring straight ahead.

Marco sat next to her and gave her a gentle nudge. 'Of course you can, you're a brilliant dancer.'

'But what about my dance classes? I can't let them down.'

'You won't have to let them down; you still get a couple of days off per week. I can work around your schedule and at least I'll know you're not lusting after me all the time.' He said, tongue in cheek. Lottie whacked him playfully on the arm. 'Come on, you won't regret it, I promise. I'll look after you.' He added, 'Tell her, Doris.'

'It is an amazing opportunity, dear, and after all, you did audition for it in the first place,' said Doris.

'Yes, but that was accidental and I never for one minute expected to get it.' She jumped up and covered her face with her hands.

'Well, now you have so come on, what do you say?' Marco's phone rang and he checked the caller ID. 'That's them now, wanting to know your answer.' He took the call.

Lottie's head felt as though it would explode from the pressure of having to decide.

'Yes, I'm with her now,' he replied, looking at her expectantly.

Lottie heard the voice on the other end of the call asking what she'd said and with butterflies the size of dinner plates in her stomach, she spread her fingers to peep through them and nodded at Marco.

'Is that a yes?' he shouted.

'Wait . . .' she hesitated. 'Who was next after me because if it's Mia I would rather she had it – she deserves it much more than I do.'

'Who was in third and fourth place?' he asked and listened patiently. He shook his head at Lottie. 'Mia didn't make the top three unfortunately. So will you take it?'

'OK, I'll do it. It's a yes,' she said.

'Did you hear that, she said yes!' he bellowed down the phone.

'Brilliant,' said the voice. 'See you later.'

'Bye,' he said before giving Lottie a hug. 'Oops, I'm sorry.'

'It's fine,' she replied, wishing it could have lasted longer.

'I've got to get back.' He stood up, swigged the last of his coffee and put the cup down on the worktop. 'I'll see you tomorrow – you won't regret this.' He touched her arm gently as he passed her and kissed Doris on the cheek on his way out. Doris turned and winked at Lottie before she left too. Lottie tried to get her thoughts in order, as from now on she was going to be even busier. She just hoped she'd be able to cope with it all.

Chapter 25

Lottie still had the first of her children's dance classes to get through before rehearsing the next day with Marco. The first class was free and she was astonished to see how many children had turned up. The age range was between five and ten, but as Lottie was collecting forms that she'd asked the parents to fill in, she noticed an older girl hovering near the door.

'Hi,' said Lottie, 'can I help?' The girl's blush almost matched the red top she was wearing.

'No, it's OK, I'll come back another day.' She turned to walk away.

'Are you sure? You can stay and watch if you like,' said Lottie, gesturing with her arm that the door was open and she should come in.

The girl turned and her face lit up. 'Can I really? Are you sure you don't mind?'

'Of course not, come along, some of the parents are watching too.' She held out her hand, 'My name's Lottie, what's yours?'

The girl took her hand and gave a gentle squeeze, 'Melissa.'

'Well, it's lovely to meet you, Melissa, come on in.'

Melissa followed Lottie into the room and sat in one of the dining chairs that Lottie had set out.

The session was very eventful and chaotic to begin with, until Lottie brought a semblance of order with her calm teaching method and sense of fun in the lesson. The parents who'd stayed seemed happy with how the lesson had gone and most of them booked for the next week. As the last one left, she noticed Melissa hovering by the door again.

'What did you think?' asked Lottie.

'Oh, I loved it,' she replied with a faraway look in her eyes. 'It's my absolute dream to be a dance teacher.'

'Oh really?' Lottie immediately flashed back to when she first knew she wanted to dance and could see the same look in this young girl's face.

'Yes, I'm studying dance at college and I've been looking for some experience in a dance school but I've been rudely rejected by some and completely ignored by others. I saw your advert and thought I'd pop along to see if you needed any help. I wouldn't need paying.' She bit her lip in preparation of facing another rejection.

'Well, that's a very interesting proposition – why don't you stay for a cup of tea and one of these cupcakes and we can have a chat.'

Melissa beamed at her. 'Thank you, I'd love to.' She reached into her bag and pulled out an envelope which she handed to Lottie. 'Here's a reference from my college tutor and I've also got a DBS check in there as I have a part-time job in a nursery too.'

Lottie made the tea and placed a plate of the cupcakes on the table. Melissa told her how she had slight learning difficulties and was painfully shy.

'My mum said that I could dance before I could walk and I've always loved music. I've been watching choreography lessons on YouTube and I've been having a go myself.'

'That sounds very interesting – how would you feel about showing me?'

Melissa blushed to the roots of her dark blonde hair. Lottie placed her hand reassuringly on top of hers. 'Don't worry, you don't have to do it now.'

Melissa breathed out a sigh of relief. 'I can show you a video.'

'Well, that would be amazing – yes, please, I'd love to see it.'

Melissa found the video on her phone and handed it to Lottie, who watched it with tears in her eyes. She felt overcome with emotion at the innocence in the young girl's face as she performed. It took her back to when she danced unashamedly without a care in the world. When she still had her mum and dad.

She dabbed at her eyes with a tissue. 'You've moved me to tears here, Melissa. Your dancing is beautiful, I'm very impressed.'

'Really?' Melissa looked as though she would burst with excitement and took a hearty bite of a cupcake.

'Yes, really, you're amazing and I'd love you to come and help out but only on one condition.'

Melissa stopped mid-chew, her eyes questioning.

160

'That I insist on paying you for your time. Now let's get our diaries together,' she said. They ate, chatted, and even got up and rehearsed a move that Melissa had been having trouble with.

Chapter 26

Mia's reaction to Lottie's news had been very supportive, much to Lottie's relief as she wasn't sure how she'd take it.

'You'd better not go falling in love with him though, remember he's all mine,' she'd joked.

'Don't worry, I have absolutely no intention of falling in love with anybody else for a very long time,' Lottie had reassured her. She would miss dancing with the group as they had all got to know each other quite well and the reality of dancing with Marco so intensely was hitting her nerves hard.

She entered the practice room and apart from a brisk hello, Marco appeared quite stand-offish.

'OK, we're going to have to hit the ground dancing as time is running out,' he said as he turned on the speaker. 'Did you manage to look through the videos I sent you?'

'Yes,' she replied. 'I'm familiar with the jive as my mum and dad used to dance it a lot and I won a jive competition when I was thirteen.'

'OK, good, well let's get started.' The look he gave her made her want to hide inside herself.

As the music boomed around the room he got into position and determined to give this everything she had, she held onto his hands and danced. After four hours of non-stop twisting and twirling, pushing and pulling, they were able to stop for a brief lunch. Marco left the room and Lottie sat outside to eat fruit and yogurt. Anything heavier would sink in her stomach and she couldn't possibly dance with the same intensity as she had done that morning. The adrenaline coursing around her body was making her feel a little sick. After a couple more sips of water, she headed back into the rehearsal room and Marco was already waiting for her. She stretched and took a deep breath as he turned the music on and they began again. The atmosphere felt very tense and the hair on the back of her neck bristled.

'I'm sorry, I just can't seem to get this bit,' she said as she stumbled slightly for the zillionth time.

'The diva couldn't do it either,' he scoffed.

'Well, if you think about it, then we maybe need to look at the common denominator,' she snapped.

He looked taken aback. 'The common what?'

'Oh nothing,' she replied, her heart heavy. 'Can you maybe show me in slow motion? Once it's in there it will stay,' she said, tapping herself on the temple with her forefinger.

'OK, let's record it,' he said, setting up the camera on his phone and leaning it against the stereo.

He huffed and proceeded to perform the steps with her slowly rather than the breakneck speed with which they were used to and after a few times, Lottie realised there was a beat where he overstepped that was throwing her off balance slightly.

They tried again at the quicker pace and she stood on his foot. He yanked himself away from her and bashed the off switch, causing a deafening silence that rang in her ears.

'I'm sorry, but you're overstepping,' said Lottie indignantly.

'I don't think I am,' he retorted. 'You're just being too slow.'

'Well let's look at the recording then for proof.' She stood with her hands on her hips defiantly.

'Good idea,' he said. He picked up the phone and they watched the dance in slow motion.

'Look there,' she said, tapping the screen. 'You overstepped.'

'You're right,' he replied, his voice filled with disbelief. He threw the phone down onto the stereo and ran his hands through his hair, leaving it sticking up in tufts as though he'd just got out of bed.

'I apologise,' he said. 'It's all my fault. I was being unfair to you. Maybe this wasn't such a good idea after all. Feel free to drop out and go back to the ensemble.'

'Why would I do that? We haven't even given it a chance yet. What's wrong, Marco?'

'Oh, I don't know, I'm just annoyed that the diva wasted so much time and I just don't know if we will be able to catch up now. We've only got two weeks until we perform for real on the telly.'

'Are you saying you've got no faith in me?'

His eyes widened and he touched her arm. 'Not at all, I've got every faith in you but I've just realised what a hard ask it is.' He smiled but she could see the frown on his forehead.

'What is it really, Marco, you're not being yourself.'

'Is it that obvious?' he replied. He slunk to the floor and sat with his back against the wall, his elbows balanced on his knees and his head in his hands.

Lottie grabbed their water bottles, handed him his and sat beside him.

'Come on, spill, or I'll tell Denni you've been mean to me.' She nudged him with her elbow.

'No, don't do that, he's my only friend,' he laughed and took a swig of water from his bottle. 'This morning I found out that my ex is also competing in the show from a different region. I didn't think I would be seeing her again after we split up and it's just rocked me. I'm sorry if I was mean to you – I just wasn't thinking straight.'

'Was it a bad break-up?' she asked.

'For her, no, but for me it was devastating, but it did make me look at myself with a magnifying glass and to be honest, I got what I deserved. As my cousin says, I met my match with Alexia – she used and abused me just like I had with all the others. I thought she was the one – she even met my family in Italy – but I wasn't the one for her.'

'When was the last time you saw her?' Lottie asked.

'Over a year ago when she left me for a director.'

'Is she still with him?'

He shrugged. 'I've no idea.'

'Are you still not over her?'

'What do you think?' he replied. 'I've never been told off for overstepping before.' He winked at her.

'Never been told off for overstepping or never overstepped?' she asked.

'Neither, I swear – my dancing is usually impeccable.'

She jumped up and held her hands out to him. 'Come on, we've got lots of work to do.' She pulled him up. 'We're going to fix that broken heart of yours and win this competition.'

'Oh, we are, are we? And just how are we going to manage that?'

'Well, for a start, I know someone who fancies you so you haven't lost your touch and secondly, we are going to practise until we get these steps right, even if it takes all night.'

She put the music on and they danced until her bones ached. At the end of the session, he turned the music off and she could still feel it ringing in her ears. She sat on a bench to change her shoes whilst Marco straightened the room up and closed the windows.

'It's you, isn't it?'

'What's me?' she replied as she filled up her water bottle and he cheekily handed her his to refill.

'The one who fancies me?' he laughed.

'No, it isn't.' She pushed him on his chest and tried to hide her reaction on feeling his firm muscles but from the way his dark eyes flashed, she could tell he suspected.

'Who is it then?'

'I'm not telling you, but it definitely isn't me.'

'Fibber.'

'How about I tell you if we get through the first round?'

'Sounds good,' he said, 'but I already know it's you.'

'I think I preferred sad Marco,' she laughed. She turned her phone on and it pinged immediately with a text.

'Oh no, is that your boyfriend checking up on you?' he asked.

'Something like that,' she replied and typed a thank you message to Doris who'd invited her for dinner.

Chapter 27

Half an hour later Lottie was sitting on Doris's recliner chair with her feet up, dinner tray on her lap as she tucked into a delicious chicken casserole. She had downed a couple of ibuprofens before she left the playhouse, and they were just taking the edge off the pain she felt in every throbbing muscle of her body.

'I'm not sure I can make it to my own bed tonight, Doris, I might have to sleep on your comfy couch forever.'

'I know how you feel, dear,' replied Doris. 'I feel the same after one of your dance classes.' She lifted her glass of squash and tapped it against Lottie's. 'It's the trials of being a dancer, I guess.'

'I think you're right, Doris. It's not easy for us professional dancers, you know, we might make it look so but it's mostly about discovering aches in muscles you never knew you had.'

'I know that feeling,' chuckled Doris. 'Anyway, I'm dying to know, how did dancing go with your hunky man?'

Lottie swallowed her food and drank a mouthful of squash as she contemplated. 'It wasn't what I expected, to be honest. I was quite nervous about it but excited too and then Marco was . . . well he just wasn't Marco – he was more like a damaged soul. He's a perfectionist at dancing yet he missed a beat – his mind was just not on it today so it made me feel a little bit down about the whole thing.'

'Oh no, that's not good. I was hoping you'd really enjoy yourself today.'

'I did in the end. He confided in me about what was on his mind.'

'I imagine that awful article in the paper shook him up a bit.'

'Yes, I think it did. I mean, he has been a bad lad in the past but he swears he's not like that anymore and I believe him. Also, the fact that he and I now have to get used to each other after he'd already been working with Davina the diva and they'd got through so much of the dancing.'

'Well hopefully it won't take too long for you two to catch up; I mean you make a stunning couple.'

'I can assure you that is the last thing on both of our minds but yes, I think we could dance well together. He's certainly keeping me on my toes – that's when I'm not standing on his, of course,' she laughed.

'You didn't, did you?'

'Oh yes I did and he wasn't happy. Luckily it was all on camera and he accepted that it was his fault so that's fine. It's going to be hard work but I think we can dance well together with practice.'

'Ooh, I bet it made your insides turn to mush having some sexy hunk hold onto you so tightly. I would probably accidentally snog him if it were me,' she said, her eyes sparkling with mirth.

'Doris,' shouted Lottie, 'you're so bad!'

'Oh, come on, you can't say you haven't thought about it, you're only human,' Doris teased.

'I might have done in the audition, but today when he appeared so cold, I didn't feel that way at all.' She felt ridiculous as tears sprung to her eyes but the tension and nerves were catching up with her, along with the disappointment of not enjoying the day as much as she thought she would. She cheered herself at the thought that they had at least ironed out some of the problem and hopefully things would be better tomorrow.

'Are you OK, dear?' asked Doris as she took away Lottie's plate and replaced it with a bowl of jam roly-poly with custard.

'I'm fine, thank you,' she replied, swiping away the tears running down her cheeks. 'Oh, my word, Doris, I won't be able to move tomorrow if I eat this.'

'Nonsense, it's good old-fashioned fare with carbohydrates to give you the energy to get through another day of intensive training.'

Lottie didn't have the strength to argue and not enough conviction to resist her favourite dessert.

'My mum used to make this for me – it's my favourite comfort food.'

'Well you enjoy it, my darling, and there's plenty more for tomorrow as well.'

Lottie had a taste and her eyes closed as the delectable

sweetness filled her mouth. She continued taking tiny spoonfuls to savour the blissful feeling.

'There's something I need to talk to you about, Lottie.'

Lottie stopped scraping the bowl and immediately snapped out of her post-food afterglow moment. 'What is it?'

'I've had a message from someone on Facebook that I wanted to show you.'

Lottie jumped into protective mode. 'You have to be so careful on social media as sometimes people aren't who they say they are and there are so many scammers out there. You haven't shared your bank details or sent anyone money, have you?'

'No, not at all. I'm not stupid.'

'I know you're not, Doris, but these scammers are so clever nowadays and very sophisticated.'

'Well, I hope it's nothing like that anyway. Can you have a look?'

'Of course I will. Let's just get these dishes done quickly.' Lottie kicked back the recliner, winced at the pain in her calves and stood up to put her bowl in the sink. Doris immediately washed it along with their plates, Lottie grabbed a tea towel to dry and Doris put the kettle on to make tea.

Once the chores were finished, Doris logged into her account and placed the laptop in front of Lottie. She clicked into the messages and saw it was from a man called Reggie McDougal. His profile picture looked relatively normal, of a grey-haired man with a walking stick standing in front of the Sydney Opera House.

'So do you know this Reggie guy then?' asked Lottie.

'Yes, we were friends for ages right through school and we started going out together a few years after we left. It got pretty serious actually.'

'Oh really, he looks very nice. What happened? Why did you split up?'

Doris looked down. 'It sounds ridiculous really now, but the thing is, he proposed to me.'

'You split up because he proposed to you? Did you love him?'

'I did more than anything, but you see his proposal came with conditions.'

'Conditions? Sounds very ominous.'

'Well, the thing is he had an amazing opportunity to move to Australia; he had family over there who could sponsor him. It was his lifelong dream.'

'Oh, I see, and didn't you fancy that?'

'I did fancy it a lot, but I was also terrified as it was so far away and not as easy to get to as it is today.'

'So you turned him down?'

'Not quite. You'll probably laugh at this because I was a grown woman but basically my parents wouldn't let me go and, in those days, we did as our parents told us. I told him I couldn't go and that was the last I saw of him. I was heartbroken. Comfort-ate for months, hardly left the house and my dad just said it was for my own good.'

'That's so sad. So you never saw him again?'

'Only once at a dance that my friend had forced me to go to. Only that's when I discovered that he'd proposed to one of my other friends and she'd said yes. They'd married earlier that day; I escaped before he could see me. Never heard from him again.'

'I'm so sorry, Doris, that must have been awful for you,' said Lottie, squeezing the old lady's hand gently.

'It was at the time but do you know, I'm not sure I would have left my parents even if I could have.' She refreshed the teacups with more tea from the pot. 'My mum said he can't have loved me that much at the time if he was so willing to go off with someone else so soon.'

'Your mum has a very valid point there,' said Lottie. She should have kept that to herself instead of rubbing poor young Doris's face in it, she thought. 'Did you ever meet anyone else?'

'There were a few dates but nothing substantial and then old Malcolm, who came to help out on the farm. We started seeing each other behind my parents' back; mind you, I was in my forties by then but it felt daring and also my way of rebelling too. After Mum and Dad had gone, he moved in here with me. It was a nice relationship but not earth-moving, not like with my Reggie, but it was companionship. Anyway, as you know, he left me a few years ago, went into hospital and never came home again.' She wiped a tear from her eye.

'I'm so sorry, Doris, that must have been so painful.'

'It was, but there you go – you live, if you're lucky you love and then you die.' She topped her tea up from the saucer where she had spilled some. 'Some people don't get to love at all so at least I must be grateful for that. But what do you think about his message? Do you think it's him or a scammer?'

Lottie read it out loud.

Dearest Doris, I hope you're well. My granddaughter put me on this social media business a year or so ago to keep me occupied after losing my dear wife. I've regularly searched for your name so imagine my surprise when you finally popped up on here. You still look as beautiful as ever, by the way. I hope that life has been as kind to you as it has to me. I'm visiting the UK next month and have been in touch with a few old friends to meet up. Do you remember Freddie Fahrenheit? He was always so red and looked as though he were about to explode when he got too excited, and he hasn't changed by all accounts. Also, Hammy Hamilton and his wife June. Quite a few of our mutual friends have passed away apparently, which is sad. Anyway, on a brighter note I just wondered whether you would like to meet up too. I look forward to hearing from you. Yours Reggie x

Lottie noticed Doris blushing profusely but decided not to tease her about it as she seemed a little nervy about the whole thing. 'That's really sweet, Doris, and it seems pretty genuine. Do you recognise the names he's talking about?'

'Yes, I do, and I've checked but they don't seem to be on Facebook so he couldn't have got them from there. What do you think?'

174

'I think it's wonderful and a fantastic opportunity to meet up with old friends.'

'I was thinking that, but then a part of me is a little bit angry now and it's raked up all my hurt feelings from the past. I'm not sure I can open myself up to this. I'm wondering if it's best to just ignore him.'

'Well, there's no rush, of course, so why not take a little time to think about it before you reply to him? It might be nice to catch up with him and the others. I wonder if whether because he was so young then that you might possibly forgive him for what he did?'

'We were so very young, it seems like multiple lifetimes ago, but the only way I can forgive him would be if he apologised, which he hasn't done.'

'Maybe he just didn't think it was the right time or maybe he wants to apologise face to face.'

'True,' Doris nodded.

'Look, why don't you sleep on it before you answer him? If you want to wait until I'm back from work tomorrow then I can help you but, in the meantime, why don't you make some notes on what you want to say?'

'Oh, you are a love – that sounds like a great idea. Thank you, darling Lottie.'

'You're welcome. I'll see you tomorrow and I'll bring a takeaway for dinner.'

'Ooh yummy, night then, dear.'

'Night, Doris. See you tomorrow.' She leaned and kissed her on her soft wrinkled cheek before leaving for a well-deserved sleep.

Chapter 28

The next morning, Lottie got to the studio early to practise some moves alone. She felt super-energised and her mind clear from the negativity following yesterday's session with Marco. Today was going to be a fresh start and she felt invincible. She wondered whether Doris had been right about the jam roly-poly; the thought of it made her mouth water. Her breakfast this morning consisted of a strawberry, banana and blueberry smoothie, which alleviated her guilt at having a takeaway and more roly-poly tonight.

'You're an early bird today,' Marco shouted over the music, stopping her mid spin.

'I know, I surprised myself. I think it's all the comfort food Doris is feeding me.'

He turned the music down. 'Look, I need to apologise for yesterday – I was a real swine, as my mum used to call me. A selfish pig, so I really do, from the bottom of my heart, apologise and I promise never to bring any problems I have on the outside into our dance sessions ever again.' He stood opposite her and took her hands in his. Tingles ran through her body as a result of his unexpected touch. She looked into his eyes and saw absolute sincerity in his gesture.

'You are a swine,' she said. A sexy one, she thought. 'But I forgive you, just this once.'

'You won't regret it, I promise. But I have an idea – I think we need a story to go with the dance to help us visualise it better.'

'What kind of story?' she asked, intrigued.

'Well, I was thinking if we give ourselves character names and create a little narrative, it might help us relate to them a bit more, which could help with our expression.'

'Oh, I see, so we can bring the dance to life?' she said as she stretched her legs.

'Yes, that's exactly it, what do you think?'

'I think we should definitely give it a go.'

'OK, so how about Elvis is a sexy captain of a ship and he falls for the beautiful lady singer called . . .' He gestured for her with his hand to think of a name that she wanted.

'Lola,' Lottie suggested.

'Brilliant, yes, and what is Lola's story?'

'Well, she's in love with Elvis but she is the girlfriend of a gangster boss who is also on the ship.'

'I like this very much, so how do they get to see each other?'

Lottie wracked her brain – she was really getting into this now. 'Her man is very possessive and dangerous, but one night she manages to drug him and when he's asleep she goes to meet the captain.'

'Don't you mean the sexy captain?' Marco teased.

'Oh yes, the incredibly sexy captain, and while they're together they dance their brains out. Then she must sneak back to her boyfriend before he wakes up and she can never be with the man she truly loves.'

'I love it,' said Marco. 'OK, Lola, let's do this.'

He turned the music up, pushed his shoulders back and held out his hand for her to join him. The beat of the music reached into her heart and pounded in her chest as he pulled her towards him. After practising for two hours, they had a breakthrough, as they both discarded any awkward moves and suddenly it clicked; they had gelled together and were both totally on the same wavelength. Their synergy was as one being; when one's energy subsided, the other provided the force to keep the movements fluid. As they fell apart dripping with sweat after the fourth consecutive unblemished routine, they held their final pose, both panting heavily, and heard a loud clap. Lottie jumped up to see Baz, one of the producers of the show, applauding them.

'Wow, that was sensational! If you two can dance like that in the show then you will be guaranteed top three at the very least. Keep up the good work, guys.'

'Wow, thank you so much. Fine praise indeed,' said Lottie. She grabbed her water bottle and downed it in one go.

Baz stayed to talk to Marco so Lottie excused herself as she had arranged to meet Mia for a quick lunch. She went into It's a Wrap and decided to wait for her near the photographs on the wall so she could study Marco's ex in more detail. She tried to read between the lines of the looks of seeming adoration in their faces, but the photo gave her no clues other than that they looked totally besotted with each other. She surmised that despite the popular saying, the camera obviously does lie because Alexia had left him heartbroken. Maybe she was a good actress.

'She's stunning, isn't she? I don't stand a chance when he can get the likes of her.' Mia's voice brought her back to reality as she had got lost in her imagination, wondering how it must feel to be in a relationship with Marco and have him look at you the way he was looking at Alexia.

'Hi Mia.' She hugged her friend. 'Don't worry, she's not a patch on you.'

'I believe you, thousands wouldn't,' she replied. 'Oh my god, I'm starving, can we eat now?'

'Yes, of course. Let's see what flavour wraps we have on offer today.' They headed towards the counter. 'Why don't you go and find a table and I'll get this,' said Lottie as she noticed the café filling up.

'OK, if you're sure, I'll have a prawn and mango wrap please and a pineapple juice.' Lottie ordered the food, including a wrap filled with tuna mayo and grapes for herself, and treated them both to a slice of homemade chocolate banana bread.

Lottie approached the table that Mia was waving to her from and set the tray down.

Mia helped her offload the food and drinks. 'So how is it dancing with Mr Grrrr,' she roared and did an impression of a lion scratching the air with its paw, then winked at Lottie as she took a hefty bite of her wrap. Lottie laughed and pointed to the corners of her mouth where Marie Rose sauce had spilled out; she handed her a napkin, which Mia took gratefully. 'You should know by now that you can't take me anywhere,' she said. 'But stop changing the subject. How is it?'

'Well if you'd asked me this question yesterday, I would have said horrible.'

Mia's mouth was too full to say anything but she raised her eyebrows in surprise. She managed to mumble something that resembled 'why', so Lottie continued.

'He just wasn't his usual friendly self. I mean, I know he's got a reputation for being an arrogant sod but I've never really seen that side of him. He's only ever been fun and flirty but yesterday I thought I'd made a huge mistake. He was quite horrible, very stand-offish, cold, and tried to blame me for getting the steps wrong when it was most definitely him.'

'Oh, that sounds awful. So, was he better today then? Could he have been having an off day?'

Lottie felt she shouldn't really divulge what he'd told her but she was desperate to talk to someone about it. 'I can tell you this because it's in the public domain but Alexia, his ex, is competing in the show. He'd just found out yesterday morning and it really knocked him off his axis.'

'Oh no, that is quite a shock for him, I imagine, but I'll always be there for him in his hour of need.' She primped herself and flicked her long braids off her shoulders. 'Oh, that's unless you've fallen madly in love with his dancing charms.'

'No way,' Lottie replied. 'I've had enough man trouble to last me a lifetime and I really don't want anymore. Besides, I thought he needed cheering up yesterday so I told him that I know someone who fancies him,' she laughed as Mia struggled to swallow her wrap.

'OMG, did you tell him it was me?' A rosy glow appeared on her light brown skin.

'No, of course I didn't, but I will put in a good word if you want me to.'

'Aw thanks, but I guess we'll have to wait until the show is over before we can let that secret out.'

'Well, we did sign contracts saying we wouldn't get romantically involved with each other,' she said in a matronly tone. 'I'm glad we're allowed to be friends though,' she added softly, tucking into her wrap.

'Yeah, me too. Oh, wow there he is. He has such presence, doesn't he?'

Lottie put her finger on Mia's chin and pushed it up gently to close her mouth. 'As my mum used to say, you'll catch flies with your mouth open like that.'

Mia giggled and wafted her hand over her face to cool herself down. 'My mum would say stop gawping.'

Their eyes followed Marco as he joined the back of the queue. 'He's such a star but look so down to earth too.'

He looked over and winked at Lottie. She realised he didn't smile much in here but when he was visiting Denni or rescuing her from ditches and wardrobes, he smiled and laughed a lot. She hoped he was laughing with her and not at her in those situations but guessed it was a bit of both.

'Omg, he just winked at me I swear,' said Mia. 'Did you see that?'

'Yes, I did,' said Lottie, not wanting to burst her bubble.

'That has made my day and this chocolate banana bread will be the cherry on the top.'

'Cheers,' said Lottie as she held her banana bread up so Mia could tap it with her own.

'Cheers, and even better, you and Marco are practising with us minions this afternoon.'

'I know, I can't wait to dance with my fellow minions, it's going to be a-ma-zing.'

Chapter 29

Doris's smile didn't look as natural or relaxed as usual when Lottie arrived at her door later that day armed with a Thai takeaway.

'Are you OK?' she asked after kissing her hello.

'I'm fine, dear, although I've poured us a glass of wine each so I can loosen up a bit before I send my reply. Oh, this smells heavenly, let's dish it out before it gets cold.' She took the plates out of the oven and they set about dishing up the mixed starters and dipping sauces. 'D'you know I've been dreaming about this takeaway ever since you mentioned it.'

'Me too,' added Lottie, taking a huge glug of red wine. 'It's such a good feeling having a day off tomorrow.'

'Oh, I bet it is! Have you got anything planned?'

'Apart from my regular chores, absolutely nothing and I'm planning to keep it that way. I'd like to spend some time with Denni; maybe I'll take a book to the field and sit with him.'

'Oh, he'd love that. Come on then, let's sit and eat.'

Lottie slid into the chair opposite Doris and began to help herself to the spring rolls and chicken satay.

'So how was dancing today? Was his lordship in a better mood?'

Lottie stifled a giggle and licked a dollop of peanut sauce from her thumb.

'He was in a much better mood and we really clicked today. There's a moment when you're with a dance partner and you just lose all inhibitions and awkwardness and you almost become one. You can anticipate the other person's moves and they yours; it's a magical feeling and we've reached that stage quite quickly. I think it's maybe because we know we have such little time now to prepare so we've panic-bonded.'

'Is it like when you're with a new lover?' asked Doris, before tearing off a piece of chicken from the skewer.

Lottie felt a drop of sweet chilli sauce go down the wrong way as she chewed on her spring roll. 'I guess it is,' she coughed. 'But it's been a long time since I've had that experience.'

'Imagine what it's been like for me. I mean, imagine if Reggie wants to meet up and do all that sort of thing. Maybe I shouldn't reply to him after all. I really don't know about all this; I mean at least you and Marco are young and sexy. I can't let Reggie see me like this. I mean, just look at me.' She gestured down her body, which was clad in her usual overall, lifted her glasses and wiped at her eyes.

'Oh Doris, don't be worrying like this. You're a beautiful woman and I'm sure Reggie will love you, but if you feel uneasy about it then you can always let him know it's just friendship you're after.'

'Yes, but if I say that then he'll think who the hell does she think she is, as if I'd be interested in anything else.'

'I promise you he won't think that at all. I really think you're jumping the gun here so let's just take it one step at a time.' She gently squeezed her hand across the table. 'If you want some new clothes, we can go shopping and get some, we can have a girly day.'

'Do you know I've never had a girly day? Some of my friends had them with their daughters and I never wanted to intrude.'

'Well, we're going to have the best girly day ever, I promise you, and we can even get your nails done. How about that?'

'I'd love that. I've always had farmer's nails so it would be a real treat.'

'Good, that's settled then. Now eat up so we can get tucked into those curries.'

After dinner and pudding and at least half a bottle of wine each, Doris seemed much more relaxed. She opened a second bottle, filled up their glasses and watched as Lottie logged into Facebook to send the reply.

Doris was a lot gigglier at this point and Lottie tried hard to keep a straight face.

'OK, so did you have a think about what to write? Remember you were going to make some notes.'

'Ah yes.' Doris made her way to the coffee table and picked up a tatty A4 notebook, found the right pages and tore them out. She handed them to Lottie, who flicked through them.

'Doris, there's about ten pages here. I think we only need to send a short note to start off with and maybe you can mention some of these other things as the conversation goes on.' Her eyes scanned the pages. 'Ah here we are, we can begin with this. *Dear Reggie, thank you for your message – it was lovely and such a surprise to hear from you after all this time.* That's a great start, I might skip the bit that says *especially after you callously ditched me and ran off with one of my friends, giving me not a moment's thought, no doubt, until you were widowed.*'

'What can I say, I hold a grudge,' said Doris.

Lottie tutted and smiled as she saw the mischievous twinkle in her eye. She carried on reading, 'Ah, here's a nice bit. *I'm glad that life has treated you kindly and that you have children and grandchildren, how many do you have?*' Lottie hesitated. 'Ah, hold on, maybe not the next bit. *Unfortunately, I spent my best years pining after you and so my womb has remained as barren as the Outback. Have you visited there by the way?* Hmm, OK, so I think we can leave the notes there for now. But I think we have enough. Do you want me to add that you would like to meet up?'

Doris thought about it for a minute and took a swig of wine. 'Oh I'm not sure I'm ready to talk about that yet.'

'OK, that's absolutely fine. How about: life has been kind to me, I'm enjoying good health and am surrounded by loving friends. I look forward to hearing from you.' Lottie typed the words as she spoke.

'Yes,' Doris clapped, 'that sounds perfect.'

'OK then, do you want to press send?' Lottie asked.

'Oh no, I can't do it,' said Doris, her finger hovering over the enter button.

Lottie tapped her hand so she pressed on it and the message sent. 'Oops sorry,' she said, covering her mouth with her hand in mock horror.

'You little minx,' giggled Doris.

'You love me really,' said Lottie.

'I do, you know,' added Doris.

'I know you do and guess what? I love you too.'

Lottie threw her arms around Doris and Doris hugged her back. 'Thanks for helping me today, darling. You're a real tonic for me.'

'And you're the gin for me: a little bit spicy with a kick like a mule,' she laughed. Now let's wait and see what Mr McDougal comes back with.' She clinked her glass against her old friend's.

Chapter 30

After her chores the next morning, Lottie could see Doris waving her over to the house. 'I've made you an omelette,' she shouted.

Lottie patted Denni and headed over to the house. She'd barely had time to kick her wellies off before Doris physically pulled her into the kitchen.

'Quick, wash your hands before this gets cold – I've grilled it just the way you like it so the cheese goes crispy.'

'Oh yum, thank you,' said Lottie, salivating at the thought. She washed her hands and Doris chucked her a towel.

'Are you OK, Doris, you're very chipper considering how much wine we got through last night.'

'Hurry up and sit down,' she said, placing the omelette in front of her.

'You're making me nervous,' said Lottie, 'although not too nervous to chew this piece of golden heaven, I must admit.'

'He's replied,' shouted Doris. 'What the hell am I going to do now?' She fanned her face with a tea towel, opened the laptop and turned it to face Lottie.

Lottie read the message. 'Aw that's lovely, two daughters, three granddaughters and one grandson, and a couple of great-grandchildren too. He's glad that you're happy . . . Oh and there's a picture of the two of you.' She turned to look at Doris. 'He kept it all this time. How sweet.'

'But look at this bit . . .' Doris tapped the screen with her fingers, 'he's coming over in a couple of weeks and wants to meet me.'

'Don't panic, you'll be fine.' She ate a mouthful of omelette and wiped her hands on a paper towel.

'It's not fine, look at the state of me — I look like a scarecrow.'

'No, you don't, but everything is going to be OK. Why don't we have our girlie day today — will that put your mind at ease?'

'Oh yes please, I was hoping you would say that! If it's not too much trouble — I can't let him see me like this. When did I let myself go? He wants me to send him a photo, look at this one he sent me.'

She thrust a piece of paper in Lottie's hand and Lottie smiled at the image of a very normal, happy-looking man.

'Doris, don't get all worked up — he looks very down to earth.' Realising that there was going to be no reasoning with Doris today, Lottie told her to get ready whilst she went back to the barn to get showered and changed.

'Right, first stop is the hairdresser's where I've booked you in for a cut and colour. While that's going on I'm going to have a facial, then we're both getting our nails done before we go clothes and make-up shopping and I've booked us both in for afternoon tea at Serendipity when we get back.'

'Ooh, is that the boat café? I've seen it but never been inside.'

'Yes, it is and there you go then – another new experience. Come on then, our pampering awaits.'

As they were about to leave the house, Lottie's phone pinged. She was going to ignore it until she saw it was Marco asking her if she was free that evening as he'd had an idea that he thought might be mutually beneficial. Intrigued, she replied that she was and he told her to be ready for eight and he'd pick her up. He ended the text *Wear your dancing shoes. Mx* The kiss at the end had her heart pounding and she felt she might go into full-on Doris's panic mode about having nothing to wear. Maybe she needed to treat herself today too.

Doris emerged from the hairdresser's a completely new woman; her messy, dirty grey hair had been lightened to platinum with a couple of bluish-purple streaks. 'Oh my god, you look ten, no twenty years younger,' said Lottie much to Doris's delight.

They both had matching pink nails and Doris couldn't stop looking down at hers. 'I've never had nails like this – these gels are miraculous.' Lottie was equally impressed with hers as it had been a long time since she'd had a manicure and the sparkly topcoat on her nails kept drawing her eye. They drove off in Petal to the nearest shopping mall and headed to a make-up boutique, where they both sat on twirly stools whilst the ladies in the shop explained what make-up went where and how to apply it. Lottie was pleased to see that Doris had really subtle shades on for a romantic natural look and her heart leapt on seeing her cry when the make-up lady held the mirror for her. 'Thank you, thank you,' was all she could say and Lottie noticed even the shop girls were close to tears.

'Can you take a selfie for me please,' Doris asked Lottie as they left the shop.

'Yes, of course, but it's only a selfie if you take it yourself – I can just take one of you normally.'

'I know, I'm not daft. I mean a selfie of me and you, I want to show Reggie my gorgeous honorary granddaughter, if that's all right with you?'

Tears sprung to Lottie's eyes. 'Of course that's fine by me; in fact I'd be honoured.'

After some serious clothes shopping, they visited Serendipity and enjoyed a delicious afternoon tea on the river. 'Do you know, Lottie,' said Doris as she spread clotted cream on a gigantic cranberry and raisin scone, 'what with shopping, make-up, hairdos and now a scone as big as my head, this has been the best day of my whole life.'

'Aw Doris, I have to say I've loved every minute too.' Lottie looked out of the window and marvelled at the serenity around her as she sipped her tea. This must be what contentment felt like, she thought.

Chapter 31

The butterflies in Lottie's stomach were multiplying with every minute she stood looking out of the window waiting for Marco's car to arrive. It's not even a date, she chastised herself, but she knew it was more apprehension of the unknown. He'd been very mysterious, with the only clue that she should wear her dancing shoes. She looked down at them; they were her favourites, the sparkles cast light all around the room. She smoothed the full skirt of the dress she had bought today from a charity shop in Hummingbird Lane; the dipped hem showed off her legs at the front. Her heart leapt as she saw his car pull into the drive, a nifty little two-seater with the roof down, music blaring a samba beat, her body wanting to gyrate to the rhythm. She grabbed her bag and took a deep breath as she waited for him to knock and when he did, she paused a few seconds before opening the door as she didn't want him to think she was too eager.

Even though she knew it was him on the doorstep, she did a double take as he looked more handsome than ever, his black hair a little ruffled from the wind on the journey here no doubt. His dark eyes, surrounded by thick lashes, could somehow see right through her into her soul. His eyes drifted over her body like a soft caress causing her to have an involuntary shiver. Her voice croaked as she spoke to him, and she had to clear her throat.

'OK, I'm intrigued, Marco – where are we going?'

His serious face broke into a beaming smile.

'Don't worry, I'll explain everything on the way. You are looking sensational, Bella.' He took her hand and kissed the back of it, which felt lovely; soft lips surrounded by bristles. The feeling remained on her skin long after he'd moved away.

'Thank you,' she replied. 'You scrub up quite well yourself.'

She closed the front door and took his arm, which he held out to her, and they walked to his car. Marco waved to Denni in the field and then blew a kiss to Doris, who was waving from her window. He opened the passenger side door for her and waited until she'd tucked her skirt in before closing the door. As he drove through the countryside, they had to raise their voices to be heard. Lottie wished she'd tied her hair in a bun as it whipped across her face but remembered she had a spare bobble in her bag so retrieved it and managed a temporary ponytail; at least she could see now. Marco glanced at her and smiled, which was a sight she realised she could never get bored of, especially when his dimples showed.

'So, the reason I invited you out is because I've been thinking that the jive we're performing is great but it's not fantastic. I think it needs something new, something a little bit special, so when I heard about this place, I wanted to give it a try.'

'Sounds good to me,' she replied, her words getting carried off in the roar of the wind.

They arrived after about twenty minutes to a location in the middle of the countryside and Marco parked alongside numerous cars, including quite a few vintage models. He came around to her side of the car, opened her door and offered his hand to help her out. Lottie felt as though she were in the middle of a dream, everything felt so surreal. Here she was, all dressed up with a gorgeous Italian hunk, and they were going dancing in the middle of nowhere to a place with a sign saying *Jive Club* on it. She could hear the sound of rock 'n' roll emanating from the building and it blared even louder as Marco opened the door to go in.

The music pounded in Lottie's chest as Marco took her hand and led her through the crowd of vigorous dancers to get to the bar. The atmosphere was electrifying as couples were swinging each other around, stepping over them then pulling them up through their legs.

'Do you want a drink first?' asked Marco.

Lottie's hips were already moving, she couldn't help herself. 'No thanks, I just want to dance.'

Marco bowed in front of her, offered his hand, and led her to the middle of the dance floor. They jived, Lottie laughing as she spun round thinking it was so much more fun than rehearsals but she got Marco's point too. They had been rehearsing for this show quite stiffly, following the dance to a tee, whereas if they could freestyle a little more, then they could bring something new to their routine that would stand out in the competition. They danced for an hour non-stop, then Marco pulled her back to the bar and ordered cocktails and water. Lottie guzzled her water and sipped at the cocktail.

'This is brilliant, Marco, thanks for bringing me here. It's giving me loads of ideas for our routine.'

'I hoped you'd like it. Look, do you see that couple over there, the way she adds almost ballet-like steps after the spin. That looks fantastic.'

'Yes, I was watching them earlier and the two guys dancing together over there almost reversing the dance back-to-back – I've never seen anything like it. We could incorporate some of this into our routine for a unique spin on the dance.'

'That's what I'm hoping for. I didn't think we'd have time to do anything like that, but you've picked everything up so quickly and we've already gelled as partners so we should give it a go.'

'I'm looking forward to it.'

'Come on, let's get back to it, throw all the rules out of the window and just have some fun.' Marco placed her cocktail back on the bar, grabbed her hand and led her back to the dance floor where they remained for the rest of the evening.

On the way back, Lottie felt exhilarated.

'Are you hungry?' he asked.

'Starving,' she replied. Marco had kept the roof down to keep them cool and Lottie pulled the bobble out of her hair and held her arms up in the air as though she were on a rollercoaster. 'Woo-hoo!' she yelled as the adrenaline coursed through her body. Marco laughed at her and put some music on; they both sang along until they pulled into the car park of a late-night chicken restaurant.

They sat at a window table eating fried chicken and chips and slurping on milkshakes. 'I don't want this night to end – it's been amazing,' said Lottie, licking the saltiness off her finger.

'I totally agree,' said Marco, eyeing up one of her chicken pieces. She gestured for him to take it, which he did and took a huge bite of it. 'It will be exciting to choreograph the dance with all of this new information, don't you think?'

'Oh absolutely, my mind is racing already. I'm bursting to put some of it into practice.' She slurped the last of her milkshake louder than she expected and giggled as Marco laughed at her. 'Oops, sorry about that.'

'Well, enjoy your day off tomorrow and then we can get back to it and hit the ground jiving as they say.'

'I can't wait. Maybe I'll do the jive with Doris and her friends too – I'm sure they'll love it.'

'I'm sure they will,' he agreed.

As they got up to leave, a rock 'n' roll song came on the radio. Their eyes met and Lottie raised an eyebrow; Marco nodded and put his arm round her waist and they laughed as they danced, much to the delight of the counter staff and the few customers in there. Some of whom took out their phones to video. As the song ended, he took her hand and they ran out of the restaurant to the sound of cheers and clapping. She was still giggling when he dropped her off. He walked her to the door.

'Thanks for a great night, Marco. I feel like I've stepped back in time and starred in a production of *Grease*. It's like I'm drunk and I literally only had half a cocktail.'

'I'm sorry I can't help it; I just have that effect on the ladies.'

'Oi.' She placed her hand gently on his chest. 'Your sexy charms don't work on me, I'm afraid.'

'Ah, so you think I'm sexy then. That's enough for me – I'm going to quit while I'm ahead.'

'No, I mean . . . some people think you're sexy but I'm immune.'

'Oh yes, you still haven't told me who your imaginary friend is who thinks I'm sexy. So, it's obviously you,' he teased.

'No,' she giggled, pushing him away.

He stepped forward and kissed her on both cheeks. 'Ciao Bella.'

'Bye Marco, and thanks again.' He waited in the car until she was safely inside and she really liked that about him. Chad would have driven off without a care in the world.

She made herself a cup of tea, had a quick shower and went to bed.

Chapter 32

Lottie was woken by the sound of a cockerel from the neighbouring farm and instead of rolling over and going back to sleep, she jumped out of bed and began practising some of the new dance moves she'd witnessed the night before. She didn't want to steal anyone else's ideas so worked on them to make them her own, and Marco's of course; they could also roll them out to the ensemble too. The moves were subtle, but enough to turn the jive on its head and make people take notice. When she felt she had perfected it, she recorded herself dancing with her V-shaped pillow with a printout of Marco's face on it as she knew it would make him laugh.

She texted it to him and a little while later, she received a reply with lots of laughing face emojis and the word *perfecto*. Followed by another one saying he loved her invention and thought that women all over the world would want to buy one with his face on.

She was still laughing to herself when her dance students started showing up. Doris was surrounded by her friends all complimenting her on her hairdo. She looked over at Lottie and smiled. Lottie felt a gentle tap on her shoulder and turned round to see Melissa standing in front of her with a glowing smile.

'Ah Melissa, you made it. Well done – I need all the help I can get with my rowdy pensioners.'

'Hi, yes, it's a big class. I'm happy to help. What shall I do?'

'OK, well first, if you join in to learn the routine then by the second half of the class you can help with any individuals who may be struggling.'

Melissa stored her bag on the couch and joined the back row.

'OK everybody,' Lottie clapped her hands together. 'Can you all get into position and we can work on the routine we are doing for Arthur's proposal, which is in just a few weeks. We'll be working on the group steps today and next week we can practise the individuals. Wow, we have twenty people here today; I think that will have to be our limit now and I'll have to set up some other slots. We've also got my lovely assistant at the back. Melissa, can you give everyone a wave.' She waved at Melissa, who waved back, her cheeks beetroot. Lottie turned on the music. 'OK, we'll start with some warm-up exercises, stepping from side to side and rolling those shoulders.'

As she ran through the routine, Lottie was impressed by how well everyone had developed in the class; they really were moving as one now, apart from the odd leg or arm that was out of sync. She really felt a sense of satisfaction that she'd managed to whip these lovely people into shape. Once Melissa had mastered the routine, she walked around everybody and helped with any difficult steps, patiently giving advice and demonstrating each step in slow motion until the person she was helping got it right.

At the end of the session whilst everyone was sipping tea and eating biscuits, Lottie slipped a twenty-pound note into Melissa's hand. 'Oh no, you don't have to pay me, honestly. The experience is more than enough for me.'

'I insist,' said Lottie. 'You were a real help to me today and it won't be long before you're up at the front taking classes yourself.'

Melissa beamed and took the money. 'Thank you so much but only if you're sure – it's almost three times what I normally get paid an hour.'

'Well, you've deserved it. Thank you so much and I'll see you at the next class.'

As Lottie waved Melissa off, Peggy joined her.

'Lottie, Arthur wants to show you something that he'd like you to add to the routine if possible. Come, he's out here.'

Intrigued, Lottie followed Peggy to the door and saw Arthur in the middle of the grass next to Denni's field.

'Are you ready?' he bellowed.

'I guess so,' shouted Lottie.

'What's that?' shouted Arthur, cupping his ear.

'Yes!' Lottie and the others who were now milling around the door yelled.

Arthur gave an exaggerated thumbs-up and then every one of the spectators stood open-mouthed as he flick-flacked, cartwheeled and somersaulted in mid-air to land on his feet just a few yards away from them.

'Oh my god, Arthur! Are you OK?' asked Lottie. 'I thought you were quite a flexible dancer but this is a complete surprise.'

'I'm as right as rain,' said Arthur, 'Do you think my Edna will be impressed?'

'I should bloody think she will be if he's this flexible outside the bedroom. God help her,' muttered Doris to giggles from the others.

'I think she will be very impressed, but how did you learn to do that?' Lottie asked.

'Oh, I've always been good at gymnastics and then for many years I was part of a troupe. We went round the world performing – I loved it.'

'Does Edna know you can do that?'

'No, she doesn't. I want it to be a surprise,' he replied, looking bashful.

'It will be a fantastic surprise, Arthur, she's a very lucky woman,' Lottie reassured him. She still felt a little uneasy about Arthur's proposal in case it raked up bad memories for her but it meant a lot to him and they'd all been practising really hard for it so she couldn't back out now. Although the flick-flacking could become problematic, she supposed.

As she waved off the final dance students, she saw a familiar car pull up in the driveway. Her stomach flipped as she saw Marco get out with a beautiful bunch of flowers in his hand. Her cheeks flushed as she anticipated him coming towards her, maybe kissing her cheek again in greeting as he handed over the flowers. But then he didn't walk towards her door but instead, after a wave in her direction, he headed over to Doris's house.

'Oh, bloody hell, I almost forgot I'd invited him over for lunch so I can ask him if he will be my honorary grandson,' said Doris. 'That way I can send a picture of us both in my next correspondence to Reggie. Do you want to join us? I'm guessing he'll hope you'll be there.'

Lottie felt a wave of disappointment wash over her, yet knew she was being ridiculous. However, the disappointment quickly turned to relief that she didn't have to explain her reluctance to be in a relationship with him.

'Oh, er, no, it's OK, thank you, but my brother has invited me to have lunch with him and Camilla. I haven't seen them in ages so I really should go and get ready.'

'Ah that'll be nice, but if you're back in time then you can always join us later if he's still here. He's offered to fix all my broken cupboard doors. Isn't that nice of him?'

'Very nice,' said Lottie.

'He's a lovely young man. Reggie said he can't wait to meet you all.'

'Ah, so you've been corresponding more then, you're getting braver.'

'I am, aren't I, but my makeover has made me feel so much better about myself.'

'I'm really pleased for you but you'd better go – that noise is Marco knocking on your door.'

'Oops, OK, I'm off, see you soon. Have a lovely time.'

'You too.'

Lottie closed the door behind Doris and leaned on it for a little bit. She felt foolish and hoped that Marco hadn't seen her reaction after thinking the flowers were for her. If he mentioned it, she would say of course she knew they were for Doris. She looked out the window and saw Doris giving Marco a hug and the memory of his mouth on her cheeks just last night came back in a fleeting moment; she had breathed in the scent of sandalwood as his lips touched her skin. She threw herself on the couch, closed her eyes and before she knew it, she was hugging the pillow that still had his face on. Then she did something that she hadn't done since she was a teenager. She kissed the photo of him right on the kisser, then she covered her mouth with her hand and giggled until her ribs hurt. She ran upstairs to get ready; she needed to get out of here and have some normality, even if it was just for a few hours.

Chapter 33

Lottie left Blake and Camilla's house with a full tummy, her laughing muscles well and truly exercised and thanks to tuition from her future sister-in-law, a little lemon bootee that she'd managed to knit and was immensely proud of. Her mum had tried to teach her to knit many years ago and she remembered sulking and folding her arms in disgust as she just couldn't get the hang of it. Her patience had obviously improved a lot since then as well as her ability to concentrate, now that her mind felt clearer. She'd brought home the needles and wool to create the other one along with fifty cupcake kisses from Camilla as a good luck gesture for everyone involved in *Truly Dance*. Each one had the show's logo printed in icing and embedded in a delicious buttercream swirl. Lottie was so touched by the support for the team and loved sharing them with everyone the next morning.

They had a busy day ahead as Lottie and Marco had to finalise their new steps and then show them to the ensemble so they could incorporate them. Lottie arrived early again and was surprised to find an eager Marco already finalising his dance moves.

'I've watched your video carefully and I think when you incorporate the ballet style movements, I should do this . . .' He demonstrated what he meant and Lottie joined him, eager to see how these dance positions would look together. They struggled a little the first few times they did it but then, like puzzle pieces, they slotted together perfectly.

'So we need to get the music to stop and change to 'Swan Lake' for twenty seconds for the dream sequence that Lola has when she imagines what life would be like without her possessive boyfriend. Then we swing back into the jive and then we're done. Is that right?' asked Lottie.

'That sounds perfecto,' Marco replied. 'Let's go once more from the beginning then we can show the others.'

They ran through it without a hitch and skipped into the other studio to show everyone else. Lottie knew they had a hit when she heard the collective gasp go up from their fellow dancers. The element of surprise had got to them and they applauded loudly as the song ended. Lottie and Marco did a playful little bow and he unexpectedly kissed her on the cheek. It felt so natural as they were caught up in the excitement of the moment. The choreographer joined them and began discussing with Marco how they could incorporate the moves into the ensemble dance and some of the female dancers surrounded Lottie and began to replicate her steps. Lottie revelled in the sense of belonging she felt in the midst of this electrifying atmosphere; the noise levels were raised and she felt all of her senses had come alive. This was what their dance had needed to give it that edge. Mia made her way through the crowd to give her a congratulatory hug.

'That was totally insane, Lottie. Well done!'

'Thanks Mia.' She kissed her friend on the cheek. 'We haven't got much time left though so are you up for the challenge?'

'I'm always up for the challenge – in fact, challenge is my middle name. We are going to smash this, Lottie, just you wait and see.'

'I guess we just need to practise as though our lives depend on it, easy peasey,' said Lottie.

'Just beware, one wrong move and . . .' Mia drew her finger across her neck and made a croaking sound, 'it'll all be over.' She laughed and Lottie laughed too.

Chapter 34

The next week flew by in a blur of costume fittings, dress rehearsals and dancing pensioners practising for Arthur's unusual marriage proposal, which was becoming less like herding cats as they became more connected with each other and with the dance moves. Melissa's assistance had been invaluable; she was a quick learner and proactive in the lessons, especially in the new children's classes as they loved her energy, most of which was spent chasing after them.

The excitement had reached a crescendo as they headed into London for the first recording of *Truly Dance*. A coach had been laid on to transport everyone and Lottie had managed to get a couple of audience tickets for Blake and Camilla, who were making their own way there. Lottie sat with Mia and they chatted non-stop the whole way.

'Are you nervous?' asked Mia.

'A little, but I just want to get it done now; we've all practised so hard for this moment and yet we could be kicked out in the first show.'

'Well, let's hope it won't come to that. Look, you and Marco have created something really special here and you deserve to win, never mind just get through to the next round. Here, I got you this for good luck.' Mia handed her a little gift bag.

Lottie held the bag to her chest. 'Oh Mia, you didn't have to do that. This is your show too, you know.'

'I know, but let's face it, you're our leading lady and you've just proved why if anyone had been in any doubt before.'

'What do you mean?'

'That dance routine you choreographed is so inspiring, Lottie; I don't think you realise that not just anybody can create like that. It takes something special and whatever it is, you've got it.'

'That's lovely of you to say.' Lottie opened the bag to find a silver bracelet with a delicate ballet slipper charm on it. She slid it onto her wrist. 'Thank you, Mia, it's gorgeous – I'm going to need all the luck I can get.'

'Don't forget we're all here for you and we've got your back.' Mia kissed her on the cheek and Lottie squeezed her hand.

'Here we go,' she said as the coach pulled into the car park. 'There's no backing out now.'

'Let's do this,' said Mia, linking arms with her as they entered the building.

Lottie's head spun at the amount of energy buzzing around the television studios; everyone moved at such a fast pace. They were herded through to the dressing rooms to drop off their belongings and then to the dazzling main dance floor where the show would be filmed live this evening. Lottie's stomach lurched at the thought of all the people who would be watching from the comfort of their homes, not to mention the live audience. It was thrilling and terrifying at the same time.

Doris had sent her a photo of her and all her friends standing around the telly just waiting for the show. They'd decided to make an afternoon of it with drinks and nibbles. Lottie wondered whether they'd be in any fit state to watch the show as some of them looked sozzled already.

After a comfort break, they were given their practice time slot and then taken to another studio where they could rehearse. Lottie's heart raced as nerves seemed to be getting the better of some of the dancers; even Mia had thrown up, which was very unlike her as she was usually the epitome of confidence.

After a few hiccups they completed two unblemished performances. High fives, fist bumps and hugs were plentiful as they made their way to the grand ballroom. This was the final rehearsal before the main show and they had to get it right. Everything was going amazingly well until just as Lottie completed her final spin, she felt a strange sensation and realised the heel on her shoe had snapped off. Her heart sank through to her stomach. Marco's face dropped and those who'd noticed held their hands over their mouths in shock, the cumulative gasp was audible over the music.

Lottie felt tears spring to her eyes and her mind went completely blank. Mia ran towards her. 'Here, take mine,' she said, unbuckling her shoes. 'We're the same size and these are so comfortable.'

'I can't do that,' said Lottie. 'What will you wear?'

'Don't worry about that – I can sit this one out. There'll be plenty more shows.'

'No, I couldn't possibly, you've been looking forward to this for ages. I can't deprive you of your well-earned place in the show.'

'You don't get it do you, Lottie? There is no show without you.'

Lottie felt a burst of love for her friend. 'If this was a cartoon, you would see lots of red hearts pumping out of my chest towards you. I can't believe you would do that for me.' She hugged her and put on the shoes; they would take a little getting used to as they were slightly higher than her own but she had a little time to practise.

She wondered where Marco was and saw him entering the room with one of the producers. She walked over to Lottie.

'Hi, I'm Caz, I hear you've had a little misfortune,' she said, picking up the broken shoe.

'You could say that,' said Lottie, as she wiped away a rogue tear that had escaped after hugging Mia. 'My friend is lending me hers but it means she can't be in the show.'

'There's no need for that. Don't you worry, come with me.'

She led Lottie to a storage area with rack upon rack of amazing outfits in clear protective covers. Shelves were heaving with boxes of shoes each with a photo of the contents on the front. 'OK, so we have these and these in your size.' She pulled two boxes down and offered them to Lottie, who felt she would burst with relief.

'I can't believe this, you're a life saver. I never would have forgiven myself if Mia had to miss out on this amazing opportunity.'

'She must think such a lot of you to do that.'

'I know,' Lottie replied, 'and the feeling's mutual.'

She tried the sparkly dance shoes on and did a couple of dance steps in each pair to see which felt the most comfortable. Fortunately, the most comfortable ones happened to be the most sparkly ones too. 'Thank you so much.'

'You're very welcome – we like to keep a few spares as it happens a lot,' said Caz. She led Lottie back to the ballroom, where Lottie handed Mia her shoes back. Mia's eyes sparkled and she put her shoes back on.

'OK,' shouted Marco, 'now that we have averted that disaster, let's give these new shoes a whirl, shall we?' They ran through again.

'They're so comfortable I feel like I'm dancing on air,' said Lottie.

'Thanks everyone! Next time you see this room we'll quite literally be dancing live on air! Let's go; costumes and make up next,' announced Marco.

Lottie linked arms with Mia and they left the room to the sound of whoops and made their way back to the dressing room. As they left, they passed another group on their way in and Lottie noticed Marco talking to one of them. Her stomach flipped as she realised the tall redhead was his ex. She grabbed Mia's arm.

'Ow, what's up?' asked Mia.

'Look,' said Lottie, gesturing to where they were up ahead.

'Oh shit, she's even more gorgeous in real life. How am I supposed to compete with that?' she laughed.

Alexia kissed Marco on the cheek and she walked off. Marco turned to watch her go, his eyes filled with pain. He remained there for a few seconds before walking off.

Lottie held her breath as Alexia walked past her talking to another girl and laughing.

'Yes, that is the famous Marco and I could have him back like that, if I wanted.' She clicked her fingers loudly.

It felt like an arrow piercing Lottie's heart. Alexia's voice was cold and cruel, her laughter shrill. She couldn't possibly know how much she'd hurt Marco, or maybe she did and didn't care. She ached to find him and make sure he was OK, but they wouldn't see each other now until they were in the ballroom. She hoped seeing Alexia hadn't affected him too much.

'Well, she sounded like a right bitch,' said Mia, breaking into her thoughts.

'She really did,' Lottie nodded.

'She's probably right though; judging by the look on Marco's face, he's still got feelings for her,' Mia tut-tutted.

Mia's words unintentionally hurt Lottie more than Alexia's did, mainly because she knew it was true, but why did it upset her so much to acknowledge it? Maybe because she'd seen the vulnerable side to Marco and not many people had. He appeared so strong on the outside as though nothing could touch him, but Alexia obviously knew how to break through his armoured shell with her barbed words and actions. Hopefully Marco could shrug this off and not let it affect his dancing. She thought about sending him a text but she didn't really want him to know that she'd seen his interaction with Alexia, nor would she tell him what she heard her say as that would be too much for him to bear. She would need to keep a close eye on him now though as this could be a tough gig for him.

Chapter 35

The moment had arrived, and as they made their way from the dressing room to the ballroom, they could hear the muffled sound of the audience cheering and laughing with the warm-up guy, along with short bursts of the theme tune for *Truly Dance*, which boomed out of the speakers periodically.

Lottie looked down at her sparkling corset and full circle skirt and felt she needed to touch something physical to ground herself as this all seemed too much like a dream, then Marco appeared next to her wearing his trademark mask, his hair in a quiff and wearing a long Teddy Boy coat with sequinned trim. He winked at her and held her hand, giving it a gentle squeeze and immediately she felt grounded. The doors opened and they walked into the ballroom to the sound of cheers and the *Truly Dance* theme tune that was being played by a live band. The dancers all found their position and Marco and Lottie climbed into the front seat of a chevy in the middle of the dance floor.

'So, let's give a warm *Truly Dance* welcome to our South-East region contenders with the fabulous Marco Abruzzo and his partner Lottie Daniels,' the commentator announced to deafening applause. Lottie tried not to look at the audience as it terrified her, but she was trembling as the music began. Marco began the routine pretending to drive them along before jumping out of the car and opening her door. He held her hand.

'Just look at me, you've got this, Lottie,' he mouthed to her. She looked deep into his eyes and he smiled and nodded; it was one of his special smiles that she felt he reserved only for her and as he began to swing her around, her stage fright disappeared and she was lost in the story they had created with their dance. She kept up with the fast beat and suddenly the *Swan Lake* music came on and Marco whipped away her full circle skirt to reveal the sparkly white tutu underneath, whilst she pulled at his jacket and revealed his skin-tight white sequinned shirt that showed off his clearly defined muscles. The sharp contrast of the enthusiastic beat with the much slower ballet moves incited an audible gasp from the audience and the strobe light helped provide the dream-like quality they were hoping for; the ensemble dancers in a circle around them created the effect of a zoetrope and elicited a spontaneous applause.

Once they'd finished, they held their pose for the required length of time before Marco jumped up and pulled her to her feet. He kissed her cheek and they bowed before waving to the audience. Then hand in hand they headed towards the judges to the sound of thunderous applause. They stood, still panting, with Marco's arm around her, and Lottie slipped her arm around the back of his waist, reassured by the heat from his body that she wasn't alone.

The presenter went to the judges one by one. 'Stanley Park, your score please.'

Stanley held up a paddle with the number seven on it.

'As you know, I'm an ex-ballroom champion myself and I'm a stickler for detail and a perfectionist. I have to say I felt you were a little shaky on your feet there, Lottie, and I was going to give you a number six but . . .'

The audience were on their feet booing and doing thumbs-down gesturing. Lottie just nodded; she couldn't possibly tell him about the last-minute shoes as that would look as though she were making excuses. She felt his criticism was justified. Marco pulled her tighter into an embrace and kissed the top of her head.

'Hold on,' said Stanley, engaging with the audience, 'I haven't finished yet. Marco, I thought at one point you were swinging a rag doll around; we can see your masculinity – you don't need to prove it. I say be a little gentler next time. Otherwise, a great dance and the extra point I've given you is for originality. That dream sequence was epic and a great surprise. I'm looking forward to seeing you two dance again.' The crowd cheered and Lottie's hands flew to cover her mouth and nose in shock and delight of the positive feedback.

'And now, Anne Field, can we have your score please,' said the presenter.

Anne was a vibrant and energetic American singer and dancer who performed in stadiums in front of thousands as well as having starred on Broadway and more recently in the West End.

'Well, what can I say? I remember seeing Marco Abruzzo in his show in New York and I thought to myself that man has got some crazy ass moves.' She moved her body rhythmically, much to the delight of the audience, who cheered her and whistled. She put her hand up to shush them. 'Lottie, you were amazing. I know this is your first time on a TV show and apart from some little nerves where you missed a couple of beats by a fraction of a second, I thought you did great. Marco, you're just a dreamboat but if you want me to remain conscious then you need to keep those muscles covered up because you just about knocked me out.' The audience screamed their appreciation and Marco blew a kiss to Anne that she pretended to catch.

'That's fine feedback from Anne Field there but I must ask you, Anne, what's your score?' the presenter laughed.

'Oh, I nearly forgot, sorry!' She fiddled with the paddles until she found the right one. 'Eight,' she announced, holding up the corresponding paddle. The audience erupted once more.

Lottie punched the air and jumped up and down before turning to face Marco, who pulled her into his arms and squeezed her. She loved the feeling of him but felt a little self-conscious as her sweat had turned cold and clammy.

'And now to our final judge and winner of *Truly Dance* last year, Matthew Street.' Matthew bowed his head and smiled as the audience clapped.

He held up his paddle with the number eight on. 'I just want to say one thing: thank god I'm bi because you two are a dancing dream and I didn't even have to pick a favourite – I could imagine myself dancing with either one of you. What beautiful people. I agree you weren't quite as sure-footed as you could have been, Lottie, but you can easily work on that and I'm looking forward to seeing what else you have to offer.'

Lottie and Marco hugged, blew kisses to the judges and ran off to enjoy the rest of the show from a separate area. Marco hugged Lottie again when they got there.

'You were amazing out there, I'm so proud of you, Bella.'

'Thanks Marco, I'm sorry I let you down over the shaky footwork.'

'Don't worry about that – it was new shoes, nerves, and the fear of the unknown. At least next time you know what to expect. Well done.'

'I couldn't have done it without you, you're a true star,' she replied. They were soon separated by the other dancers congratulating them during an ad break.

Chapter 36

All went quiet again as the other contestants performed. Lottie looked on in admiration at some of the moves she witnessed and could tell they were better than her and Marco's performance; on the other hand, she could also see some were not as good. The scores reflected her thoughts. They had twenty-three points, which she felt was a fantastic score, especially for her first effort. Another team did quite badly at only nineteen points, another got twenty-two and the leaders had twenty-four.

Now it was Alexia's turn to perform and Lottie and Marco had to stand close together for the performance so they could be seen on camera. His arm was draped over her shoulders and hers around his waist. She felt his body tense against her as Alexia and Dafydd, her partner, entered the stage. She looked stunning in an emerald-green sequined full circle dress with sweetheart neckline. She reminded Lottie of Jessica Rabbit as she filled the dress in all the right places. Her performance was impeccable and the judges rewarded them for it with nine and two eights, which received standing ovations from the crowd. They were now in the lead. Lottie could feel Marco's heart almost beat out of his chest and she felt an unexpected burst of envy. She looked up at him and he kissed her forehead and winked at her; the familiar sparkle wasn't present in his eyes though and that saddened her. She kissed him on the cheek and he turned to her, his eyes wide in surprise. He smiled, showing his dimples and that lifted her heart immensely.

The final contestants performed and received twenty-two points, which meant that Lottie and Marco had made it to the untouchables board and would be dancing again next week. The three teams with the lowest scores had to dance against each other in the elimination round to see who was knocked out. Lottie's heart pounded for each of the contestants who had to go through this ordeal as she wasn't sure her nerves could take it. Everyone watched with bated breath as the dancers gave the performances of their lives. Lottie cheered loudly for the ones who got through and commiserated with those who got knocked out. The atmosphere was extremely camp and panto-like and such great fun.

After the show was over, they only had time for a quick change before heading back to the coach exhausted but happy. Lottie sat with her head resting on Mia's shoulder as she flicked through the congratulatory texts she'd received. She showed Mia a picture of Doris and friends all standing by and kneeling in front of the telly whilst Lottie and Marco's faces were paused on the screen. They both laughed at the joy in the older ladies' faces, and Doris looked so proud. Blake had texted a congratulatory message saying how proud he and Camilla were and he'd naughtily snapped a pic of her and Marco mid dance. Lottie couldn't quite equate that the person in these images was her and that she'd actually been on the telly and performed in front of millions of people. It was extraordinary.

Chapter 37

She roused herself later than usual the next day and was about to rush out in her pyjamas to sort Denni out when she noticed a note had been slipped under her door saying not to worry as Doris had seen to him and the chickens, seeing as they had such a busy day ahead. She breathed a sigh of relief but then realised it was the day of Arthur's proposal and she was going to need all the strength she could muster. She filled the kettle to make a good strong coffee and feeling ravenous, she made a toasted cheese and ham sandwich and sat with her feet up on the couch to eat it.

After showering and putting on make-up, she slipped into her rented police uniform and texted her group of pensioners to ensure everyone had their props and costumes. She then headed over to Doris armed with a speaker to see if she was ready. Doris answered the door in her Mrs Mop outfit, complete with headscarf, a roller in her fringe and an overall on.

'Good morning, officer,' she said, carrying the mop bucket out to the car like a handbag. Lottie helped her load the mop and bucket, along with the speaker, into the back of Petal and they drove off to pick up Peggy,

Edie and Arthur. The ladies, both dressed as nuns, giggled excitedly. 'It was two for the price of one in the fancy dress shop,' said Peggy when Lottie looked from one to the other with a smile on her face. Arthur, dressed like a British fighter pilot with a leather jacket and cap with goggles, looked deathly white.

'How are you feeling, Arthur?' asked Lottie, glancing at him in the rear-view mirror.

'Bit nervous if I'm honest,' he replied.

'You'll be fine – your outfit is brilliant.'

'Oh, thank you dear, my Edna is a huge fan of Biggles.'

'And we're all huge fans of yours, aren't we, ladies?'

'Yes,' they replied in unison before chanting, 'Arthur, Arthur.'

Lottie shook her head and smiled. 'Right, let's get on our way then shall we.'

They soon arrived at Flowerpots, the garden centre where Edna worked and where she was going to be giving a talk on flower arranging. Peggy and Edie went to sit amongst the small audience that had gathered ready for the talk. Arthur was safely ensconced in the potting shed waiting for his moment and Lottie winked at some of the other ladies, including Melissa, as they milled about in various disguises. Doris began cleaning and some of the others acted like customers checking prices on things whilst Edna began her talk. Lottie sat in the outdoor coffee shop, nursing a cappuccino whilst waiting for the right moment. As the talk came to an end, Lottie approached Edna with a small notepad and pen. Edna took one look at the uniform and looked slightly concerned. Some of the audience members who had been about to leave sat down again.

'Excuse me, is your name Edna Joyce?'

Edna looked stunned. 'Yes, it is – is there something I can help you with?'

'And do you have a licence to create flower displays?' Lottie continued.

'Well, no, but I'm sure my boss does.'

'That's good, but I must report that I've got a message for you from Mr Arthur Blight.'

'Arthur? What is it?'

Lottie clicked the remote for the speaker and the music began blaring out; this was the bit she'd been dreading as Arthur had chosen the same song that she'd played at her own almost-wedding, which seemed another lifetime ago now.

Poor Edna looked bewildered as the fake audience members and the whole of the dance troupe joined in with the street dance moves, Doris incorporating the mop wonderfully into her routine. Even the real audience members joined in, as well as lots of bystanders, and the garden centre workers began clapping along to the rhythm. Then Lottie watched Edna's eyes light up as she saw Arthur appear out of the shed and join in with the routine without faltering on any of the steps. He danced away from them getting further and further back until he turned and performed his piece de resistance and flick-flacked, cartwheeled and somersaulted in the air to land on his feet just in front of Edna. He immediately got down on one knee and produced a ring that he offered up to her. Edna's hands flew to her face as she gasped out loud and tears ran down her cheeks. She looked a little unsteady so Lottie offered her arm, which she took gratefully.

'My dearest Edna, I do love you so much, will you do me the greatest honour of becoming my wife?'

'Yes,' she replied. 'Yes, you crazy wonderful man.'

Arthur put the ring on her finger and stood up to embrace her. She gave him a little peck on the lips and everybody clapped.

'What did you think of our little flesh mob?' he asked.

'Flesh mob?' repeated Edna.

'He means flash mob,' Lottie corrected. 'The surprise dance routine we just did.'

'Ah I see, I loved it! Thank you, everybody.'

'Yes,' said Arthur, 'thank you to each and every one of you. I hope I'm still allowed to continue with the dance lessons as they've brightened up my life, they have.'

'Of course you are, Arthur – you're one of us now and you can never leave,' Lottie joked.

'I love that, thanks Lottie. Now come on, everyone, I've booked us all into the café for lunch with tea and cake. I think we've all earned it. My treat.'

Lottie was relieved that whenever she heard that song again, she could think of this fun and happy moment, which could erase the uneasy and uncomfortable feeling she'd had before. Lottie threw her arms around Arthur and congratulated the happy couple.

Chapter 38

Lottie still had a kids' dance class to get through before she could relax and then the next day, she was back on the hamster wheel with Marco. This time they only had one week to come up with a new routine and the theme was the cha-cha-cha. She figured she would show the kids some easy cha-cha-cha dance steps as that would be great fun. Melissa arrived and after the chaotic lesson, she stayed for a cuppa. Lottie found her an enthusiastic person to be able to bounce ideas off and they both practised together. Melissa was able to point out a couple of areas where Lottie could improve.

'You're going to make a brilliant dance teacher one of these days,' said Lottie. Melissa's face lit up like the fountain in Market Square.

'Do you really think so?' she asked.

'I don't just think so, I know so,' said Lottie. 'You're amazing and have given me lots of ideas on how to improve the dance. Marco will be impressed and I'll be telling him tomorrow that it was your idea.'

Melissa's face burned brightly. 'Will you?'

'Yes, of course I will,' said Lottie. Melissa looked as though she would burst.

'Oh, hold on a minute, don't tell me you've got a crush on him as well. I thought it was bad enough that my best friend was infatuated with him but not you too,' she teased.

'I can't help it, he's gorgeous and . . .' she paused.

'And what?' asked Lottie, intrigued.

'I've got a poster of him on my wall at home,' she mumbled quickly, her hands clasped over her mouth.

'Marco is on a poster?' Lottie's eyes opened wide.

'Yes, he was in a show at our local playhouse and he played the baddie, then he was the star of a musical in New York called *Latino*. The Bramblewood magazine did a feature on him and his cousin, and I cut out the page and stuck it on my wall,' she giggled.

'I knew he was going to be in a film but I didn't know there was a poster. You'll have to send me a picture of that,' laughed Lottie. 'I bet you kiss it every night!'

Melissa covered her face with a cushion and shrieked into it.

'You do, don't you?' she laughed.

Melissa nodded and laughed hysterically until tears rolled down her cheeks. The more Melissa laughed, the more Lottie did too and it felt so good. She hadn't realised how much pent-up tension she had until the laughter relieved it.

'Do you want me to show you something funny?' asked Lottie.

'Yes please,' said Melissa, wafting her hand in front of her face as though trying to cool it down.

Lottie picked up her V-shaped cushion and turned it round, showing Melissa the picture of Marco stuck on the other side.

Melissa burst into uncontrollable laughter. 'What? You too?' she asked with a raised eyebrow.

'Oh no, nothing like that really. I was just making myself laugh, teasing Marco and trying to get in the dancing mood.' It was Lottie's turn to blush.

'Oh yes, I believe you, thousands wouldn't,' Melissa chuckled, then looked at her watch. 'Ooh, is that the time? I must go. Thank you for letting me help and well done again for getting through to the next round. I'm so proud of you.' She kissed Lottie on the cheek on her way out.

'Oops, I almost forgot, here's your wages,' said Lottie, handing her the money. 'Bye and thanks again.'

'Thank you, although I have so much fun here, I really feel as though I should be paying you. Bye.'

Lottie marvelled at the difference in Melissa since she first met her; her confidence was growing with each session and it was a joy to see.

After Melissa had gone, Lottie felt a wave of exhaustion wash over her and lay down on the couch cuddling her Marco cushion, smiling at the thought of Melissa's face when she saw it, and before she knew it, she'd drifted into a deep sleep.

She woke totally refreshed a couple of hours later when Doris rang her to tell her that dinner was almost ready. She quickly sorted Denni and the chickens and arrived as Doris was dishing up a delicious-smelling lamb roast.

'Oh Doris, I have to say I'm ready for this. I feel as if I've just been spat out of a whirlwind – I really don't know which way is up.'

'Is that Lottie?' asked a man's voice, causing Lottie to almost jump out of her seat.

'Yes, it is, say hello to my honorary granddaughter. Isn't she gorgeous?' said Doris, picking up her laptop from the worktop and placing it on the dining table opposite Lottie. Lottie caught sight of herself on the screen and noticed her hair looked as though the chickens had been laying eggs in it. She tried to smooth it with her hand and licked her finger to wipe away mascara from under her eye.

'Hi, you must be Reggie,' she said to the beaming face on the screen.

'Yes, that's me,' he said. 'It's lovely to kind of meet you at last. Doris has told me so much about you.'

'Yes, you too,' Lottie replied. 'How are you?'

'I'm very well, thank you. I just wanted to congratulate you on your performance yesterday.'

'Oh, thank you. Did you see it then?'

'I was on a video call with Doris and her friends and was able to watch on her TV, albeit a few seconds behind, but I loved every minute of it and it was so good to see Doris absolutely bursting with pride.'

'That's so lovely,' said Lottie, smiling as Doris stood behind her chair and gave her a squeeze.

'Anyway, I'll let you go as I can see you've dished up now. Looking forward to meeting you properly and I can't wait to try one of your delicious roasts, Doris.'

'It won't be long now,' replied Doris. She picked up the laptop and put it back on the worktop where she blew a kiss to Reggie and he signed off.

'Well, it looks like things are going very well with you two.'

'Yes, I think they are,' agreed Doris, with a wistful look in her eye that warmed Lottie's heart.

'Aw I'm so happy for you. So when is he coming over?' She cut into her tender lamb and added a chunk of crispy roast potato to the fork. 'Mmm, this is delicious as per usual,' she declared.

'Next week.' She pulled a nervous face. 'I'm starting to feel excited now, although still very nervous. I mean we get on wonderfully over the video but it's not quite the same in real life, is it?' She poked her fork into the roast lamb and dipped it into the puddle of mint sauce on her plate.

'You'll be absolutely fine, Doris, the look on his face when he mentioned your name proved to me that he is smitten with you.'

Doris's fork hovered by her mouth.

'Do you honestly think so?'

'Yes, I do, he was *head over heels* or should that be *heels over head* seeing as he's in Australia.'

'Oh Lottie, you are funny, and Reggie was right, I am so, so immensely proud of you, my darling.'

'And I'm proud of you too, Doris. Thanks for everything.'

'No darling, thank you – you've changed my mediocre little life and made it into something quite special.'

'Ditto,' Lottie replied.

Chapter 39

Marco's excitement was almost tangible when Lottie entered the dance studio the next day. 'Good morning, Bella, and how are you today?' he boomed over the music. 'Are you ready for your photo shoot?' he asked.

'What photo shoot?' she replied, self-consciously smoothing her hair, which was in a tight bun.

'You haven't checked your emails, have you?'

Lottie shook her head and reached for her phone; her email notifications were on silent and she hardly ever checked. She opened the app and saw emails from the producers of the show. She opened one up.

'Oh, don't read them all now – I'll simply tell you. The local press wants to interview us and take photos because of our success. We're booked in to speak to them at one so we have a few hours to practise and then we can freshen up for the interview, but we'll have to stay later tonight to make up the time. How does that sound?' he asked.

'It sounds good. What are they?' she pointed to some garment carriers hanging on the back of the door.'

'They're your dresses to try on for the shoot.'

Lottie pulled down the zips to peek at the most

sensational ball gowns. 'These are gorgeous but I just wouldn't know which one to pick.'

'Well, I think you will look stunning in all of them so wear them all.'

Lottie gave him a funny look.

'No, not all at once, one at a time. It's going to be a double-page spread so I'm sure they'll need lots of pictures.'

'Mmm, good point and thanks for the compliment by the way. I'm sure you'll look stunning in your outfit too. That's if you've got one.'

'They want me to wear my mask and cloak one – remember the one I wore for the auditions?'

Lottie gulped and her eyes opened wide. She had a flashback to how sexy he looked, just like Zorro, mysterious and edgy. Tingles ran down her spine and she shivered involuntarily just at the thought of him.

'Are you OK? You look a little pale,' he said, his face filled with tenderness.

'Yes, I'm fine, thank you,' she replied, taking a sip from her bottle of water to cool herself down and to avoid having to look into his dark and sensual eyes, which were having a curious effect on her.

'OK, so I got you a present for this week's rehearsals as the cha-cha-cha involves a lot of flexibility, as you know.'

'A present for me. What is it?' she asked.

'Close your eyes and hold out your hands.' Hesitantly she did so, then opened them again quickly, 'Are you playing a trick on me?' she asked.

'No, I'm not and I promise you, you'll like it.'

'OK, but if you tickle me, I'll scream.' She pointed a finger at him in warning.

'I'm not going to tickle you,' he laughed. 'Trust me.'

She closed her eyes again and soon felt something long and thin in her hand. She had a quick peek to see a glittery hula hoop and noticed Marco had one that he was doing tricks with, moving it from his waist to his arm. 'We have to be completely in sync for this dance so I thought we could practise with these.'

Lottie hadn't played with a hula hoop for years so had fun getting into the rhythm and having contests with Marco to see who could keep spinning for the longest. She tried doing the legwork of the dance whilst still spinning the hoop on her waist and laughed as it crashed to the floor.

'It's a bit like trying to pat your head with one hand and rub your tummy with the other,' she giggled. Marco lost his rhythm and his hoop fell to the floor.

'Yes!' said Lottie, 'I'm the winner. Hey, why don't we try to do one together?' She lifted the hoop up, stood in front of Marco and pulled it down over both their heads and began to gyrate. Not to be outdone, Marco joined in and they managed a few rotations before she suddenly realised how close he was to her. The hoop kept them perfectly in sync but the closeness of his body to hers, with the occasional touch, sent electric shocks right through her, the intimacy of the situation becoming apparent, it felt so much more intimate than when they were dancing.

'Er, maybe that's not such a good idea after all.' Breathlessly, she quickly pulled the hoop back up, tossed it to one side and walked away from him.

'It's certainly one way to discover if we are compatible,' said Marco. 'In dance, I mean.'

'Oh yes, of course, in dance,' said Lottie, her face burning. What on earth had she been thinking? She didn't know where to look, so appeared mesmerised by the hula hoop as it circled the room before spinning to a stop like a giant coin on the floor a couple of inches away from her. She shoved it further away with her foot, more to distance herself from the embarrassing situation than anything else.

'OK then,' said Marco. 'What do you think our story should be this time?'

'I think you should be Diego and I will be Sofia; my father owns most of the hotels in Cuba,' said Lottie.

'That's good, and Diego works in the kitchens and has no money but what little money he does have, he uses to care for his grandmother.'

'He sounds very caring and kind.'

'He's also incredibly sexy,' teased Marco. 'He always wears a mask to protect his identity because he is like Robert Hood.'

Lottie looked confused. 'Who's Robert Hood?'

'You know him – he steals from the rich to give to the poor.'

'Ah Robin Hood, yes I love that.' Lottie clapped her hands together.

'Diego and Sofia meet at a dance and they fall in love but her dad won't let them be together so Diego plans to rob her father and he kidnaps his daughter. With her consent,' he adds after seeing Lottie's smile slip.

'Ah I see, yes, and then they elope and live happily ever after with lots of children.'

'And a donkey,' added Lottie.

'But of course, and don't forget the chickens.'

'How could I, we . . . I mean they all come as a team.' Her temperature had risen a few degrees just imagining Marco as Diego and her as Sofia and she'd found herself totally absorbed in the story.

'OK then, this is for Diego and Sofia – are you ready to cha-cha-cha?' He put on the music and Lottie's body rippled in time to the beat, she just couldn't resist. She looked up and saw the fire in his eyes as he took her in his arms; she laid her hand delicately on his shoulder and they began. She noted that their bodies were now slightly further apart than they had been inside the hula hoop. By the time they wound up the session a few hours later, Lottie felt that there wasn't an inch of floor left that her aching feet hadn't touched. She and Marco had matched each other's movements with razor-sharp precision, and exhilaration coursed through Lottie's bloodstream.

'That's not bad at all for day one of practice, Lottie. Are you ready for the interview?'

'No, I'll need to pop home first to freshen up. I haven't even got a brush with me.' Lottie looked at her watch, 'Oh god, is that the time?' She grabbed her bag and car keys and headed off. 'I'll see you soon then,' she said to Marco.

'I'll be waiting,' he replied.

★

Lottie showered as quickly as possible and picked up some clean dance gear as she would be rehearsing again after the interview. She took out her bun, leaving her hair to fall in loose tendrils around her shoulders. Then she applied a light moisturising foundation and artfully used a smoky eyeshadow to highlight her eyes. She didn't have time for eyeliner so added a couple of coats of mascara and a pale lip gloss to finish off the look. She pressed her lips together with a piece of tissue in between them and threw it in the bin.

'You'll do,' she said to herself in the mirror.

Once back at the studio, she tried on the dresses and chose a beautiful magenta silk with sequins and black tassels that swished as she walked. She imagined they would look amazing when she danced. She entered the room and stopped dead as she saw Marco in his masked outfit; he took her breath away and a pull deep below her belly drew her to him.

Through the mask, she could see his dark eyes drifting up and down her body leisurely before focusing on hers; she tried to avoid his carnal gaze but couldn't tear herself away. Her imagination went into overdrive and she envisioned him in these swashbuckling clothes defending her honour with his sword, whilst pulling her up on his stallion and carrying her off into the night to be ravished by him.

'Oi, what are you up to?' the angel on her shoulder interrupted her daydream. 'He can't be ravishing you, he's a heartbreaker.'

'Is he though?' Lottie asked, 'or is he actually the heartbroken?'

'Don't fall for his charms,' said the angel, 'your heart is precious and I'm in charge of looking af—'

'Just one little kiss wouldn't do any harm, would it?' interrupted the devil on her other shoulder. 'Even a little fling could be just what you need.'

'Lottie, are you OK?' Lottie snapped to attention and realised the photographer was talking to her.

'Oh, I'm so sorry, I was in a world of my own there.'

'No problem. I wondered if you would mind posing with Marco as though you are mid-dance.'

'Yes of course.' She walked over to Marco and into his waiting arms.

'You look spectacular,' he whispered, his hot breath tickling her ear.

'Thank you. You don't look so bad yourself.'

'That's perfect, absolutely magical,' said the photographer. 'If you can keep looking at each other like that for a couple more seconds . . .' He took the shot. 'Brilliant, thank you, and I just need to get some close-ups of you separately but I can do that whilst you're being interviewed and I can get some really good candid ones of you dancing too, if that's OK.'

'Yes, sure,' said Marco.

They danced part of their routine whilst the photographer took his shots. He then introduced them to the interviewer, who invited them to sit down. A table of light refreshments and cold drinks was laid out in front of them. Lottie took a drink of water to ease her throat, which was dry with nerves.

'So can you remember your first meeting?' asked the interviewer.

'I'll never forget it,' Lottie replied.

'I found her in a ditch,' said Marco. The interviewer laughed. 'Very funny.'

'It's true,' said Lottie. 'I was trying to save a donkey.'

'Hold on, so let me get this straight. Who was in the ditch – you or the donkey?'

'Both of us,' laughed Lottie. 'Marco saved us both and our friend Doris too.'

'So there were three of you, possibly four in the ditch?'

'No, Doris was in the house but that's a whole other story,' replied Marco.

'Well, I knew this interview was going to be fascinating but I never expected it to be this much,' she laughed.

During the interview Lottie discovered that she knew so much about Marco without even realising it and she was stunned by the number of things he knew about her. Favourite food, favourite drinks, annoying habits. Where they most wanted to go on holiday. They could practically answer each other's questions and Lottie found herself laughing when the interviewer compared their interview to a game of Mr and Mrs.

'I guess when you're spending nearly every minute of nearly every day wrapped in each other's arms, you tend to pick little bits up about your partner,' said Marco, pausing. 'I mean dance partner.'

'It sounds romantic,' said the interviewer.

'It is,' said Marco, 'very romantic.' He looked at Lottie and smiled.

Lottie nudged him with her shoulder then linked her arm through his. 'You're just a big softy.'

'You're obviously very close. What do you like best about Marco?' asked the interviewer.

'Well, he has this special smile that not many people get to see. I like to think it's reserved just for me and when I'm feeling exhausted at the end of a gruelling dance session, just seeing that smile gives me a boost and it gives me the energy to keep going.'

'And what about you, Marco, what do you like best about Lottie?'

Marco clasped her hand in his and raised it in the air.

'Well, I mean, just look at her for a start.'

Lottie blushed and nudged him with her elbow.

'She's stunning, intelligent and talented,' he continued. 'She's one of the best dancers I've ever had the pleasure of being partnered with and she is full of sass and doesn't let me get away with anything. She keeps my feet firmly on the ground and I need that.' He squeezed Lottie's hand and she turned to face him, just as he turned to kiss her on the cheek. His lips landed on hers, sending a thrill right through her body. She kissed him back just with a peck as it seemed rude not to. The photographer snapped a picture just at that moment.

'Oops sorry,' whispered Marco.

'It's fine, don't worry,' she replied just as quietly, a rush of affection for him bursting from her heart as

239

he smiled awkwardly at her, showing those devilish dimples.

'Sounds like the perfect partnership,' said the interviewer, whom Lottie had forgotten was still there. 'Well, thank you both – I think we've got everything we need for now and if not, I'll be in touch.'

'Yes, me too,' added the photographer, looking gleefully at his camera screen. 'Bye for now.'

'Bye,' Lottie and Marco said in unison.

Marco cleared his throat. 'So I guess we should get back to work, what do you say?'

'I say let's do this,' said Lottie, 'but I'd better get changed first.'

'Oh yes,' he replied. 'Me too, if we must.'

Lottie tried to hide her disappointment as she rather liked looking at him in his wickedly attractive outfit.

'Well, I suppose we could always leave them on just this once – we could consider it a dress rehearsal. What do you think?' The devil on her shoulder said nothing but gave her a thumbs-up whilst the angel sat shaking her head.

'I think that's one of the best ideas I've heard all day,' he replied with a wink.

Chapter 40

It was either doing the interview together or sharing the close proximity of the hula hoop that had altered something between them. Maybe it was a bit of both, but either way, Lottie had discovered that she really liked Marco as a person. She didn't recognise him as the man he'd been described as by the girls who first gave her the leaflet about the show; they'd said he was arrogant but the only arrogance she'd seen was his jokey side when he bigged himself up. She figured his sense of humour was so dry that not many people got it. She knew his cousin Gabe did as she'd seen them laughing together and she did too, or at least she did now.

Looking back to when she first met him, she'd been the arrogant one, blaming him for not looking after Denni when it was nothing to do with him. He could have got annoyed with her and put her straight but he didn't; his immediate concern had been to laugh at the situation and then immediately jump into action mode when they discovered Doris lying on the floor. Much as she had fought against her feelings for him, she couldn't deny that she liked him. His qualities shone from him like rays of the sun: loyal, caring, funny, a family man, strong, sexy, handsome. She could go on extolling his virtues but she had to change the subject as she could still feel the sensation of his lips on hers and if she didn't distract herself, she might be unable to resist going back for seconds.

The beat of the music filled the room and her body began to sway and gyrate as he held his hand out to her.

'Wait for me,' he said, masterfully pulling her towards him. She felt she couldn't look into his eyes in case he saw the burning lust in her own. As they began to circle the room, he put his finger under her chin and gently tilted her face until her eyes met his. She could almost hear the electricity crackling as it sent a jolt through her body. She exhaled as the intensity of his gaze bored into her soul. His face remained serious and she became conscious of his lips being just inches away from her own as their hips gyrated simultaneously in time to the music. She looked back up to his eyes and noted they were fixated on her lips, which were now slightly parted. She swallowed and an invisible pull drew them together like magnets. She realised the dancing had stopped and her heart raced as his lips grazed hers, his touch as soft as a butterfly's wing. His eyes closed as did hers and she felt the warmth of his face as the magnetism pulled once more. Time stood still, the anticipation driving her crazy; all she knew for certain was that any second now she would be melting into his kiss.

'Are you ready for the ensemble yet?' Mia knocked and opened the door in one fell swoop. 'Oh, I'm sorry.' She turned to go.

Lottie and Marco leapt apart, their kiss incomplete. What would have been a perfect moment fragmented and was lost. Lottie's heart pounded out of her chest; she felt speechless and overwhelmed with disappointment after such an intense build-up.

'Yes,' said Marco, recovering quickly. 'We're ready . . .' he paused the music, 'for the ensemble, I mean,' he continued. He took off his hat and mask and lay them on top of the stereo. 'I just need to . . . see a man about a donkey.' He pressed his mouth into a fake smile and left the room, passing all the other dancers who were coming in chatting excitedly.

'Oh my god,' said Mia, linking her arm through Lottie's. 'You're a dark horse – were you two canoodling?'

Lottie put her finger to her mouth and ushered Mia to the edge of the room. 'No, shhh. It wasn't like that – we were just dancing closely,' she said.

'As my gran used to say, I'm not as green as I'm cabbage looking, or something like that.'

'What does that even mean?' asked Lottie.

'I'm not sure, but I think it meant something like I wasn't born yesterday. No idea what it has to do with cabbages though.' She laughed then covered her mouth. 'I can't believe you're stealing my man.'

'No, I'm not honestly, Mia, I would never do that to you. We just got carried away with the dancing and . . . oh, I'm such a rubbish friend.'

'Relax, I'm joking. I mean, he is gorgeous but the truth is my heart belongs to someone else. My infatuation with Marco was my attempt at trying to forget about this other person but it's not working, so feel free. Fly my little bird to your one true love.'

'Stop,' giggled Lottie, trying to cover up Mia's mouth with her hand.

'Don't worry, I'm not going to tell anyone. You're my best friend and he was never mine to begin with so we're all good, I promise.'

'Are you sure? I'd never hurt you in a million years. We were just lost in the moment. You won't tell anyone, will you?'

'Of course not. So what's next for you two?'

'Nothing can be next, can it, as we're contractually obliged to stay away from each other. Besides, I don't want a relationship. I guess I'll have to go back to Canada soon and neither of us want a fling.'

'You could always stay?'

Lottie's heart leapt at the very thought of it. Bramblewood, Mia, Doris and Marco had all worked their way into her heart and Blake and Camilla were here, leaving them would be the hardest thing she'd ever do. Much harder than leaving Chad had been.

'Besides, no one says it has to be a relationship, but I guess you can work all that out once the show is over,' suggested Mia. 'Or you could always throw the show on purpose if you decide you do want to be together.'

'You're so bad,' laughed Lottie. 'Anyway, tell me all about this person who has stolen your heart.'

A shadow passed over Mia's face. 'He's my ex, still

244

in Spain. I thought by running away I could forget about him but it's harder than I thought.'

Lottie saw the pain in Mia's eyes.

'You still love him, don't you?' she asked tenderly.

'I do, I'm afraid, but he's better off without me.'

'I'm sure that's not true.'

'It really is, I'd only spoil his fun.'

'You're one of the most fun people I know, why would you spoil his?'

'Because . . .'

'OK,' said Marco as he arrived back in the room, having changed into his joggers. 'Let's get going. Positions everyone please.'

'Great, now I look ridiculously overdressed,' Lottie whispered.

'You look gorgeous, don't worry.'

'Thanks pal. What were you about to say?'

'Oh nothing. Let's have a catch-up tomorrow after work.' She touched her arm tenderly.

'Sounds good,' said Mia with a troubled smile.

Once home, Lottie received a text from Marco.

I'm so sorry for what happened today, it was so unprofessional of me. Complications are the last thing either of us needs. I hope you forgive me. Marco.

She held the phone to her chest. Thank god Mia had walked in when she did or things could have gotten very problematic. She couldn't stop thinking about that kiss but felt embarrassment burn through her that Mia caught them. She wondered what was going on in Mia's life as she looked troubled lately, yet she was normally so upbeat. She was obviously having difficulty getting over her ex. She looked forward to seeing her tomorrow so they could have a good chat. Lottie read the text again from Marco and noted the lack of an x at the end of it. He was obviously drawing a line in the sand and she wouldn't cross it. She typed her reply.

There's nothing to forgive, it was a stupid mistake with no one to blame. Let's just move on. Lottie.

Chapter 41

Feeling a little awkward the next morning, Lottie trotted into work as usual to find Marco already there practising.

'Hi, how are you?' he asked her.

'I'm good, thank you,' she replied, filling up her water bottle and trying her best not to make eye contact with him.

'Look, Lottie, I . . .' he began.

'No, please let's forget it, it was just a silly moment.' She twiddled with the lid of her bottle.

'I just wanted to say I'm sorry. I'm not that man anymore, who takes advantage of every woman that he meets.'

'Well, if it's any consolation I didn't feel that you were taking advantage of me – I was a willing participant.' Her cheeks were on fire.

'Are you sure because that's what Alexia accused me of – she said I deserved to be treated badly because of the way I was.'

'I'm sure you've broken more than a few hearts in the past, Marco, I mean haven't we all? I walked out on my own wedding and left my ex standing at the altar.'

'I know,' said Marco, his eyes widened. 'You must know now that that was the right decision, despite being incredibly tough.'

'It was, very tough.' Her eyes filled with tears at the thought of what she'd done to Chad. 'I just left him standing there. He must have been so embarrassed. So, using your logic, do you think I deserve for someone to treat me badly because of what I did?'

'No, of course not,' Marco replied.

'Then why do you think that you deserve to be treated badly? We can't change what we did in the past, but we can learn from our mistakes and hope to grow from them. Don't let Alexia define who you are – just be the man you want to be, the man you are inside. You've got a big heart, Marco, and while I must admit I couldn't quite figure you out at the beginning, I can safely say that me, Doris and Denni are three of your biggest fans, not to mention John, Paul, George and Ringo – they always lay much bigger eggs when you collect them.'

'Do they really?' His head tilted slightly and he frowned. She waggled her eyebrows and comically moved her eyes from left to right a couple of times.

'Oh, you had me there for a minute,' he sniggered. 'But seriously, thank you for saying that. It means a lot, as does your friendship. I'd hate to lose that.'

'Me too. Now let's get on with this dance instead of sitting here feeling sorry for ourselves.' She turned up the music and they began to practise.

'How did the women you hurt react when you apologised to them,' she asked as they spun around the studio.

'Some ignored me, some said no hard feelings as I wasn't that special, and my childhood sweetheart married someone else but her dad said he will still knock my block off if he sees me again. Do you think you would send an apology to your ex?' he asked.

'I don't know whether he'd appreciate it actually but I'll give it some thought. I'd hate to set him back if he was already over it. I hear little snippets about him from one of my friends and I did ask her to tell him how sorry I was.'

'Do you regret leaving him?' he asked.

'Not at all, my only regret is letting it get as far as it did. It was an expensive mistake to make too as most of my money is going on paying them back. I just feel like I made such a mess of everything. Thank god I had my brother to visit and help to bail me out; I've now got to prove to him that I can make it on my own.'

'You're doing a great job and I'm sure your brother is proud of you.'

'I think he is and I dread to think if he hadn't been at that wedding, I may have gone through with it. I was just carried along with all the madness.'

'What happened, if you don't mind me asking?'

'No, I don't mind, although I wasn't able to talk about it for ages. Basically, he asked his dad to give me away even though I wanted my brother to do it. When Blake appeared at the church and saw Chad's dad about to lead me up the aisle, his face just dropped and it broke my heart, even though he knew he wasn't giving me away I think it hurt him when he physically saw someone else do it. I felt as though I'd really let my parents down – Blake is my flesh and blood. I shouldn't have let Chad's parents make that decision for me. They guilted me into it because Chad's dad hadn't got any daughters so wouldn't be able to walk anyone up the aisle. Then,' she looked down, 'it probably sounds stupid now, but I'd arranged to do a flash mob with my dancing friends.'

'Now that sounds perfecto,' said Marco.

'Exactly, it was amazing, they made it look like I was in a carriage and everything. I thought that because I couldn't have my brother walking me up the aisle then I would dance up the aisle instead. It was my only contribution to the whole thing; I was so excited and thought he'd love it but as I got closer, I saw Chad and his mum exchange a glance and roll their eyes. Also I discovered he was very controlling; I'd had a couple of red flags like telling me what to wear, even down to my wedding dress, which was his mother's, and much more conservative than I would have chosen. But the final straw was when he pretended to be me and turned down my perfect job.'

'What?' Marco said. 'That's unforgivable, what is wrong with those people?'

'I know,' she said. 'I think he was embarrassed as all their yacht club friends' sons married very well; their daughters-in-law are accountants and lawyers, doctors and surgeons, and then there's little old me, a dancer. I think he was only with me to annoy his parents but despite him thinking he was nothing like them, the look he gave me and the way he spoke to me made me realise he agreed with them. Especially his mother; she never thought I was good enough for her precious son.'

'It sounds like the other way round to me: they were nowhere near good enough for you. My mum would absolutely love you.'

'Would she? Is she Italian?'

'No, she was born in the Caribbean and then lived in England for a while. She met my dad on a holiday to Italy and eventually moved there. She and my cousin Gabe's mum are twins.'

'It's great that you're so close. Do you have any brothers or sisters?'

'Yes, I have two brothers and one sister, all younger than me. Dante, Rafe and Lucia. We also have two donkeys called Caldo and Freddo, lots of chickens and a couple of goats.'

'Caldo and Freddo, that sounds lovely and romantic in your accent.'

'Well, I hate to burst your balloon but it just means hot and cold.'

Lottie laughed, 'I think you mean burst my bubble, and yes, it doesn't sound quite as romantic in English.'

'Do you know I think the music finished ages ago and we've been dancing to the sound of our voices.' He looked at the clock. 'It's time for lunch but I think we have perfected this routine already.'

'I'm looking forward to working with the rest of the gang this afternoon.'

'Me too. Thanks for the chat,' he said.

'You're welcome. I hope you feel better about things now because, well I do,' she replied. 'We're not bad people and we need to remember that.'

'We're definitely the good guys,' Marco replied and smiled.

Chapter 42

Partway through the afternoon during a pretty hectic dance sequence, Lottie noticed that Mia had disappeared. Not long after, one of the producers of the show came into the rehearsal room.

'Lottie, Marco, can I see you both for five minutes, please.' They followed him to his makeshift office that the playhouse had provided for him. Once they were all in the room, he closed the door.

'OK, sorry to have to do this to you guys, but it's been brought to our attention that you two are seeing each other romantically. I just need to know if there's any truth in that?'

'None at all,' said Lottie, her pulse racing at this spurious accusation.

'You have my word,' said Marco, 'there is absolutely no truth in this whatsoever.'

'Who said it?' asked Lottie, her heckles raised.

'I'm afraid I can't say, but I trust you both so if you say it's not true then it's not. I don't think this helped though.' He turned his computer screen around to face them and they saw the photo of them kissing in the online version of the local magazine.

Marco and Lottie glanced at each other and then back to the screen.

'Ah no, that was an accidental brush of the lips,' said Marco. 'I turned to peck her on the cheek just as . . .'

'Yes, he did, just as I turned to look at him.' Lottie nodded vigorously, her cheeks aflame as they both spoke at the same time.

'Relax,' said the producer, 'I believe you.' His phone rang and he answered it, nodding at them to let them know they could go.

'You don't think it was Mia, do you?' Marco asked, though she could tell by his tone that he didn't believe it for one second.

'No way – she wouldn't do that.' Lottie felt one hundred per cent certain of that.

They had reached the studio where everyone was still practising, but there was no sign of Mia. Lottie grabbed her bag and went outside for a breath of fresh air. She pulled her phone out of her bag and dialled Mia's number but there was no answer. She tried again but to no avail. A voice message pinged and Lottie played it to hear two words: 'Lottie, help.'

With an uneasy feeling in her stomach, Lottie headed to the car park and drove round to Mia's house; her car was there but there was no answer.

'She's gone in an ambulance,' said a woman who'd popped her head out of the upstairs window of the house next door.

Lottie felt blood pumping around her temples. 'Oh no, do you know what happened?'

'I saw her collapsed on the floor outside the house so I called them. I hope she's OK. Her family are away.'

'Me too,' said Lottie. 'Do you know which hospital they took her to?'

'He said they were going to Nexton.'

'OK, great, thank you. I'll head over there now.'

'Lovely, I'll tell her mum – she's heading back but will be a couple of hours.'

'Thank you.'

Lottie raced to the hospital and managed to find the ward Mia was on.

'You're a little bit early as visiting hours don't start for another five minutes but as she's in a private room, I'll let you in,' said the nurse.

'How is she?' asked Lottie as the nurse led the way.

'She's absolutely fine – she just needs to rest.'

'What happened?'

'She'd passed out after a nasty infection but thankfully the baby's OK.'

Lottie nodded, too surprised to comment. Mia was pregnant? A lady walked past pushing a trolley with snacks for sale. Lottie picked up the biggest box of chocolates she had and paid for them.

As she approached Mia's bed, she was taken aback at how washed out she looked. Her eyes opened when she heard Lottie say her name.

'Hi, how are you?' asked Lottie.

'I've been better,' she replied.

'What happened?'

'I don't remember much. I felt really ill in rehearsals,

came home and then as I got out of the car I remember feeling pain in my side. Then I felt dizzy before everything went black. The next thing I knew I was in an ambulance.'

'You poor thing.' Lottie handed her the chocolates. 'Here, I got you these to cheer you up.'

'Lottie, there's something I need to tell you.'

'I already know – the nurse slipped up.'

Mia picked at the cellophane on the box of chocolates. 'I think it's because I've been in denial.'

Lottie held her hand. 'How many months are you?'

'Five.'

'Oh my god, you don't look it, there's nothing there.'

'I know; I guess I'm lucky like that.'

'Does your ex know? Tell me to mind my own business if you'd rather not answer.'

Mia shook her head. 'Kevin. No, he doesn't. I told you before I don't want to cramp his style; he's having a brilliant time in Spain and I don't want to be the one who puts a spanner in the works.'

'But what if he doesn't see it like that? You've already said you still have feelings for him. You might be giving up the chance of true happiness and a beautiful family. Surely you both deserve to make that decision together.'

'I don't know, but what if he hates me? I won't be able to keep up with the lifestyle we had there. We had so many plans and none of them involve a baby.'

'I'm sure that's very unlikely. Believe me, if you hated his guts, I would never ask you to consider talking to him but I've seen the anguish in your face lately. Don't give up on the chance of true love, Mia. I know it sounds corny, but not many people get the opportunity to find "the one" and it sounds like you have. Has he tried to contact you at all?'

'I don't know. I left without telling him, just changed my number and closed all my social media accounts down so he couldn't find me. I didn't want to burden him.'

'I'm sure he won't see it like that. Why don't you give him a ring?'

'I must admit having this happen has really made me want to be with him. I'm so nervous though, it's making me nauseous.'

'But they've said the baby will be OK, haven't they?'

'Yes, thank God and I must admit Kevin was the first person I wanted to see when I woke up here.'

'How would you feel in your heart if he turned up right now?' asked Lottie and smiled as Mia reached for her heart.

'Oh, I don't know . . . I've probably left it too late. I'll have a think about it.'

'OK, well make sure you get plenty of rest.'

'I will. The trouble is I'm going to have to give up the show. I knew it was only a matter of time but I think it's now.'

'That's not a problem, you can help me out with dance lessons. I mean it's not much at the moment but maybe you can take them over when I go back to Canada.' Lottie was struck with a sinking in the pit of her stomach at the thought of leaving her dance students behind but it couldn't be helped.

'I would love that, thank you, Lottie, but I'm still going to hound you to stay, even if I have to get down on my knees and beg, although spoiler alert, I think you'd have to lift me back up again.'

'The most important thing at the moment is for you to get yourself better. I've got a lovely new assistant called Melissa who has been an absolute godsend. I've also had so many enquiries for the dance school, especially since this article appeared online. I checked my emails and they've literally blown up.'

'That's fantastic news. They said they're keeping me in for one night and I can go home tomorrow. I'll be bored stiff doing nothing so I can answer the emails if you like and set up some sessions if you let me know your availability.'

'That would be a brilliant help. This dance show has come at a bad time really, but at least it can help me to pay my share of the wedding back, amongst other things.'

'It's good fun as well though, isn't it? I'm so glad I managed to make one of the live shows. It was a fabulous experience – I just didn't realise how much it was taking out of me,' Mia yawned.

'OK, you need your rest so I'm going to go.' Lottie kissed Mia on the cheek and waved goodbye to her.

Chapter 43

The next live show had arrived before she knew it and Lottie missed her friend so much on the way there but she smiled when she received a text from Mia.

I called him and he was in England looking for me. He saw me on the show last week on the telly, can you believe that? He's with me now. Break a leg honey.

She looked at the attached photograph of Mia and Kevin smiling broadly. Lottie's heart fluttered at the look of love in their eyes.

Their performance went reasonably well but the other contestants were so much better and she and Marco found themselves in the bottom three and therefore were required to dance again. Lottie felt that Stanley had summed up their routine quite well when he described it as lacklustre. Marco had stood with his arm round her through the scoring but she felt throughout that they had both held each other at arm's length during the dance.

Luckily, they scraped through the dance-off and another couple were eliminated. Lottie felt relieved but not particularly excited. She sat next to Marco on the way back.

'I think we need to talk,' she said.

'I think we need to dance better,' he replied, swigging from a bottle of beer.

'Marco, last week I felt as though we were on fire and totally in tune with each other, then because of that . . .' she hesitated.

'The almost-kiss, you mean?' he smiled, flashing his white teeth.

'Yes.' She looked around to make sure no one could hear them. 'The trouble is, I think we've pushed each other too far away; our dancing has become more rigid and too regimented. We need to get that fire back in our bellies and go for gold.'

'OK, let's say we won – what would you do with the prize money?'

'That's easy – I would pay off my debt for the wedding that never was. Maybe move here permanently and officially open up my own dance school, treat Doris and buy my new niece or nephew something special and Mia's baby too.'

'Sounds like you've got it all mapped out.' He offered her his beer and she took a swig from the bottle.

'Oh, I have, and even if we don't win, I'm still planning on doing all those things – it will just take longer, I suppose. What would you do with the prize money?'

'I don't know really; maybe have a decent holiday and treat my family back home or maybe I'll invest in your dance school.'

'Would you?'

'Yes, I would. I can see how passionate you are about it so I'd love to help. Maybe I could come and join you occasionally.'

'That would be totally amazing.' She smiled at him and their eyes connected, sending shock waves deep within her.

'OK, so back to work. I guess what you're saying is we have to get that passion back and keeping our distance just doesn't work,' said Marco, putting his arm around her.

'We owe it to the public really, don't we?' said Lottie, resting her head on his firm chest. He pressed a kiss on the top of her head, which filled her with warmth.

'Yes, I think we do. Let's not fight it anymore. The passion between us is electrifying until we try and dull it down.'

'In some ways I think maybe we should just do it and get it over with just so we can both get on with being normal.'

'Are you saying what I think you're saying?' said Marco, almost choking on his beer.

'What?'

Marco wriggled his eyebrows in reply.

'No, not that.' She slapped his arm.

'What then?'

'The kiss. If we can just get it over with, then we can stop wondering what it would be like and maybe we can concentrate on the dance more.'

'Well, if you think it will help, I'm happy to oblige.' He looked around to the back of the coach where most of the dancers were either asleep or playing on their phones.

Lottie couldn't believe she was being so brazen but she looked upon it as an icebreaker. Since seeing Mia almost lose out on the chance of true love and happiness, she'd been thinking about what she wanted in life and realised that Marco was becoming harder and harder to resist.

She lifted her face up to him and he pressed his lips onto hers. She drifted off to a heavenly place as his warmth, his delicious smell, and the feeling of his strong arms around her played on all of her senses. She parted her lips and his tongue explored her mouth, sending wave upon wave of tingles through her body. She'd never been kissed like that before, ever. What she had thought would be an icebreaker could have melted a whole iceberg.

The coach came to a standstill and Marco ended the kiss with a couple of pecks then smiled at her. Her heart was pounding out of her chest whereas he looked as cool as ever.

'Well, that was even better than I imagined it would be,' he said.

'What? Do you mean you've been imagining kissing me? Since when?'

'Since I saw you in that ditch covered in mud like a potato.'

'Oi you!' she laughed. 'Well, now that that's done, we can get on with dancing, resume the passion and know that we're not missing out on anything.' She winced as she saw a look of hurt in his eyes and hated herself for lying. The truth was she'd loved that kiss and wanted it to go on forever.

They alighted the coach.

'Can I ask you something?' Marco said.

'Yes of course, what is it?'

'I wondered, after the shows are finished, if you'd like to go out for a meal or something.'

'Oh, what like a wrap party with everyone?'

'No, I mean a date with just you and me.' His eyes looked sparkly from the reflection of the streetlamp in the car park.

'I think I'd like that. Very much.' His eyes lit up then dulled as she continued. 'I'm just not sure it would be such a good idea.' She couldn't understand why she'd said that, other than she couldn't trust herself not to hurt him and after the way that kiss had affected her, she worried for her own heart.

Chapter 44

With passion reignited, Marco and Lottie set the dance floor on fire. Mia had come in to see them and said she felt as though she would get an electric shock if she touched one of them.

The paso doble was an intensely sensual and demanding dance; Lottie was grateful to be utterly drained after training. Knowing that they could potentially become more than dance partners in just a short time if they wanted to, allowed her to pour her passion into the dance and it seemed to be the same for Marco – the pressure was off. They could be affectionate with each other now, both in and out of the studio, and even snap at each other when steps went wrong. That kiss had just given them a taste of what was to come and Lottie was torn between dying to find out what else Marco had to offer and sheer terror at the thought of hurting him or having her own heart broken.

Doris had invited both Lottie and Marco to dinner after work so they could meet Reggie. Marco turned up a little earlier and popped over to see Denni. Lottie spotted him and invited him in for a cold drink before they went over to Doris's.

'Poor Doris is so nervous,' said Lottie. 'She won't let me help with the dinner or anything and the place is absolutely sparkling; she practically washes the cup before you've finished your coffee,' she laughed. 'Oh, who's that?' she said as someone knocked on the door. She answered it to see a flustered Doris standing there wringing her hands.

'Come on you two, what are you waiting for? He's just messaged me to say he's on his way. He'll be here any minute.' She took the glass of beer out of Marco's hand just as he was about to have a sip of it and put it on the draining board.

Lottie giggled at the look on Marco's face and slipped her shoes on.

Marco handed Doris a gift bag with Belgian chocolates in it. 'Here these are for you.'

'Oh, thank you, darling, but you didn't have to do that, they look ever so expensive.'

'Only the best for you,' he replied. 'Might I say, Doris, that you look absolutely beautiful.' He kissed her hand before linking it through his arm.

'Aw you, you're such a charmer,' she said. 'Isn't he, Lottie?'

'He certainly can be,' Lottie agreed. 'Right, let's go.'

Lottie linked her other arm and they escorted her over to her house to be greeted by the delicious smell of her speciality: roast lamb with all the trimmings.

Lottie heard a car and looked out of the window.

'Here he is,' she said, as the taxi pulled into the drive. Reggie got out of the car carrying flowers and champagne. Doris took a deep breath and opened the door.

Reggie handed over the gifts and greeted both Lottie and Doris with a handshake and a gentle kiss on each cheek.

'Welcome Reggie, it's been a long time,' said Doris.

'It really has and you're looking even more radiant than ever,' said Reggie. Lottie noticed Doris was blushing to her silver roots.

'Marco is in charge of drinks, so what would you like?' asked Doris.

Marco jumped to attention to assume his nominated role.

'I'll have a whisky and dry please, young man,' said Reggie.

'And what would you ladies like?' asked Marco.

'Pink gins and lemonade for us please,' said Lottie. 'I'll help to put the fruit in.'

Doris led Reggie into the lounge and Lottie followed with some nibbles in bowls, which she placed on the coffee table in front of him. Marco brought in the drinks for everybody, including a beer for himself.

Once everyone was acquainted, Doris called them into the dining room where she had laid out smoked mackerel pate on her best china, which Lottie had never seen. She really was pulling out all the stops to impress Reggie. Lottie felt a warm feeling spread through her chest just looking at Doris but wished she could be less nervous and just enjoy herself.

She did seem to relax a lot more once the champagne started flowing and the main course was served up, even getting quite giggly.

'So, how's your dance school doing, Lottie? asked Reggie. 'I know Doris and her friends have said it's been a life-changer for them.'

'Oh really, that's so lovely to hear,' said Lottie. 'It's really starting to take off; my friend Mia is now helping me with it as the show is taking up so much of my time right now. I have Tuesdays and Sundays off so Mia has arranged for the new lessons to fit around them and a couple of evening sessions which I can get to. We've had so many enquiries thanks to the show and an interview Marco and I did for a local magazine. Also, Mia has come up with a fantastic suggestion of wedding dance classes. You know, for those couples who want to impress their guests when doing their first dance?'

'That all sound terrific, well done and good luck with it all,' said Reggie.

'How is Mia now?' asked Doris.

'She's doing great, Doris, thank you. Also, Kevin proposed to her so she is literally over the moon.'

'Oh, what happy news, she's such a lovely girl.'

'She really is.'

'It's great that we're having so much new interest but I'm just finding it all a squeeze now, so I think we might need to look for new premises, especially as we have the staff. Melissa has been amazing too.'

'Doesn't the playhouse have any rooms you can hire?' asked Doris.

'Unfortunately not – they're always booked solid. I've tried a few places but no such luck.'

'Well, my offer for the bigger barn still stands – you could convert that into a studio?' said Doris. 'There's plenty of room in there, you could probably even fit two rooms in there, and there's even space for a little office upstairs if you needed one.'

'It sounds like a fantastic idea, Doris, but it would take a lot of hard work and, I imagine, be expensive to get going.'

'Well, you've never been afraid of hard work and I'm sure we could round up lots of people to help.'

'I'd certainly help and I'm sure my old mates would too,' said Reggie. 'We may not have the strength we once had but we sure ain't afraid of hard work.'

'I've got friends and cousins that are quite handy too,' said Marco. 'I think it's a great idea.'

'Thanks everyone, I just need to think of a way of getting the money to do it. I mean if we win the show, the prize money would help but I can't rely on that.'

'Well, this would be something that could benefit the community so why not get the community to help out? Arrange something that could get everybody involved,' said Marco.

'What about a barn dance?' suggested Lottie. 'With all the proceeds going to the dance school?'

'Oh, I haven't been to one of those in years but I love them,' said Reggie.

'Me too,' said Doris. 'How exciting and what a wonderful idea.'

'We could turn it into a huge celebration,' said Lottie. 'Maybe have some stalls there for good measure. We could charge the stall holders for the slots. We could have dance exhibitions as well.'

'Denni could do donkey rides, he'd love that. He used to love the sound of children's laughter,' said Doris.

'Oh, that reminds me, I saw this picture the other day on Twitter,' said Lottie, picking up her phone and swiping through it.

'Ah, here it is'. She held up her phone to show them the image and everyone laughed.

'That would be brilliant,' said Marco.

'It would, wouldn't it? When shall we do it?' asked Lottie.

'How about the Sunday after the finale?' said Marco. 'It won't give us much time but it'll hopefully be long enough. It could be a double celebration or commiseration, depending on what happens with the show.'

'I'm so excited I want to rush off and make a list of things we need to do,' said Lottie.

'Not before pudding,' admonished Doris.

'Of course not! Come on, Marco, give me a hand with these dishes.'

Marco helped her carry the dishes out and filled the sink full of soapy water. He started washing the plates and Lottie grabbed the tea towel to dry.

Doris joined them and began to dish up her apple and pear crumble with custard.

'What do you think of him?' She dug Marco in the ribs with her elbow.

'He seems like a lovely man, dear Doris.'

'He is, isn't he,' she replied with a sparkle in her eye. 'Not bad-looking either.'

After pudding, Marco and Lottie said goodbye and left a very content-looking Doris and Reggie listening to the record player playing old songs they loved many moons ago.

Marco walked Lottie to her door and leaned in for a kiss but against the advice from the devil on her shoulder who was urging her to go for it, she held her finger to his lips much to the relief of the angel, who nodded her approval with a smile.

Chapter 45

Lottie jumped out of bed bright and early the next morning, and rushed out to feed Denni and sort the chickens. As she turned towards the house with the freshly laid eggs in the basket, she saw a tired-looking Doris charging towards her.

'Have you got time for a chat, love?' she asked.

Lottie looked at her watch; she didn't have long as she had to get ready and go to rehearsals. 'Of course I have – is everything OK?'

They walked to Lottie's's kitchen and Lottie put the kettle on. Doris sat in the chair and fidgeted until Lottie brought the drinks over and joined her.

'Has something happened?' Lottie asked.

'Yes, it has, me and Reggie . . .' She stopped and looked from side to side. 'We kissed last night.' Doris's hands flew to her mouth as if trying to cover the evidence.

'Ooh, get you,' said Lottie, realising that Doris didn't know that she and Marco had also kissed. 'What was it like?' she asked.

'It was rather lovely. The thing is he told me something that's taken me by surprise, which has upset me.'

She blew her nose on a hankie she retrieved from the cuff of her cardigan.

'Oh no, what is it?'

'He said that my dad warned him off me all those years ago. My dad was happy when he first proposed but not when he told him we would be going to live in Australia. I feel quite hurt that my mum told me he couldn't have loved me because he went off with someone else, but apparently my dad had got quite aggressive with him and scared him off, threatened him and everything.'

'Oh no, I'm so sorry, Doris, that's awful.' Lottie put her arm around her older friend.

'He said that although he'd had a happy life, he'd always wondered about me and to him I was the one that got away. That's why he kept the photograph of us both for all that time.'

'That is so romantic, I love it,' said Lottie.

'But what about all those wasted years?' said Doris. Her lip quivered and then the dam burst.

Lottie reached for a box of tissues and pulled a handful out to give to Doris to mop up her tears. She put her arm around her and gave her a reassuring squeeze, holding her until her sobs subsided.

'Everything will be OK, Doris, that cry has probably been long overdue.'

'It really has. I've been so lonely and yet I could have been happily married with children and grandchildren for all these years. It really hurts, Lottie.'

'I can't even imagine how painful that must be for you and you need to take the time to grieve that loss.

Here, let me get you some more tea.' She stood up to refresh the cups. 'You can't change what's happened in the past. All we have is the present and the future.'

Doris gratefully took the tea from Lottie. 'That's what he said. The thing is, he's asked me to go back to Australia with him. He would have offered to stay here with me but he can't bear to leave his children and grandchildren.' She sniffed. 'We feel as though we've really got to know each other now, what with the video calls, and when we met last night, it was like the years had melted away and he was the young man who'd proposed to me.'

'Oh wow, that was quick – it's an amazing opportunity though. How do you feel about it?'

'Well, as he said, we have to be quick; enough time has already been lost and what are we waiting for?' She blew her nose. 'I can't stand the thought of him leaving me again but the thought of going so far away is terrifying. What do you think I should do?'

She looked so lost that Lottie's heart ached for her. 'Have you had breakfast yet?' she asked.

Doris shook her head.

'Right, let me make you some and we can have a chat.' She put the eggs on to boil and filled the kettle again. Doris would normally be busying herself about the place laying the table and cleaning up, but she sat clutching onto her tissue and staring into space.

Lottie texted Marco to tell him she would be late and then popped the bread in the toaster. She retrieved a notepad and pen from the drawer and handed it to Doris.

'While you're waiting, why don't you make a list of pros and cons of going to Australia?'

'I made one first thing this morning,' Doris replied. She pulled a crumpled page out of her pocket and handed it to Lottie. 'What's this?' She held up the notebook to Lottie, who felt her cheeks burn.

'Oh, you know, just idle doodling, ignore that.'

'Lottie Abruzzo? Hey, looks like I'm not the only one who's been dreaming of romance – those names look good together.'

'Well, you know all my single mates are dropping like cherry blossom petals. First Mia and now you,' Lottie laughed nervously. 'Seriously though, it would never work. Marco wants to settle down and I . . .' she paused. 'Well, I just don't know what I want but I know I'm no good for him, look what I did to Chad – it was unforgivable and humiliating to leave him standing at the altar.'

'Yes, but he wasn't right for you and it was pretty awful of him to try and humiliate you when you were trying to express yourself and give yourself to him as you are. If he didn't like that, then that's his problem and not yours.'

Lottie knew this was true but still had a hard time digesting it.

'That's true, and what he did to me was pretty unforgivable too.'

She got on with preparing the breakfast. Once ready she put the plate of boiled eggs and soldiers in front of Doris, along with a mug of tea. She then brought her own over and sat down.

Doris began cutting off the top of her egg and sprinkled salt over it.

'OK, so let's have a look at your list?' said Lottie, eager for a change of subject. She opened the page and placed it on the table, smoothing the creases out with her hand she began to read it out.

'Pro: You can't bear the thought of losing him again and this way you get your chance of love.

Con: It's so far away.

Pro: You've always wanted to go to Australia.

Con: What if you don't like it when you get there?

Pro: You get a readymade family.

Con: What if his family don't like you?

Pro: It's the most exciting thing that's ever happened in your life.

Con: It would the scariest thing you've ever done.

Pro: You love him.

Con: You will miss your friends, especially Lottie.

Aw Doris, we will miss you too, but this is your second chance at a once in a lifetime opportunity.' She squeezed her hand gently. 'Has he mentioned his family at all?'

'Yes, and he's introduced me to them all on the video. They all seem lovely and he's mentioned to them that he's asked me to go with him.'

'And what did they say?'

'He said that they're all excited about meeting me.'

'Then really I've just got one thing to say to you,' Lottie smiled.

'What's that?' Doris swallowed nervously.

'What are you waiting for?' said Lottie. 'Pack your bags and fly high, little bird.'

Doris smiled and sighed with relief.

'That's what I hoped you were going to say, except I need to ask you something first before I make my final decision.'

'What's that?' asked Lottie, intrigued.

'Well, my main con is who would look after Denni for me and see to the chickens and this place. So, I wondered if you could do that for me?'

'Oh, I see.' Lottie realised that all the signs seemed to point in one direction. Her destiny seemed to be in Bramblewood. Even thinking about leaving her dance classes was too painful to contemplate, she adored each and every one of her students, but she knew if she left, she could, albeit reluctantly, leave the school in Mia and Melissa's capable hands but Denni was another matter – he was a permanent fixture here. She couldn't just abandon him to anyone, she loved him. She enjoyed living in the barn and she enjoyed her life here. Lottie realised that her journey here had led to this very moment and perhaps it was time to sort herself out and make an executive decision.

Lost in her thoughts, she realised Doris was staring at her, nervously awaiting a reply.

'You look troubled, my dear. I think you should take your own advice.'

'What's that?' asked Lottie.

'Write a pros and cons list.'

'Oh yes, of course, why didn't I think of that?'

Doris grabbed the pen and wrote 'Pros and Cons for Lottie to stay at Bramble Farm'. across the top of the page.

'OK, first of all, a pro?'

'I get to stay with Denni and look after him but con: you won't be here.' Doris wrote everything down as Lottie spoke.

'Pro: I could really work on setting up the dance school and turn it into a professional organisation, which seems to be needed in this area. Con: I suppose it could fail miserably.'

'Nonsense – it'll be fantastic and hugely successful.'

'And you're not biased at all, are you, Doris,' she chuckled. 'Pro: I've made lovely new friends here and I would hate to leave them. Con: I still have great friends in Canada and I won't get to see them.'

'You can always FaceTime your Canadian friends or visit occasionally,' added Doris.

'Surprise, surprise, I think I can see which side of this debate you're coming down on, Doris,' she smiled. 'Pro: I get to live in this lovely barn conversion. Con: it might be a bit much having to look after the house as well.'

'Oh no, that won't be a problem – I'm thinking of renting it out so that I have some regular income coming in and if you're happy to rent the bigger barn from me, then that would be a huge help.'

'Oh yes, of course I would – that's if I stayed, of course.'

'Well, there's no pressure from me.' Doris wrote a word down.

'Oh no, not much,' Lottie laughed. 'Anyway, what's that you're writing down?'

Doris turned the page to face her and she saw a name written in capital letters under Pro.

'Marco?' said Lottie. 'I've already included him in the friend's suggestion.'

'He could be more than a friend if you would just let your barricade down.'

Lottie felt her face burn. 'I'm not sure I can. Doris. I really like him but he's still quite torn up about his ex. I still feel shitty about what I did to mine and I don't know whose heart I'm more worried for. I know I like him far too much to want to break his.'

'OK, so, Pro: Marco – I like him too much,' Doris wrote.

'Con: Marco – I like him too much,' Lottie added. Doris's eyes met hers and she nodded in understanding.

'Finally,' Lottie cleared her throat. 'Pro: if I stay, then I get to be the best auntie to my future baby niece or nephew and provide my brother with family close by.

Con: well, what can I say, there really is no con for that is there?'

'I really don't think there is, Lottie my dear. I can only see happiness for you in that regard.'

'Well, that makes my mind up then . . .'

'It does? And what's the verdict?' Doris had her fingers crossed.

'Of course I'll stay to look after Denni – he's my soulmate,' laughed Lottie. 'If it weren't for him, I would never have met you.'

'Or Marco,' added Doris. Lottie's heart fluttered at the mention of his name. 'Thank you, Lottie. I mean, I might hate it and want to come back after a couple of days, but if I don't try, I'll never know.'

'I'm sure you'll love it but if you just look at it as a holiday at first, then it might make it a bit less daunting. Try seeing it as a wonderful adventure.'

'I will do, darling, thank you for everything. Now I feel I can eat my breakfast without a lump in my throat.'

They enjoyed their breakfasts together whilst both considered their new lives, then Lottie rushed off to rehearsals and told Marco about Doris's news, does this mean that you'll be sticking around for definite?' he asked, his eyes sparkling.

'I'm thinking about it,' she replied. This was a conversation they could have some other time.

Chapter 46

Marco had expressed his happiness for Doris before they moved on to discuss the dance.

'My suggestion for our story for the paso doble is about a bullfighter called Lorenzo who falls in love with a girl called Elena,' said Marco, his voice full of passion.

'Is Lorenzo incredibly sexy by any chance?' Lottie teased.

'He's the most handsome and sexy bullfighter you have ever met,' said Marco, gesticulating with his hands and standing up straight with his elegant dancer's poise.

'OK, but the conflict is that Elena is not only a vet but a vegetarian as well, and to win her heart he mustn't kill the bull.' Lottie wagged her finger at him from side to side.

Marco face-palmed his hand, but then looked up as he'd obviously had another idea. 'OK, I see what you're doing there, but just to add to the tension a little more, Lorenzo is then ironically gored by the bull and Elena has to save his life.'

'Touché,' said Lottie. 'However, I've got a better idea.'

Marco looked up at her, his hair flopped over his eyes, and he smoothed it back with his hand. A sense of relief shot through Lottie as had it stayed there any longer, she would have been sorely tempted to brush it away herself.

'I'm intrigued, what could be more powerful and sexy than Lorenzo and Elena?' Marco emphasised the names in his Italian accent.

'Something much sexier and much more powerful,' she smiled as he gazed at her expectantly. 'Last week we tried to be other people and, as fun as it was, we ended up in the dance-off and could have been booted out.'

He raised his eyebrows and nodded.

'OK, I get that. So how do we remedy it?'

'It's easy – we remain as ourselves, Marco and Lottie. If we want to win this show, what is the one factor that we need to excel as dancing partners?'

'That's simple – passion.' He stamped his feet and clicked his fingers above his head in emphasis. 'The paso doble oozes passion – it cannot be successfully executed without it.'

'No,' replied Lottie, smiling at his animated movements, then laughing at the look of shock and confusion on his face as he stopped in his tracks.

'What are you talking about? How you can say there is no passion in the paso doble?' He ran his hand through his hair, leaving tufts sticking up.

'Well yes, of course passion is necessary, but that's not it.'

'Romance?' he said, pointing a finger in the air.

'Nope,' Lottie shook her head. He opened his mouth to speak but she got in first.

'Again, yes, the dance is screaming romance, but that's not it.'

'Sexiness, fire and strength,' he retorted.

'Yes, yes, yes, but no, no and no. All of these are fabulous and necessary qualities but the most important thing for me is . . .' she paused for dramatic effect and because she was enjoying seeing him hang on to her every word, 'trust.'

'Oh of course trust, but that goes without saying. You trust me, don't you?' He searched her eyes.

She gazed back for a little but then looked away; she feared he would get inside her soul and she would be lost to him forever.

'Yes, I do trust you, Marco, you know everything there is to know about me but my question is, do you trust *me*?'

Marco did a double take as he looked taken aback.

'Of course I do, you know everything about me.'

'I know your parents' names, even your donkeys' names and where you're from. I know your favourite ice-cream flavour is mint choc chip and I know you had your heart broken by a beautiful redhead but I don't know your deepest darkest fears and what makes you tick.'

'Do I know yours?' He searched her eyes.

'Yes, I think so, well actually, I'm only just putting a name to my problems. Getting away from my old life has helped me see things much more clearly. I think I have abandonment issues. It sounds weird but my clinging on to Chad came about after my brother left Canada. Chad promised me companionship and fun, lots of fun and excitement; we fed off each other's impulsiveness, almost daring each other to do crazier things – jumping out of planes, jet skiing – and once we'd started the marriage ball rolling, it became impossible to stop. I basically handed over the responsibility for myself to Chad and his mother instead of staying in control of it myself.'

'Do you regret being with him?'

Lottie thought for a minute before answering, a couple of errant tears stung her eyes. Marco put an arm around her.

'I don't. My dad always told me that regrets were negative, useless and unnecessary. He said we should use mistakes as opportunities to learn from.'

'He sounds a very wise man.'

'He was, and very protective, then Blake took over when he died. I guess I just rebelled, which is stupid because I only ended up hurting myself more. So no, I don't regret meeting Chad – he was handsome, could be very charming and despite how it ended, we did have a great time together. He was as broken as I was really. His parents never had much time for him and he had an elder brother who was hugely successful. Chad could never live up to him so he filled his life with one adrenaline rush after another. Both of us should have been made to stand on our own two feet.'

'First rule of dancing: stand on your own two feet and not your partner's,' Marco quipped.

Lottie laughed. 'You're never going to forgive me for that, are you?'

'Never,' he joked. 'I'm glad you're sounding more positive though.'

'Life is certainly becoming a lot clearer for me. Bramblewood and the people in it have seen to that.'

'So, you're staying then.'

'The idea is becoming more and more appealing and besides, I can't leave the love of my life, especially if Doris does go.' She didn't feel ready to tell him for definite just yet in case he expected her to commit to more.

'Ah yes, our handsome Denni.' He turned his head to face her. 'Wait, what do you mean, if Doris goes? Isn't it definite?'

'It is, I think, but I don't know, she seems so nervous about it – I'm just not sure that she'll go through with it. I hope she does because it's everything she ever wanted, a husband and a family, although I don't think he's proposed yet.'

'Sounds too good to resist.'

'What about you? What are your plans for the future?'

'I don't know . . . I'll be finishing the last bits of filming soon for the movie so that will take me to America for a little while but you know, I think I'm going to need someone to keep my feet on the ground and my mama has said there is a beautiful woman back home that she'd like to introduce me to. She knows I'm ready to settle down and maybe that will be the best thing for me.'

'You'll go back to Italy?' Lottie hadn't expected that. She also hadn't expected her stomach to sink as low as it had.

'Oh I don't know . . . My mama has been trying to get me to go back there ever since I left.'

'When was the last time you were there?'

'A few months ago. I'd not long got back when I met you.'

'Did you have a nice time?'

'As well as can be expected. Unfortunately it was for a sad reason that I was there.' He rubbed at his temple and closed his eyes.

'Oh no. Are you OK?'

'I'm fine, it's just . . .'

'Just what? What happened, Marco?'

He swallowed. She stroked his back gently.

'My uncle, he died.'

'I'm so sorry.' She hugged him tightly and felt the strength leave his shoulders as they dropped just for a minute. He pulled away from her and brushed the tears away from his eyes before they had a chance to fall.

'Thank you, I'm fine. My uncle was always very proud of me, even if sometimes my father was not.' He swigged from his bottle and clapped his hands. 'And now we must dance.'

'But . . .' Lottie hesitated, wanting to know more.

Her heart felt lighter after unleashing her thoughts onto Marco, as though she'd tied each little problem or guilty thought to a helium balloon and released them into the sky. She had shown she trusted him implicitly and although she knew he was still holding something back, she had begun to peel the layers back and get to the heart of the matter.

Three hours later, Lottie had decided to cool off outside during lunch after the particularly steamy dance session. Marco stamping his feet like a matador had raised her temperature significantly. She checked her emails and opened one from Mia.

Marco appeared and sat on the bench next to her, and drank a pint of water down in one. 'It's thirsty work, the paso doble, isn't it? I think it's the sexiest dance of them all.'

'I can't deny that, Marco – I might add it to my wedding dance repertoire.'

'Good idea. I'm sorry for interrupting you on your phone.'

'Oh, that's OK. I've had an email from Mia, she's so excited about the plans for the barn dance and has offered to do all the admin work and sort out any permission we might need from the council. She's also discovered that there are community grants available that we could apply for with regards to the dance school. That's very kind of her as she knows how busy I am with rehearsals and everything.'

'Sounds fantastic, she's a lovely girl. I'm glad things are working out OK for her.'

'Me too. Also, Kevin has offered his services. He's a DJ and all-round entertainer and he's got loads of experience with barn dances.'

'That's great news. Did you tell her about the plans for Denni?'

'Yes, I did, and she laughed a lot but she loves it. D'you know, Mia's enthusiasm has motivated me to get started on clearing out the barn. I'm thinking of organising a meeting this evening for anyone who might want to help. What do you think?'

'I think it's a fantastic idea.'

'Will you come?'

'Yes, of course, and I'll bring my cousins Gabe and Franco if they're free.'

'Thanks Marco, I really appreciate that.'

She typed out an email to all her local contacts and pressed send.

'Come on then, Marco, our ensemble awaits.'

Marco stood up and stretched. She tried to avoid looking at the muscles rippling under his T-shirt but did manage a sneaky glimpse.

Chapter 47

Lottie's excitement increased a hundredfold at the number of people who turned up that evening despite such short notice. Her little barn was soon bursting from the rafters with friends and volunteers. The buzz of chatter escalated as more people turned up. She was grateful for the number of paper cups and bottles of squash and beer she'd bought as she had never expected so many lovely people to be interested.

She stood on a chair and tapped a glass with a spoon to attract everyone's attention. The conversations hushed and she felt a little self-conscious as all eyes were on her.

'Firstly, I'd just like to say a huge thank you to all of you for coming along and giving up your time to help out. In case anyone doesn't know, my name's Lottie and I have started a little dance school. I've already met some wonderful people through running my dance classes and I want it to be a part of the community. Once it's running properly, I'd like to be able to offer bursaries so that children whose parents can't afford luxuries like dance classes don't have to miss out.' The room reverberated with the sound of applause.

'Thank you. Now I don't know if it's anything to do with a little dance show on the telly you may have heard of called *Truly Dance*,' she smiled and paused as a cheer went up, 'but the number of people who would like to join my dance classes has skyrocketed since the publicity went out about it. Usually, I hold the classes in here but, as you can see, I need to expand.' She caught Marco's eye in the crowd and he winked at her, which spurred her on to keep going.

'My lovely friend Doris has offered me the larger barn just next door so we thought it would be a lovely idea to hold a barn dance there to raise some cash for the dance school. We will also be selling pitches to any local stallholders too. So, this is where you all come in if you're willing. We just need a hand to empty out the barn and ensure it's safe enough to have the dance there. My brother Blake has checked it out and has a list of jobs he thinks need doing. So, clap your hands if you want to go over and see what the job entails?' The applause resumed and Mia helped Lottie down from the chair. She led the way to the bigger barn.

Once inside, she got a shock as she saw the farmer from the farm next door drive the beaten-up old tractor away. For a moment, she wondered whether he was stealing it until she saw Doris waving him off with a huge smile on her face.

She held up a thick envelope.

'What's that?'

'Open it,' instructed Doris.

Lottie opened it to find a thick wodge of cash.

'It's going towards the conversion.'

'Doris, I can't possibly take this, there's thousands of pounds here. I don't expect you to go selling off your stuff.'

'I know you don't, dear, but it's no use to me and it's one in the eye for my dad as that tractor was his pride and joy. Don't worry, I kept some for myself to pay for my trip to Australia and to keep me going for a little while.'

'Are you sure, Doris? I don't want you to do anything that you'll regret.'

'I regret nothing. My dad treated that thing better than he treated me. I'd much rather it went to a good home.' She rubbed her palms together as if washing her hands of it.

'Thanks Doris, you're amazing. I must admit I never quite realised how expensive tractors were.'

'I know, shocking isn't it. But we had no use for it, not since Dad sold most of the land off, but I think the money is going to a great cause. I'm the landlady of the barn so I think it's only right for me to pay something towards the conversion.'

'Only if you're absolutely sure, that would be fantastic, thank you.'

'I'm definitely sure. Look at us, two little lost souls going on amazing adventures,' Doris replied.

'D'you know, Doris, I have to say for the very first time since my mum died, I don't feel like that lost soul anymore.'

'Me neither,' said Doris, 'not since you came into my life.' She gave Lottie a gentle hug.

'Ah, there you are,' said Reggie. 'I've been looking all over for you. What do you want to do with the bits and pieces of farm machinery in the far end of the barn?'

'I'm going to photograph it all and put it up for sale on the internet, as I made an absolute killing on the tractor. Come on, Reggie, let's get snapping so we can make some holiday spends.'

'OK, but there're some items that people want to buy now.'

'Well let's go and take a look,' said Doris, slipping her arm into his.

Lottie smiled as the happy couple walked off. She looked around at all the people who had come to help and her heart burst with warmth. Blake had brought along some of his workers, Marco his cousins and friends, Melissa had brought her dad and brother along, Mia's boyfriend had a couple of mates with him, and even Reggie and his pals turned up and some of those from the pensioners' dance class had brought along husbands too. Not to mention many of the dancers both from the show and from the Bramblewood Amateur Dramatic Society.

Melissa's dad wanted to get stuck in immediately.

'We can't thank you enough for what you've done for our Melissa,' he said. 'She's gone from a shy and timid little mouse to a young woman bursting with confidence. Nobody else would give her a chance but you've completely brought her out of herself.'

'Melissa is a delightful and extremely talented young woman and I'm proud to have her on the team.'

'Well I'd like to help you with any plans that need drawing up for the conversion, just to show my gratitude.'

'That would be absolutely amazing, thank you,' said Lottie, overcome by his generosity.

At this rate the place would be ready in no time, she thought. She joined in with the clearing out and used Doris's rusty old wheelbarrow to transport the rubbish to a skip that Blake had organised for her.

By the time she collapsed into bed, she ached from top to toe but her heart soared at the outpouring of love, support and friendship that she'd experienced today.

Chapter 48

Clearing out the barn had been exhausting but Lottie was still determined to help the volunteers each day after work and was pleased that apart from a few hay bales, it had finally been emptied in just a few days. Marco had joined her to see what else needed doing.

'It's looking great in here. Well done, Lottie.' He gave her an affectionate nudge with his elbow.

'It really is, though not much to do with me − it's absolutely down to all these wonderful people helping.'

'Yes, but they wouldn't be here if it wasn't for you. You have reached beyond the stars to make your dreams come true. I'm truly in awe of you.'

'Oh you,' she said, elbowing him back. 'You always seem to know the right thing to say. Sometimes I worry that I've taken on too much and I'll burn out and be good for nothing. I'm so tired, I fall asleep on the way upstairs to bed.'

'Don't worry, I won't let you burn out − I'll look after you.' He put his arm around her shoulders and she hugged him, resting her head on his chest. He put his other arm around her and encircled her in a beautifully warm embrace that she never wanted to end. He kissed the top of her head like he did at the shows when they awaited their scores. Electric shocks made their way down her body; she closed her eyes briefly until the delicious feeling passed through her. As though attracted by magnets, her face lifted up to him and as her eyes met his, she was hit by a bolt of realisation. She gasped silently and watched as his dark eyes blazed a trail to her mouth, and she licked her lips in anticipation. His eyes met hers again, full of unspoken questions; his long lashes seemed to blink in slow motion. His black hair flopped forward as he dipped his head towards her. Her eyes closed again as his lips brushed against hers, awakening every one of her nerve endings and rendering resistance futile. She pressed her lips to his only for him to pull away, leaving her mouth searching and bobbing like a goldfish out of water.

'Hi Gabe, how are you?' he said.

Lottie's eyes popped open wide and her soaring heart crashed back to earth with a disappointed bang. Gabe and his girlfriend Poppy stood in front of them. Marco shook his hand and kissed Poppy on the cheek.

'I'm good thanks, cuz. Just to let you know that there's a journalist here who wants to speak to Lottie about the new dance school. I thought you might want to know,' he added after obviously registering the panic on both of their faces. 'Don't worry, I sent him over to meet Denni first.'

Lottie blushed furiously and on seeing a sparkle on Marco's lower lip, she instinctively went to wipe away the evidence of her lip gloss but stopped herself just in time when she realised how intimate that would have looked.

'Oh, you have a little something on your lip,' said Poppy in her Liverpool accent. She handed him a tissue from her bag and winked at Lottie.

'Hi, I'm Lottie, I've seen you in the café in the playhouse.'

'Yes, that's right, and I also have another business called the Posh Pannier. I was hoping to book a stall on the day of the barn dance if there's any still available?'

'Yes, that would be brilliant, the more the merrier.' She took out her phone to take Poppy's details.

'Did you manage to secure the stage and PA system from the playhouse?' Marco asked Gabe.

'Yes, that's all done,' he replied. 'I just need to do a quick measure of the area if you've got a couple of minutes.'

'Yes, of course,' said Lottie and led them to where she wanted the stage to go.

'You must be so excited about your plans for the dance school.'

'I really am,' said Lottie, 'I can't wait to get stuck into it and welcome all my new students here.'

'So what's the plan for this place?' asked Poppy.

Lottie gestured to the middle of the room. 'I'm going to get folding doors right across here to make two rooms for classes but then we can open it up for when we want to have shows on. We should also be able to have the hayloft converted to a little office.'

'That sounds wonderful. The playhouse often runs out of room for things so I'm sure they would like to book the rooms out when they're free for extra practice.'

'That would be great. We need all the money we can get at the moment. The community have been brilliant coming together like this and as a thank you, I'm donating time in the hall for community meetings and I'm offering free dance classes for those who can't afford it. I really want to give something back.'

'I think that's amazing and I just wanted to wish you all the luck in the world with it and with the show on Saturday – you're doing great.'

'Oh, I don't know about that, we scored pretty low last week – it was so scary.'

'Yes, but if you don't mind me saying, I think you and Marco didn't have that spark last week – it was like someone had thrown a bucket of water over you both. But after what me and Gabe just saw happen between you two just now, I'd say that spark is more of an Olympic torch and it looked pretty inextinguishable to me.' She laughed as Lottie blushed.

'We're not together,' said Lottie.

'I know, but from what I've seen, you bloody well should be,' Poppy smiled. 'I've seen his eyes following you around the room in the playhouse and his face light up like a beacon when you walk into the room and when you dance together, my god, you could set the place on fire. Marco is well and truly head over heels in love with you, and me and Gabe are made up about that after him getting his heart broken.'

'By Alexia?' Lottie asked.

'Yes, she's a bit of a diva, but honestly, I think it was for the best. Marco needed to understand how he treated women wasn't right and he learned the hard way. He's a different man now. He always seems so sure of himself but I think it's mostly bravado he's a big softy underneath it all. He's not quite himself at the moment but he'd never tell you if he had a problem he just hides behind a façade. But I can honestly say I've never seen him look at anyone the way he looks at you, and even Gabe agrees.'

'That's nice to know,' Lottie replied.

'What do I agree with?' asked Gabe, putting his arm around Poppy.

'Everything I say,' Poppy joked.

'That's true,' said Gabe, kissing her gently on the lips before turning to Lottie.

'OK, so I was thinking of the stage being this big,' he gestured to where he had laid rope in a rectangle on the floor. 'Which should be able to fit in the DJ and are you having a band?'

'Oh, that would be brilliant, yes, my friend Mia's guy Kevin is supplying the DJ set and disco lights, and he knows a professional ceilidh band – we're just waiting on confirmation for that.'

'Sounds great, and we've got miles of fairy lights you could borrow to go round the barn itself for some atmosphere if that helps.'

'That would be amazing, thanks,' said Lottie.

She caught Marco's eye as he turned to leave with Gabe and he gave her a mischievous smile, her stomach flipped as she remembered that glimpse of a kiss which had left her longing for more.

'So, are you two going to get together? After the show, I mean?' asked Poppy.

Lottie felt that even though they'd only just met, Poppy, with her warm personality and cheeky sense of humour, was someone she would love to get to know better.

'I'll just say watch this space,' she teased.

'Yay, we can be cousins-in-law,' whispered Poppy. 'He's a lovely guy and they're a lovely family. We have so much fun together. Anyway, I'd better go, but it was lovely to meet you properly and good luck with everything.'

'Thanks, and it was so good to properly meet you too. Bye.'

'Bye,' said Poppy, waving as she walked off to join Gabe.

'Lottie Daniels?' asked a guy standing in front of her.

'Yes, that's me. How can I help?' she replied.

'I'm Neville Jones from the *Bramblewood Echo* and I was just hoping to ask you some questions about your new dance school, if that's OK.'

'Yes, of course.'

'Also how does it feel to be featuring in *Truly Dance* with the amazing Marco Abruzzo? What's your relationship like?'

'Oh, we're not in a relationship – we just dance together.'

'Yes, that's what I meant.' He looked surprised that she would think anything different.

Lottie flushed slightly and hoped he didn't notice. She guessed it was just her guilty conscience affecting her; after all; she could hardly tell him that she was having trouble keeping her hands and lips off her drop-dead gorgeous dance partner.

She enjoyed the interview and concentrated as hard as she could on it, but her mind kept drifting back to what Poppy had said about Marco being in love with her. She wished more than anything that this show would hurry up and be over so they could decide once and for all whether they should get together properly.

Chapter 49

The paso doble was a roaring success as Marco, dressed as a matador and accessorised by his trademark mask, and Lottie in a sparkly black and transparent flamenco style gown, held the audience in the palm of their hands. Lottie wasn't familiar with the dance but Marco had explained that he would be the matador and she would be representing the swish and swirl of his cape using a step called the chasse cape. Lottie had the fluid movements down to a tee and her heart pounded in time to the beat of 'Don't Stop the Music' by Rihanna, as Marco swirled her from one side to the other. His movements were strong and powerful, whilst hers were sensual and seductive; every time Marco performed the appel, which required him to stamp his feet, the audience would cheer and the carnal movement and sound would go straight to Lottie's heart and melt it even more.

The judges were on their feet clapping ferociously when they stopped, with Lottie inches from the floor looking straight into Marco's dark sensual eyes. His breathing was heavy as he pulled her to her feet and she felt her pulse racing as they waited for the results.

She had high hopes but daren't believe that they could come anywhere near the top.

The scores were in and Lottie screamed then covered her mouth with her hands as they received three nines and got twenty seven, becoming joint first with Alexia and Dafydd. Marco lifted her off the ground and spun her around, which set off the crowd once more. Lottie noticed the camera had focused on Alexia's face and she looked furious with the result, plastering on a fake smile that looked more like a grimace.

Chapter 50

Lottie felt as though she would never come down from the high that she was on, which was probably a good job as every muscle ached on Sunday. She and Marco and the rest of the crew had drunk champagne straight from bottles on the way home after the show. The atmosphere on the coach was electrically charged as they celebrated their impressive score.

'So, what do you think about the theme for the rumba next week in the final?' asked Marco on the way home.

'The rumba is quite good; I won a trophy in a dance competition when I was a teenager.'

'Oh really,' Marco laughed, 'well, I'd better make sure I don't end up spoiling it by stepping on your toes if you're the expert.'

'Oh no, *I* didn't say I was the expert – that was *you!*' she giggled as the bubbles fizzed up her nose.'

'I've just had a thought.'

'What's that?'

'I'm going to miss dancing with you when this show is over.'

'Me too, but then who says we've got to stop dancing? You can join my dance school if you want.'

'Oh, can I? That's very kind, thank you, I do enjoy teaching dance.'

'No, I meant as a student and I'll teach you how to dance properly,' she teased.

'Oi you, cheeky!' he laughed and then time seemed to stand still as his face bent down to kiss her. As much as she wanted to, there were far too many people sitting close to them, so she decided to be sensible and taking a deep breath, she held her champagne bottle to his lips instead.

'We've only got one more week to go.'

'You're absolutely right,' he agreed, after taking a swig from the champagne, 'and I will consider myself a winner no matter what the outcome of the show is because I will finally be able to ask out a sensational, beautiful woman who has come to mean a lot to me lately.'

'Oh really, you will have to introduce me to her sometime.' Lottie laughed at the unexpected look on his face. 'Marco, you're so easy to wind up!'

'I know, I have a rubbish poker face because my emotions are here and they come out here.' He pointed to his heart and his face respectively. 'Let's change the subject. What song do you fancy doing for the rumba then?'

'Oh, I love "Despacito" so that might be good . . . or no, no I've got the perfect one. What about "Señorita"? I could be Camila Cabello and you can be Shawn Mendes – what about that?' she said excitedly. 'He's my favourite male singer followed by Justin Bieber.'

'Justin Bieber?' he snorted and shook his head.

'Hey, don't diss the Biebs – us Canadians have to stick together, you know.'

'You won't catch me dancing to Justin Bieber, not in a million years. But Shawn Mendes I like.' Marco looked thoughtful as he swigged from the bottle and passed it back to her. She shook her head; she'd had enough and didn't want to make any regrettable decisions tonight as the more she looked at Marco, the harder she was finding it to resist him.

'I think that will be perfect, even though I would normally call you signorina. So yes, a very good choice.' He played the song on his phone and they took an earpiece each. Lottie leaned on his chest as the mellow beats relaxed her and fell asleep listening to her new favourite song.

The next morning Lottie opened the door to her seniors' dance class and revelled in all the congratulations.

'We've brought cake for after the class for our winners,' said Edie as she and Frances walked in carrying tins.

'Well technically we were joint winners,' said Lottie as she peeked inside one of the tins and the fresh smells of coffee and walnut and lemon drizzle cakes wafted into the air.

'Well we don't know them so you're our winners. Can you take a piece to Marco, please,' said Frances shyly, her face turning pink.

'Yes, of course, he'll be delighted with it. Thank you, Frances.'

'You're welcome, dear.'

'Aw, here's our winner,' said Peggy from underneath a huge bouquet she was carrying. She handed it to Lottie, along with a sparkly pink gift bag. 'This is just a little something from all of us.'

Lottie looked around the room and her heart glowed at the love and support she felt from her senior class, now surrounding her with proud smiles on their faces. Every one of them was an absolute joy to teach and despite the age difference, she felt they were friends too.

'We think you're amazing and when you win on that stage it's not just for you, it's for all of us,' said Arthur.

'Thank you, Arthur, but I think you're the amazing ones, especially with all the help you've given in tidying up the barn.'

'That's not just any old barn, Lottie, that's our new dance school and we love it and can't wait to get started in there. Anyway . . .' he patted the gift bag, 'open your presents, these are to wish you and Marco good luck in the final,' he replied.

Lottie pulled out a soft package covered in tissue paper. She carefully unwrapped it to find two knitted dolls, which were obviously herself and Marco, he with his mask and hat, black trousers and see-through shirt and she, wearing a black and silver sequinned dress.

'Oh, these are wonderful.' She cuddled them to her chest then at arm's length so she could admire every little detail. 'Thank you so much, they're gorgeous. Who made them?'

'Arthur did,' said Doris. 'Isn't he clever?'

'You really are, Arthur. You've even got my sparkly dance shoes down to a tee.' She kissed him on the cheek.

'My fiancée taught me how to make them, she said I needed more hobbies, but they are from all of us, along with the flowers,' he blushed.

'Well, I love them and I can't thank you enough, all of you. These will most definitely be coming with me to London next weekend. She put the dolls down on the table, patted them affectionately then clapped her hands and turned on the music.

'OK everyone, let's get dancing! We're going to do the salsa, so let's get those hips swaying as we have a lot of cake to get through at the end of this session.'

After the session was over and most of the cake had been eaten, Lottie flopped onto the couch; she really needed some downtime as next week's rehearsals would be the most important since the show began. She couldn't wait to show Marco the dolls; she lay down and admired the amazing detail in each one then gave Marco's one a kiss before cuddling them to her chest as she drifted into a deep and satisfying sleep.

Chapter 51

Lottie popped over to see Mia before rehearsals and handed her a gift bag full of her favourite chocolates.

'What's this for?' she asked suspiciously.

'For helping me out with the dance classes. I just feel as though I'm spinning too many plates at the moment and in some ways, I can't wait for the show to be over.'

'Oh, you don't have to get me anything. I love taking the little one's classes and Melissa is a wonderful help too; it won't be long before she'll be able to take her own classes. What a lot of talent she has.'

'She's brilliant, isn't she? I'm so pleased she came to me for work experience.'

'The waiting list is so long that I think it's going to keep all three of us busy when we can move into the new premises.'

'I can't wait,' said Lottie.

'Congratulations on your success on Saturday. I must admit you and Marco were literally on fire, you make such a gorgeous couple. What's going on with you two?'

'Nothing yet.' Lottie could feel heat rising up her face.

'What do you mean "nothing yet"? Does that mean that something is pending?'

Lottie covered her face with her hands then peeked over the top of her fingers at Mia and gave a slight nod.

'Oh my god, what's happened, tell me everything – shall I put the kettle on?' she shrieked, then put her hand on her tiny bump. 'Ooh, I think the baby just jumped when I screeched, or he or she is kicking me to find out more info about your dalliance with a sexy stud muffin.'

Lottie laughed. 'I wish I had time to come in for a chat, but unfortunately I'm already late for rehearsals and we'll be hard at it all week.'

'Oh yes,' Mia scoffed.

'No, not like that.' It was Lottie's turn to shriek.

'You've got to give me a hint,' said Mia.

'OK, well, as you know we've actually kissed but then we were interrupted and on Saturday night he was going to kiss me again but I said we had to wait. Anyway, he's going to ask me out when the show is over.'

'Yes!' Mia clapped her hands. 'I can't think of anything that would make me happier right now.'

'Me too,' said Lottie. 'Although I'm still a little worried about getting into the whole relationship thing again so I need to be sure.'

'You'll be fine and I think you'll be very happy together. I could literally see the sparks flying off you both on the telly.' Mia pretended to wipe sweat from her brow.

'Really?' Lottie's stomach fluttered at the sexiness of the dance they did.

'It was so obvious; the sexual tension was lighting up the screen and the look on his ex's face when you drew. What a diva – did you see her?'

'I did catch a glimpse and she didn't look happy.' Lottie's heart sunk at the mention of what she thought of as Marco's Achilles heel. Deep down she worried that he would drop everything to get back to the woman who had broken his heart.

'She was fuming. She looks like a nasty piece of work. I wonder what he saw in her?'

'Well, she is beautiful.'

'Yes, but she doesn't hold a candle to you. You're a stunner, Lottie, and you have a gorgeous personality to match.'

'Thanks, love.' She leaned over to give Mia a hug. 'I've really got to go before Marco sends out a search party.'

'Bye love, see you soon and don't worry about the classes this week.'

'Thanks. Bye then.' Lottie blew a kiss, waved, and walked down the path to Petal.

'Ah there you are – is everything OK?' said Marco when she walked into the studio.

'Yes, sorry I'm late,' she said, a little breathless after running from the car park. 'But to make up for it, I've got a surprise for you.'

'A surprise?' Marco looked intrigued.

'Yes, so close your eyes and hold your hands out.'

He did as she asked and she took a moment to admire his thick dark lashes. She wondered how it would feel to just kiss him now on his deliciously soft lips but it wouldn't be fair as she stopped him from kissing her the other night; also it wouldn't be fair for the competition either – the rules were clear. In less than a week they could kiss to their hearts' content, she thought. She placed a package in each hand and his eyes opened wide. 'Some cake, very nice, it smells lovely – thank you.'

'Yes, it's from a couple of my senior students, Edie and Frances – they made it for the class to celebrate our win and she specifically asked me to give a piece to you. You'll love it – it's delicious.'

'Ah, please thank Edie and Frances for me, and what's this?' He looked at the dolls and laughed louder than she'd ever heard him before; it was a lovely sound that made her want to laugh too. She regarded his perfect white teeth and those dimples. 'It's you and me,' he smiled, 'or should I say Camila and Shaun.'

'Talking of which,' she flicked on the music, bent forward and tossed her hair back before dancing towards him, her exaggerated twisty steps swinging her hips in time to the music.

'Come to me, señorita, and bring those perfect Cuban motion hips with you,' said Marco, his eyebrows raised and his dark eyes fixed on her as he held out his arms for the dance. Soon they were in perfect sync as they glided around the dance floor and Lottie's heart pounded to its own beat due to the close proximity of this gorgeous man. They could definitely have both fitted in the same hula hoop with this one, and the thought sent flutters through her entire body. They stopped for a drink.

'So, I've thought of a story for this dance,' said Lottie.

Marco was halfway through gulping his entire water bottle but raised his eyebrow at her.

She took it as a signal to continue. 'So this story is very interesting. Ramon is a famous rock star and he barely notices his backing dancers, but when he goes to a bar one night, he sees this beautiful woman join her friends at a table and they all drink wine together and are happy.

'Then, as the music plays, the ladies get up to dance but a man tries to get too friendly with Maria. She tells the man to get lost and then her eyes lock with Ramon's and *she* calls *him* over like this.' She stepped a few paces away from him before winding her wrist and seductively inviting him over to her.

Marco's eyes widened and he gathered pace as he moved towards her. 'Hold on, hold on,' he gasped, breathless from swigging all of the water. 'I thought we weren't doing the stories anymore – didn't you say you wanted it to be just me and you?'

'I did, but you still haven't told me your story, Marco, so until you do, I need to keep making them up and you will forever be Ramon, unless you're ready to open up to me.'

Once he stood in front of her, she flicked her hair again from side to side and held her hand out. He pulled her towards him, stroked her arm sensuously and they danced seductively once more. 'What do you want to know? he asked.

'It's not what I want to know, it's *who*. Poppy told me you're not yourself, that you're hiding behind bravado, a façade.'

He laughed as he swung her around but Lottie could tell it wasn't genuine; she knew that much about him.

He pulled her towards him and looked deep into her eyes. He opened his mouth to speak but then faltered and she saw the light reflected in unshed tears in his eyes. 'My uncle, I told you about him dying.'

She nodded; his pain jolted in her heart.

'I was named after him, he was my father's older brother, he was the man I wanted to be. His world was glamorous, a world of designer watches, fine wines and fat cigars, and always with a beautiful woman on his arm. My nonna doted on him, everyone did, but especially me. I love my father but his world seemed so boring compared to Uncle Marco's. He lost touch with us for a while, we thought he was living the high life, but when my father found him again, he was all alone, and very ill. He brought him back to die with dignity and with his family, and the look of gratitude on his face as he took his last breath will stay with me forever.

'I've always been proud of my father but never more so than when I looked at him with fresh eyes. I've taken too long to grow up too. Alexia broke my heart, yes, but that was nothing compared to seeing the man I'd strived to be, the man who had left a trail of broken hearts behind him, lying there with no special someone by his side. It was a glimpse of my future and I didn't like what I saw. Then I looked from his deathbed to my father and mother and I realised who had the best life of all. That's why I vowed to have no more insincere relationships.'

'I'm so sorry. Are you OK?' said Lottie, slightly breathless from both the dancing and the emotion of Marco's story. She kissed him softly on his cheek and felt the moisture of a teardrop on her lip. She couldn't tell whether it was hers or his.

'Come on, pull yourself together, Marco, we've got a dance to do here,' he said, pretending to slap himself on the cheek. Then he turned to her. 'So how about at the end of the dance, you pull away from me and we end up back-to-back. Like this.' He spun her round and she landed perfectly behind him.

The unexpected movement took her by surprise and she laughed.

'Brilliant, Lottie, we should hopefully break a few hearts with this performance.'

'I hope so, thank you,' she said, squeezing his hand. 'What for?' he asked.

'For trusting me,' Lottie smiled and winked at him.

He winked back before setting up the music again so they could start from the top.

Dripping with sweat and exhausted, Lottie drove home to find a note under her door from Doris inviting her to dinner and the relief of not having to cook flooded through her. She jumped in the shower, got changed and picked up the leftover cake to take with her.

She could barely keep her eyes open by the time she'd demolished Doris's delicious toad in the hole with mustard mash, veggies, and her homemade thick gravy, rounded off by tea and cake. She filled Doris in on how the rehearsal had gone and Doris shared her news, which was mainly gossip about her friends. One of whom had a toyboy, it seemed.

'Oh, I nearly forgot – this package came for you today,' said Doris, handing over a brown parcel.

'Thank you,' said Lottie and laughed when she opened it and saw the contents. She held it up for Doris to see.

'Denni will love this,' Doris giggled.

'I hope so,' said Lottie. 'If there's any discomfort, we won't do it.'

'I'm sure he'll be fine but yes, we can play it by ear.'

'I can't believe you're going a week today,' said Lottie, feeling a little choked.

'I know, dear, it's quite scary, isn't it?' said Doris.

'Exciting too though, right?'

'Yes, of course. I'm going to miss you though, and Denni and Marco, and my lovely friends and neighbours.' She sniffed and tears started to run down her face.

'I'm going to miss you too.' Lottie handed her a tissue and gave a little sob, followed by Doris's sobbing.

'Oh my god, look at the pair of us,' said Lottie.

'Good cries are like busses aren't they? You don't see one for ages then they all come at once,' said Doris, blowing her nose.

'They certainly do,' said Lottie. 'It's all been too much and I'm really truly happy for you.'

'Thank you, darling. As I've said before, I owe it all to you – you changed my life so much for the better when you landed in that ditch and I'm sure Marco thinks the same.'

Lottie's cheeks burned at the mention of his name as memories of their first meeting resurfaced.

'Anyway, talking of Marco, let's celebrate our friendship with those posh choccies he bought me. Go on, love, you can open them – they're on the coffee table. I'll put the kettle on.'

Lottie spent the rest of the evening reminiscing with Doris as they drank tea and ate chocolates and she had never felt so at home. As she was about to leave to go to bed, she received a text.

'Thank god I haven't been drinking – I've got to get to the hospital,' she said, grabbing her keys.

Chapter 52

Half an hour later, Lottie was sitting in Camilla's private hospital room about to cuddle her brand-new baby niece.

'Here's your Auntie Lottie. Lottie, meet Iris May Daniels.' Blake gently placed the baby in her arms with tears in his eyes.

'Oh, how lovely, named after our mums and she is just as beautiful as they were. Congratulations both of you.' She stroked the silky-soft skin of Iris's cheek and marvelled at her tiny fingers. 'How are you, Camilla? You're looking fabulous.'

'Thank you. My body feels a bit bruised but my mind is on a high; I literally can't stop looking at her.'

'I'm not surprised – she's absolutely gorgeous.' Tears sprang to her eyes as the height of emotions in the room became almost tangible.

Iris half opened one eye before tentatively opening the other and as Lottie gazed into galaxies of the deepest blue, she felt as if this tiny being had all the answers to all the questions on earth. Her heart erupted with a flood of emotion and love for this baby girl she held in her arms and she knew she would do anything for her. She smiled at Blake and their tear-filled eyes met; they exchanged a look that both understood. There should have been two grandmas and one grandad in that room welcoming this new life to their family. Not for the first time, Lottie felt grateful that she had come to live near Blake. They were a family.

As Iris began to grizzle a little, she placed a gentle kiss on her soft downy hair and carefully handed her back to Camilla who held her to her breast. 'Thank you for letting me meet her so soon, but I'd better go in case you get into trouble for sneaking me in.'

'We wanted you to be the first to see her,' said Camilla.

'I feel very honoured, and remember, whenever you need a babysitter you know where I am and let me know if you need any other help too.'

'We will do, thank you. See you again soon and thanks for the gorgeous presents and balloons.'

'You're very welcome.' Lottie kissed Camilla and Blake goodbye and went home exhausted but elated. She'd never felt broody before but if the surge of love she got from holding Iris and looking into her eyes was just a taste of what having her own child would be like, then she was all for it.

Chapter 53

Another week of rehearsals flew by and Lottie's heart was opening up to Marco more and more. Thankfully the plans for the barn dance were a great distraction and everything was now in place.

Mia popped round after work one day for a catch-up. Lottie made them mugs of tea and they wandered into the barn and sat on a couple of haystacks.

'So, following the article by the journalist who you spoke to the other day and the distribution of leaflets all over Bramblewood and surrounding areas by the senior dance students, the ticket sales have gone through the roof, or in this instance, the hayloft,' Mia chuckled.

'Mia, you have been an absolute godsend in helping with the arrangements,' said Lottie. 'Thank you so much – I couldn't have done it without you.'

Mia waved her hand to brush away the compliment. 'No worries, this is a team effort. Now where are you up to with everything?'

Lottie picked up her notebook and flicked through the pages until she got to her list.

'Well, I met Poppy for lunch in the playhouse and she has offered to supply chicken or fish and chips in a basket at a discounted rate. Camilla has offered the cupcake van to transport the food to the venue and her assistant Angela will be selling cupcakes from it at the event.' She tapped each item with a pen as she read them out. 'As you know, Blake gave me contact details for builders and suppliers and the quotes have been coming in thick and fast. I just need to sort through the paperwork when I get a minute. Oh yes, and Doris has ordered extra hay bales for seats and decorations.'

'Sounds like you've got it all in hand and yay for Doris, she's amazing. What a brave thing to do moving to the other side of the world to be with the man she loves.'

'I know, it's such a lovely happy ever after for her, isn't it? She told me that the barn dance has been a brilliant distraction for her and was keeping her busy as she prepares for her big adventure.'

'I'm so happy for her. And how's Camilla doing and little baby Iris?'

'They're doing so well – here, look.' Lottie picked her phone to show Mia her new background picture of a wide-awake little Iris trying to chew on her fist.

'Oh, she's just too adorable – I love her.'

'Me too,' said Lottie smiling as she looked at the picture lovingly. 'My heart almost bursts every time I see her. She's really brought it home to me how much I'd love a family one day and I've never thought of that before.'

'Maybe that's because you've never met the right man before,' she casually winked.

'Maybe,' Lottie answered noncommittedly.

'And just maybe you have met the right man now.'

'Maybe,' said Lottie as her heart burst again but this time with a different kind of love.

'Talking of which . . .' Mia teased as Marco, Gabe and the playhouse team arrived to install the stage and the reams of fairy lights they'd brought. They all shouted their hellos and Lottie blushed as she walked Mia out to say their goodbyes, which took ages as each found something new to talk about.

After waving her off, Lottie entered the barn just as Marco turned the switch on for the lights. Lottie's hand flew to her mouth and Marco put his arm around her shoulders.

'Are you OK?' he asked.

'Yes, I'm fine, thank you. This looks so enchanting and magical.'

'It does, doesn't it? It reminds me of the farm back home in Italy – we often had dances like this. We would have our families round, all sitting at long tables pushed together. Uncles playing guitars and everyone singing.'

'It sounds perfect. Have you got a big extended family?'

'We have a reasonable number of cousins and my three siblings, but when I say family, I include friends and those who worked in the farm and in the restaurant. We were one big family. I miss that.'

'Well, you can be part of *our* little family; there's a whole little community here for you and we've even got the donkey and the chickens.'

'Thank you, Bella, I'd like that.' His eyes sparkled as he looked at her and he planted a kiss on her forehead.'

'Are you ready, Marco?' shouted Gabe.

'I must go. See you tomorrow.'

'Bye and thank you, thank you Gabe and everyone – you've all been amazing,' she shouted to them on their way out. She watched them leave and her heart fluttered as Marco turned around to wink when he got to the door. She blew a kiss to him and watched his mouth break into a smile as he left.

The barn looked enormous now that it was emptied out and she could start to visualise how it was going to look after the renovation. The quotes had been much more reasonable than she'd expected because she still wanted to retain the characteristics of the barn; the main costs would be the sprung flooring and the floorboards on top of that, the addition of toilets and a wet bar, and the room separators that could be folded away to make one huge room. The mirrors and barre wouldn't cost that much and as the dance school progressed, so Lottie could add to the new features.

A sense of anticipation rippled through her at the thought of her dream coming true and of how proud her parents would be of her. She had a quick flash to the future and imagined little Iris in a tutu pirouetting around this room; she could see Blake and Camilla sitting in the audience along with the other parents, Mia and Kevin with their little one – all were welcome. She smiled as her mind even had the audacity to visualise Marco sitting in the audience watching their twins performing. Wait, twins? She interrupted her own fantasy – where did they come from? But her mind had obviously held onto the fact that his and Gabe's mum were twins so it could be a possibility for the future. As she left the barn, she turned off the lights and packed her little vision for the future safely into her heart.

Chapter 54

The final show had arrived, and the atmosphere in the London rehearsal rooms was fraught with anxiety. Firstly, one of their backing dancers had sprained her ankle and had to be replaced. Lottie's heart broke for her as she had cried, not just from the pain but because of missing out on such a fabulous opportunity. She was soon ensconced in the front row with her ankle bandaged and seemed happy to at least have the best seat to watch from.

Lottie almost broke down in tears as she and Marco just couldn't get the ending right, despite having practised all week and despite it being perfect for ninety-nine per cent of the time, there was just something not quite hitting the mark.

'I think it's just my nerves getting the better of me,' said Lottie, her hands shaking as they stood stage side listening to the previous contestants getting slaughtered by the judges then encouraged back up again.

'I think I know what it is, said Marco, looking dangerously sexy in his trademark mask and hat, also wearing the cape that she'd first seen on her audition. His dark purple shirt open to the waist and trimmed with sequins showed off his rock-hard abs, Lottie was engulfed by a strong urge to drop to her knees and lick her way up them to his firm chest before clamping her mouth onto his and wrapping her legs around his waist. She snapped out of her daydream.

'What?' she asked, hoping he couldn't see what she was thinking written across her face.

'It's the final story – we need to get it straight.'

'I thought we agreed no more stories,' she replied.

'This one is an important one.'

'Then I'm all ears,' she smiled.

'I am Marco, a handsome, actor slash dancer slash Italian farm boy who meets the future love of his life in a ditch. Her name is Lottie, she is an ambitious, brave, stunning and beautiful dance teacher with an extraordinary love for donkeys.'

He was interrupted by the presenter's voice coming over the microphone and thanking the judges for their scores, and as the audience clapped, Marco continued with the story.

'Marco tries to be friendly with the beautiful girl but he is nursing a broken heart from an evil vixen and the beautiful Lottie cannot forgive herself for leaving her ex at the altar so closes her heart to love.' He spoke faster, his hot breath in her ear sending trembles through her body.

'And now let's give a big *Truly Dance* welcome to our next finalists The Masked Man, Marco Abruzzo . . .' the presenter's voice echoed round the building.

'And what happens next?' asked Lottie as Marco took her hand to lead her out for their final performance as the audience clapped and cheered.

'. . . and his partner Lottie Daniels,' the presenter continued.

'Fate brings them together again and their love of dance, donkeys and eventually each other decides their destiny forever.' Lottie's heart soared as he made her laugh but she could also tell there was a serious message there.

'Oh, they love each other, do they?' she murmured.

'Oh yes, she is besotted by him,' he teased, smiling broadly.

She nudged his arm. 'And what about him?'

'He's not that bothered,' he replied. 'I'm joking, I'm joking,' he added quickly on seeing her mock sulky face. 'He fell in love with her the first time he saw her covered in mud like a potato but she shouted at him for not looking after his donkey. And that is the story he will tell their grandchildren in years to come.'

'Do you know, I think she is besotted by him after all,' said Lottie, the urge to kiss him flooding her veins with enough adrenaline to fire a rocket to the moon. 'This one's for Uncle Marco,' she whispered. He nodded his thanks.

They got into position and the sultry tones of 'Señorita' began to play. Lottie looked deep into Marco's eyes as she walked towards him, her exaggerated foot-steps causing her hips to wiggle sensuously. She flicked her hair and smiled as she saw Marco swallow; he looked like he never wanted to tear his eyes away from her. He pulled her towards him and spun her round the room effortlessly; all the nerves and awkwardness that had troubled her earlier had melted away, and every nerve-ending in her body sparked with his touch.

'The result of the dance competition becomes irrelevant as they both win at love,' he whispered.

'I love you,' Lottie mouthed to him.

'I love you too,' he mouthed back before spinning her away from him so they could end their piece back-to-back. Lottie panted both from the exertion of the dance and from the wonder of what had just happened between them. There had been a seismic shift in their relationship and she could feel it in every cell of her body. They stood still, apart from their chests heaving for the required amount of time before they were able to move and stand before the judges, who were all up on their feet dancing.

'Stanley,' said the presenter, 'what's your verdict?'

'My god, I think we should call 999 as you two have set this place on fire! I'm surprised the sprinklers haven't gone off considering the heat you've just created on this dance floor. The footwork was stylish and your synchronisation absolutely spot-on. This dance requires perfect precision and today you two were the masters of that.' He held up his paddle to screams of elation from the audience. 'Ten,' he proclaimed before sitting back down again.

Marco was holding onto Lottie so tight that she could feel his heart doing the tango with her own. Still a little breathless from the dance, she covered her hands over her face in shock and stared, eyes wide open at Marco, wishing she could just lean across and kiss him on his perfectly formed lips.

'Well, what can I add, I can honestly say in all my years of dancing and judging, I've never seen anyone perform the rumba with that much raw energy before. I mean the sexual chemistry between you two is off the scale,' said Anne as she undulated her hips.

Lottie stood with her back to Marco with his arms around her. His lips brushed her ear with the softest, sweetest kiss, which sent tantalising shivers through her body. 'Good luck, Bella,' he whispered. She loved the intimacy of only her hearing what he was saying and in fact, at that moment, nothing and nobody else mattered. She squeezed his arm as Anne continued.

'You certainly had me up dancing and Marco, I really wish that you could call *me* señorita because I know I'd definitely love it.' The audience cheered and whooped. 'Ten!' she shouted, raising her paddle.

Lottie's excitement was affecting every part of her body now and she felt she would explode just waiting for their final score.

Matthew stood up and the audience fell silent. Suddenly he got down on one knee. 'Marco and Lottie, what can I say but will you marry me please? Both of you!' The audience cracked up, Lottie laughed and nodded at him as he stood up again. 'Lottie, your seductive come hither motions at the beginning of that dance were so convincing I almost joined you on the dance floor myself.' He rolled his body, sensuously performing some of the movements as he spoke.

'You both have that natural magnetism, perfect synchronisation, grace and a winning performance as far as I'm concerned. It's a ten from me as well.' He waved his paddle in the air and then pretended to spank himself on the bottom with it.

Lottie spun round to face Marco and he lifted her in the air as she hugged him tightly. She wanted to laugh, cry, scream, dance and run away all at the same time. Suddenly she became acutely aware of how close he was to her. They were only usually this close when they danced and their professionalism kicked in. However, now there was skin-on-skin contact with his rock-hard frame, she gasped as sparks shot through her body. He nuzzled into her neck and she in his and for just a few moments she felt weightless as she floated in the warmth of his embrace. She reluctantly pulled away from him as they had to exit the stage for the next performers, she caught a glimpse of his face and could tell that he hadn't wanted this precious moment to end either. They ran into the holding room where they were greeted and hugged by the other dancers.

They watched silently as Alexia and Dafydd began their performance. Alexia appeared aggressive, her face set in a grimace. The dance was spectacular but Lottie felt that they just didn't have the spark between them and it seemed somewhat lacking from her point of view, but then she was biased. Marco reached for her hand as the presenter spoke to the judges.

Stanley stood up first.

'An absolute triumph and one of the best rumba performances I've seen for a while but Alexia, you looked like you wanted to kill your partner rather than make love to him.' The audience booed. 'Nevertheless,' he continued, enjoying the pantomime baddy role he always played, 'the dance was impeccable – I give you a ten.'

'Alexia and Dafydd, I have to say that dance was impeccable and you had me up on my feet cheering you on from the first episode. It's another ten from me,' said Anne. Lottie's eyes met Marco's and he smiled, giving her hand a little squeeze; she knew what he was thinking and she felt exactly the same. It didn't matter who won the competition; all that mattered was that they could now be together.

Matthew stood up and ran his hand through his hair, smoothing it down. Frown lines appeared on his forehead. 'Oh, I feel as though I've got the weight of the world on my shoulders here now but I know that I must go with my heart and my head. This show is based on pure talent and how these wonderful dancers perform and whether we can decipher the story that they want to tell.' He shuffled his paddles around and held up a number nine. The audience erupted, and Alexia looked as though her face would crack with the effort of plastering on a fake smile and Dafydd's attempt to hug her looked mechanical.

'So that means that the winners of our *Truly Dance* final are Marco Abruzzo and Lottie Daniels! Congratulations, come up on stage, you two,' announced the presenter.

Lottie's heart leapt out of her chest and did a little jig before leaping back in again. 'While Marco and Lottie make their way onto the stage, I have some breaking news. Our winners and runners-up have the opportunity to go on tour around Europe for the next three months to compete in the Eurodance championships.'

Lottie remembered something in the contract about possible extension periods to the show but she hadn't really thought much of it at the time. Feeling dazed, as though everything around her was in slow motion, she held tightly onto Marco's hand as they made their way to the stage where they were presented with an elegant trophy of a golden couple in the rumba position and the *Truly Dance* logo at the bottom. As she felt the weight of it in her hand, Lottie had a flashback to holding a trophy for a dance competition when she was younger and looking over at her parents' faces as they beamed with pride. She hoped they were looking down on her now and were feeling as proud of her as she was.

After lots of photos they were led offstage into a room with a press junket. Bottles of champagne were opened and shared and Marco's agent joined them, congratulating them both profusely.

'This is excellent, Marco my boy – we've got the European gig now just before the release of *Latino* so this will bring in the European fans. This will literally explode your career and propel you to stardom.'

Marco smiled. 'What do you think, Lottie, a tour round Europe?' He put his arm around her shoulders. Lottie looked at him in disbelief.

'I can't go on a three-month tour, Marco!'

'Why not? It will be amazing – we can go sightseeing in between the shows.'

'I'm sorry, I just can't do it. I've got responsibilities now; I've got to look after Denni and I'm just about to launch my dance school. Also remember the rules of the competition.'

'Well, surely those things can all wait – this is really important for Marco's career,' his agent piped up.

Marco shot him a look as if to say pipe down.

'I could help you sort everything out; maybe Doris could put off her trip for a little while.'

Lottie shrugged his arm off her shoulder. 'I think Doris has waited quite long enough for her chance at happiness with her one true love and I wouldn't expect her to wait a minute more.'

'What about Mia then, she can run the dance school for you until you get back. This is a once-in-a-lifetime chance for us.'

'Mia has got enough on her plate – she's going to have a baby to look after soon. Do you know what, Marco, I've spent most of my adult life shirking my responsibilities and I'm not going back to the old me.'

Lottie felt her heart would break as she saw the despair in his eyes but he had royally pissed her off expecting her to take advantage of her friends' good natures. It was like he had no concern for her whatsoever.

'Lottie, I'm sure we can work something out.'

'No, I'm sorry, I'm going home.' She headed towards the door.

Marco jumped up and started following her.

'No,' she said sharply, 'don't bother following me. My decision is final. Enjoy Europe.' Her heart hurt as she saw a look of pain and confusion on his face but she was too angry and upset to deal with it all now.

'This gig is important for you, Marco, you'd be a fool to turn it down. Let her cool off; I'm sure she'll calm down,' his agent said.

She stormed out of the room, angry tears stinging the back of her eyes; she didn't feel as if she'd ever calm down.

'You could always pair up with Alexia as the two of you together would up the price considerably.' She felt a twist in her gut as the agent's words escaped the room just before the door slammed shut.

'Lottie . . .' she heard Marco's voice echo down the corridor.

'Don't follow me, I'm fine,' she called back. 'I'll call you tomorrow.'

'Is Marco in there?' asked Alexia as she passed her in the corridor. 'I'd love to reminisce with him about the last time we were in Europe together.'

'Help yourself. I hope you have the time of your lives,' she managed to gush before the lump in her throat made it difficult to speak.

'By the way, I hope I didn't get you into trouble when I told the producer about yours and Marco's little secret,' she smirked.

Lottie took a deep breath. She should have known it was Alexia with a touch of the green-eyed monster. This should have been the happiest day of her life, nothing to do with winning the show, but because she thought that she and Marco could be together. The organisers had provided rooms for them all for the night but Lottie couldn't face that now and got one of the runners to arrange a car for her instead. She turned on her phone to see if there were any messages from him but there were so many texts and messages from well-wishers that she turned it straight off again. Well, it didn't matter anymore because he was going to Europe with Alexia and that was that – she hoped they'd be very happy together. Once home she got into bed and threw herself down on the pillow, and although she expected to toss and turn all night, exhaustion quickly caught up with her and she fell into a deep sleep.

Chapter 55

The next morning arrived before she knew it and there was no time for moping as she had to prepare for the barn dance. She jumped out of bed at the sound of knocking, only to find Doris standing at the door with a beautiful flower arrangement.

'Congratulations,' she said, 'this is from me and Reggie.'

'Thank you, Doris, it's beautiful.'

'Also, I obviously watched the show last night and I wanted to let you know I've decided to postpone my trip, seeing as you'll be going round Europe on the tour.'

'No, Doris, I'm not going – I'm staying here.'

'But why? You and Marco can go dancing off into the sunset together?'

'Has he asked you to do this?' asked Lottie.

'No, not at all. Are you all right?'

'Yes, I'm fine. I specifically told him I wasn't asking you to postpone your trip so I'd be very annoyed if he did. OK, that's good, so it's all sorted – I'm staying here to look after Denni and open my dance school and you, my lady, are off to Australia as planned.'

Doris's shoulders dropped in relief. 'Are you sure, dear? I have to admit Reggie would have been so disappointed and having finally plucked up the courage to go, I was feeling a little disappointed myself, but if you're sure . . .'

'Doris, I had a realisation and if I don't do this now, open up this dance school just like I'd planned, then I never will. There'll always be something that seems more exciting and will stop me from doing what I really want to do. I want to lay down my roots, maybe have a family one day, who knows. But I've found a home and a life here and I thought I'd found something else too but never mind. I knew it was too good to be true.'

'So, I don't have to cancel my flight for tomorrow then?' said Doris, her tone much lighter.

'No, you don't, now let's go and get Denni into his costume.'

'Oh yes,' giggled Doris.

Lots of helpers and stallholders milled about, busy setting up their individual spaces as they headed over to Denni. The farmer next door had allowed them to use his field for parking and he was busy hammering a sign up.

Lottie and Doris put on Denni's saddle and outfit, which consisted of a sparkly silver horn with rainbow hair and wings. Lottie had printed a sign that she stuck to the fence: DENNI'S DONKICORN RIDES £1.

'So will you be OK manning or should I say woman-ning this stall then, Doris?'

'Yep, I've got my camping chair and my flask so all will be fine, and Denni will love being with the children again.'

Doris was interrupted with a ping on her phone; she pulled it out of her overall pocket, typed something in and raced off.

'Won't be long, dear, just off to help a friend with a non-emergency, emergency. I'll be back in time before things get started.'

'But—' Lottie began.

'Don't worry, I won't be long.' Lottie watched as Doris ran off, jumped into Petal, and drove off. She'd never seen her move so fast.

Lottie spent the next couple of hours helping everyone get set up. Kevin would be DJing until later on when the band would kick off the barn dance. She was relieved to see Doris eventually return in one piece with Edie, Frances, Ruby and Peggy, all of whom seemed to be holding large black bags. They shuffled off into Doris's house.

Soon the sun was shining on what Lottie thought was the perfect countryside event. Arthur and his fiancée had arrived at the same time as Doris and were now manning a stall filled with the little dolls they had knitted in the shapes of footballers and soldiers, ballerinas, chefs and doctors – there was something for everybody.

Camilla and Blake turned up pushing baby Iris in the pram and Camilla introduced Lottie to her friends: Lucy, from the Signal Box Café, who was serving delicious-smelling jacket potatoes with various fillings, and Gracie, who owned an art gallery and was selling her artwork of local views. Lottie saw a perfect painting of Doris's house complete with farm and barns and donkey so she bought it for Doris as a leaving present. The music began blaring out of the speakers as Kevin set up his equipment and she could see the ceilidh band arriving.

As the customers began turning up, Lottie looked around and tried to take in the wonder of the scene laid out before her. Happy smiling faces, the children delighted with their gentle rides on Denni the Donkicorn. She waved at many of the guests whom she'd got to know and who had not hesitated to help her make her dream come true, a community that had welcomed her without hesitation. Her heart felt full of warmth, but there was just one thing that would have been the cherry on the top. However, there was no use crying over the man who was no doubt the love of her entire life – that ship had definitely passed.

She noticed Mia waving her over to the barn so she headed over to her. Mia kissed her and gave her a gentle squeeze.

'OK, the dance is about to begin. Kevin thought you might want to say a few words to welcome everybody.'

'Oh yes I do, thank you.' She made her way over to Kevin, who handed her the mike.

'When you've said a few words, I'll play a couple more songs and then the band will come on.'

Lottie looked out to the smiling faces in the crowd.

'Hi everyone, I just wanted to say a quick thank you to everybody for supporting this new venture. As many of you know, we will be offering bursaries to those in the area who can't afford dance lessons and we hope to be an active part of this wonderful community. I would also like to say a special thank you to my wonderful friend Doris, without whom none of this could have happened. It is my pleasure to announce that the barn dance can now begin.'

'Has anyone seen Doris?' she asked, putting her hand over her eyes to block out the glare from the disco lights. The music started up and then came to an abrupt stop as a police officer entered the barn.

'Can I speak to Lottie Daniels, please?' he bellowed. Lottie was horrified to see Doris holding her arms up to reveal she'd been handcuffed.

'What seems to be the problem, officer?' asked Lottie as everyone appeared to be frozen to the spot.

'Do you have a licence to play music in public?'

'Yes, I'm sure we do.' She looked around for Mia to confirm.

'Can you come down here please,' said the policeman.

'Yes, of course, I think I recognise you – weren't you at the planning meeting we had here?'

The officer looked shifty. She climbed down from the stage.

'I'm afraid I'm going to have to arrest you for being in possession of offensive music.'

'What?' asked Lottie, trying to make sense of everything.

The officer broke into a dance move as Kevin began playing a Justin Bieber song she recognised but couldn't quite put her finger on the title. Lottie wondered if she was possibly still asleep and dreaming this scenario as she happened to notice two nuns dancing amongst the crowd. When she saw Arthur dressed in his Biggles outfit walking in on his hands, she knew something was up.

All she needed now was to see a couple of cleaners shaking their stuff and, lo and behold, Edie and Frances appeared wielding their mops in time to the music. Doris began salsa dancing in her handcuffs and Lottie realised it must be a flash mob send-off that the seniors had planned for Doris as she was leaving. Her face broke into a smile and she began clapping and dancing too. She even recognised the song now: 'Sorry' by Justin Bieber.

The dancers had multiplied as more and more came through the door and now included Gabe and a few of the playhouse group who were encouraging all the guests to dance.

Then she saw him, just standing there in black jeans and a tight-fitting black T-shirt showing off his muscley brown arms. Her heart pounded in time with the music. Now the song made sense. Marco slid into the barn on his knees before jumping up and just mouthing the word *sorry* along with the song as he danced towards her. He reached out for her hand, pulled her towards him and they danced as the music changed to 'Despacito', whilst everyone clapped and cheered.

'I'm truly sorry. I love you and I'm never leaving you.'

'But what about Europe?' she asked as his sensual brown eyes stared deeply into her own, sending trembles through her body.

'We can do Europe together sometime in the future when the time is right, as a holiday. My place is here with you,' said Marco, his eyes pleading.

'What about Alexia?' she asked as he spun her round.

'Alexia who?' he shrugged. 'I always thought that she broke my heart but now I realise she just showed me that I had one. You're the one who has shown me what love is and you're the one I want to be with for the rest of my life, to dance with, to laugh with and to love with. His eyes focused on her lips as he pulled her masterfully towards him. 'Now please can we just kiss already.'

Lottie's heart exploded like a sparkly confetti gun. Her mouth broke into a beaming smile as the angel on her shoulder danced with the devil in celebration – at last they agreed on something. Lottie tilted her head upwards and wound her arms around Marco's neck as he, the absolute love of her life, finally crushed her lips with his.

Chapter 56

Exactly one month after the barn dance, Lottie stood in front of the awaiting crowd.

'Hi everyone and thank you for coming to the launch of Lottie's School of Dance.' She pointed proudly to the hand carved wooden signage above the door that Marco had presented her with as a surprise. She'd been unaware of this talent and had been suitably impressed but then they were discovering lots of wonderful new things about each other since getting together. She cut the thick red ribbon across the door to cheers from the awaiting crowd.

'Hold on, I can't see properly,' Doris piped up.

Marco held his laptop higher and Lottie waved at a beaming Doris and Reggie on the screen.

'Congratulations my darling Lottie, we're so proud of you,' said Doris. 'And we have a little bit of news of our own . . .'

'Thank you both, I'm missing you a lot. What is it?' Lottie asked.

'Me too and that's why we've decided on a compromise. As much as I'm loving being here, we've decided we're going to pop over there for three months every summer so we really can have the best of both worlds.'

'Oh Doris, that's just the best news, I can't wait for that.'

'Me neither! Have a lovely day and I'll see you again very soon.'

'Bye Doris.' Lottie blew a kiss to the screen and Marco snapped the laptop shut and smiled at her, causing her heart to flip.

He tilted her chin slightly upwards and pressed his lips to hers,

'Now come on, Miss Lottie, we have a show to put on.' He wrapped his arm round her and they walked into the studio together. Mia and Melissa were rounding up little girls in tutus and boys in dinosaur costumes whilst parents and the senior dancers sat expectantly in their seats. The music began and Lottie took her place on the stage to a round of applause.

Acknowledgements

I can't believe this is now my fourth published book, thank you to all at Orion Dash, including my lovely editor Rhea Kurien and my fabulous cover designer Rose Cooper. My covers just get more beautiful each time which I didn't think was possible and this one really captures Lottie's passion.

Thanks once again to my wonderful friends, some of whom are also my first readers. I'm so grateful to all of you for believing in me and encouraging me; Kay Davies, my rock, who's been with me from the very beginning when becoming an author was just a dream that we talked about on our many walks along the river; my lovely Auntie Margie Morris who has always been by my side, the fabulous Sandra Woods, Barbara Stone and Katie Nash.

Thanks to my dearest school bestie Michelle (Ansloos) Clarke for all the advice on Canadian dual citizenship, I've borrowed Rachel's name for Lottie's Canadian bestie.

Special mention to my beautiful nieces for whom this book is dedicated to, Camilla Kutschker and Darcy Ward. Thank you for bringing me joy and laughter.

I love you both so much and making memories with you both is one of my favourite things.

Lots of love to Peggy my beloved Nana and her sisters Edie, Doris and Frances after whom I've named some of the special characters in this book.

To my lovely writer friends Debbie Johnston and Jenni Keer, Denni the donkey is one of the main characters in this book and he's named after you both, you know why. Thank you for the giggles.

To the Muses; Tara Cullen, Alison French, Paula Fleming, Julie Vince, Lynne Shelby, Maryam Oliver, Kathleen Whyman, Sophie Rogers and Giulia Skye thanks for all your wonderful advice and support especially when I'm dealing with the tricky bits.

To all the amazing authors and bloggers who have encouraged and supported me on my writing journey, there are far too many to mention but special thanks to Milly Johnson, Kim Nash, Linda Hill, Anne Williams, Kirsty Clifton, Karen Hilton Claire Knight, Vicki Bowles, and Dawn Crooks.

To Debbie Garrod, one of my oldest and dearest besties, there'll always be a special place in my heart for you.

Last but definitely not least, thank you to my beautiful daughter Lydia for your wise words of advice and for your constant patience when you stop what you're doing so I can read my book aloud to you. I love you.

Love and thanks also to Johnna, Jake and Damon for all the cups of peppermint tea you supply when I'm writing and for your love and encouragement.

For my readers, I will always be grateful to you for deciding to pick up and read one of my books. I love receiving messages from you all telling me how enjoyable and uplifting you found them. This book is filled with music, dancing, friendship and love and I hope you enjoy reading it as much as I enjoyed writing it.

Love
Annette x

You can follow me here:
  Annettehannah.com
  Twitter @annettehannah
  Facebook @annettehannahauthor
  Instagram @annettehannah

Printed in Great Britain
by Amazon